STOLEN ANGEL

A SINGULAR OBSESSION BOOK THREE

LUCY LEROUX

PUBLISHED BY: Lucy Leroux
Copyright © 2014, Lucy Leroux
http://www.authorlucyleroux.com
ISBN: 978-1-942336-06-8

First Edition.

❀ Created with Vellum

DISCLAIMER

This book is a work of fiction. All of the characters, names, and events portrayed in this novel are products of the author's imagination. Any resemblance to actual events or persons, living or dead, is entirely coincidental.

This eBook is licensed for your personal enjoyment only and may not be re-sold or given away to other people. If you would like to share this book with someone else, please send them to the author's website, where they can find out where to purchase a copy for themselves. Free content can be downloaded at the author's free reads page.

Thank you for respecting the author's work. Enjoy!

TITLES BY LUCY LEROUX

Knight Takes Queen
The Millionaire's Mechanic
Burned Deep - Coming Soon

Writing As L.B. Gilbert
The Elementals Saga
Discordia, A Free Elementals Story
Fire
Air
Water
Earth

A Shifter's Claim
Kin Selection
Eat You Up
Tooth and Nail
The When Witch and the Wolf - Coming Soon

Charmed Legacy Cursed Angel Watchtowers
Forsaken

CREDITS

Cover Design: Robin Harper
    http://www.wickedbydesigncovers.com

Editor: Rebecca Hamilton
    http://qualitybookworks.wordpress.com

Readers: Thank you to all of my guinea pigs! Thanks to Leslie, Kenya, Evelyn, and anyone else I might have forgotten! Special thanks to Jennifer Bergans for her editorial notes. Extra special thanks to my husband for all of his support even though he won't read my sex scenes!

CHAPTER 1

*S*ergei paused behind his open office door and listened. Ada was chatting with Kelly. It was a normal, everyday conversation...except that they were laughing and joking like they were old friends. A week ago, Kelly had been gunning for Ada, determined to make her look bad in front of him. And now this. But he wasn't really surprised anymore. That was just Ada. She could turn anyone into a friend.

Marveling silently, he went back to his desk for the latest report Ada had prepared. He could pretend to have a question about it. It gave him an excuse to talk to her. Slightly disgusted with himself, he put the report back down. It was—as usual—exemplary. Pretending it was unclear did her a disservice. Ada did her job as his executive assistant far too well.

Sighing, he picked up the coffee cup his other assistant Tim had fetched and took a long sip. It was already a little cold. Cheered by the thought of having a plausible excuse to leave his office, he opened the door wider to make his way to the break room.

Sergei passed by Ada's desk, this time making an effort to avoid eavesdropping on her conversation. He already felt like a stalker. He listened in on her a little too often. But sometimes he couldn't help himself. Ada didn't talk to him the way she talked to everyone else. He was her boss, and she treated him accordingly.

She looked up from her desk and nodded at him with the habitually distant and professional manner she used around him. He gave her a small nod back as he walked past. A few minutes later, he passed again, checking in with Tim about the time of his next meeting.

"Is everything clear in my analysis?" Ada asked from her neighboring desk.

She'd whipped together a summary for today's meeting in little more than an hour. The equivalent amount of work, with the required figures and statistics, would have taken anyone else the better part of a week. She'd been a spectacular hire, one he'd poached from one of his junior personnel. If only she wasn't such a distraction.

"It was clear, thank you," he said stiffly before retreating to his office, berating himself for his awkwardness.

It wasn't like him at all, but he couldn't seem to relax around her. He sat at his desk, wondering how things had gotten to the point where he was spying on his executive assistant and making excuses to see her.

Calen and Alexandros would laugh their asses off if they could see him now. Or at least Calen would. Alex was married now. After hearing the story of how Alex had met his wife, Sergei thought he would have some idea of where he was coming from.

What he needed was a distraction. Maybe he wouldn't be obsessing over his assistant if he got laid more than once every six months. Decision made, he flipped on the intercom.

"Tim, extend an invitation to Mz. Worth for this Saturday night."

Tim's perpetually earnest voice came back from the speaker, "You have that charity benefit on Saturday."

"I don't think acquiring a second ticket will be a problem," he said dryly.

Sergei was one of the children's charity's largest donors.

"Of course. I'm on it, Mr. Damov," Tim replied, getting to work with his usual competence.

Tim had been his social secretary for almost four years, and without him, Sergei's life would grind to a halt. Ada had only been working for him for seven months, but she had quickly become equally indispensable.

He remembered the first time he met her. One of the senior VPs on the twenty-third floor had pissed him off. Trevor Jones was usually a half-way proficient executive, but his report on one of Damov Industries' subsidiaries was two days late. It wasn't the first time, either.

Sergei had swept down to the twenty-third floor to put the fear of god into Mr. Jones, only to find the man in question tearing into a subordinate in the conference room before taking off for lunch a half hour early. A three-dimensional model of a new hybrid engine one of his subsidiaries was developing had been destroyed—by Jones himself. But the hapless junior executive had gotten the blame for not informing him that the model wasn't glued together.

Sergei had stayed out of sight, taking the opportunity to see Jones in action. He soon found himself angry enough to contemplate firing the man. His senior VP was one of those executives who blamed everyone else for their mistakes and covered their incompetence with shows of temper.

"This better be fixed by the time I come back or you're done here," a balding and sweaty Jones had hissed before he'd stomped off.

The junior executive had looked tearfully at the jigsaw pile of pieces before a petite brunette had placed a comforting hand on his shoulder.

That was the first time he'd ever seen Ada. Her dull, dark brown hair was pinned in a neat bun, a grey wool dress hugged her figure, and thick black plastic-framed glasses dominated her small face. She was nothing special—not until she'd looked in his direction. Her startling, dark blue eyes were almost purple in the afternoon light. Attention piqued, he'd moved in for a closer look. Neither she nor the junior executive noticed him

"Go clean up, Mark. I've got this," Ada said.

The panicked executive shook his head. "He'll just tear your head off, too. We've got to send this back to R&D for reassembly."

"No, really. I've got this. Go," she'd asserted with a smile, giving him a little shove.

A grateful Mark took off. Once the little brunette was alone, she paced around the conference table. She examined the pieces from all sides and closed her eyes as if she was comparing it to a mental image of the model before disaster had struck. Then she'd dived in and started putting the thing back together.

Sergei was prepared to help when she inevitably failed. The model was too complex for someone without an engineering background to reassemble without directions, a copy of which were on his phone. But, miraculously, the scattered pieces started to coalesce into a coherent whole under her small hands. Soon, the pile of parts resembled the schematic he'd been sent the week before.

Fascinated, Sergei walked into the conference room to watch her finish. She was done before finally noticing she had company. He'd introduced himself, impressed as hell with the level of concentration that would lead someone to completely ignore the CEO of the company they worked for. Not to mention the memory and attention to detail she had to possess to put the complex model back together in a matter of minutes.

Ada hadn't even realized who he was at first. She'd been caught off guard when he introduced himself, hesitating for a second and flushing a rosy pink before her usual unflappable confidence had returned. She shook his hand and cleared the table, offering him the use of the conference room without mentioning the scene that had led to the broken model in the first place.

The next day, he promoted her to a position created specifically for her. She had started as one of three aides, but his most senior PA, Edith, had retired soon after. Now Ada and Tim were his only assistants. Ada oversaw all of his corporate accounts and research, while Tim organized his daily schedule and any social events he needed to throw as the head of a multi-billion dollar enterprise.

Noting the time, Sergei turned his attention to the work on his desk. A few minutes later, Ada knocked, announcing the arrival of his four o'clock meeting. She sat unobtrusively in the corner, taking notes and feeding him information whenever he asked it of her. When the meeting ended, he focused on his departing guests, forcing himself not to watch his assistant leave.

But the image of her blue eyes and delicate features stayed in his head anyway. These days, he even saw them in his sleep.

ADA SAT at her desk with a little exhalation. Back to back meetings made her days long, but she appreciated the work. It kept her busy, and generally that was a very good thing.

Sergei Damov was the best boss she'd ever had. He had recognized her innate intelligence and had promoted her from the relative obscurity of the twenty-third floor after their first meeting. Working for him was exhausting, but Ada usually rose to the occasion. And Mr. Damov's appreciation extended to her paycheck. She was finally building a little nest egg on her own, or at least padding her emergency fund.

"I understand, Mrs. Worth, I'll send the car for you on Saturday," Tim was saying into his headset.

Ada smiled sympathetically. Neither of them much liked the divorced socialite that Mr. Damov used as a backup escort when he was between girlfriends. When Ada thought about Mrs. Worth resuming her visits to the office, it almost made her miss Ivanka, the bitchy supermodel he'd been dating when she'd started working for him. At least Ivanka had ignored her and Tim, but Fiona Worth thought of Sergei's assistants as her own. She had expected Ada to drop everything she was doing to run errands for her. Mr. Damov had to intervene once when the overly groomed woman had thrown a fit the time Ada refused to stop working to go pick up her dry-cleaning.

"I don't see why she always insists on Sergei picking her up. She has her own driver. She got him in the divorce," Tim grumbled when he hung up.

"If she used her own driver, Mr. Damov might be inclined to ditch her should he run into another supermodel at one of those events," she murmured quietly.

Tim snickered and offered to refill her coffee.

"I've had enough for today," Ada said easily, avoiding eye contact.

She liked Tim, but she didn't want to encourage another dinner invitation. In the last few weeks, she'd already turned him down twice and was hoping not to have to do it a third time. Under other circumstances, she would have liked to say yes, but keeping people at arm's length was necessary.

Turning to watch his tall form as he left, she smiled wistfully. It would have been nice to be able to spend time with him after work. Tim Moss was one of the nicest people she'd ever met. And he was cute.

Hours passed as she prepared for Sergei's upcoming business trip. She wouldn't have to attend this one, which was just as well. Ada had finally convinced him to hire back a third assistant, and she was going to be conducting some preliminary interviews while he was away. However, Tim still had to go; Sergei never went anywhere without him.

Dinner was delivered to their office at eight that night, just as Tim was getting ready to leave. He lingered for a while and was still talking to her when Sergei stuck his head out of his office door and ordered him to go home. When their boss retreated to his desk, leaving the heavy wood door ajar, Tim looked at Ada and frowned.

"You know, he never used to leave the door open," he said as he reluctantly put on his coat.

Ada was too tired to pay his comment any attention. She stretched in her chair. "Go home. I would be out the door if I was done."

Her sleepless night was catching up with her. And she didn't like to talk with Tim when she was tired and her defenses were down. Which made his habit of trying to coordinate their departure times so they could share a cab a little annoying. Especially lately. Time alone might mean another dinner invitation she couldn't accept.

Tim finally left, and Ada ate her solitary meal at her desk and went to the break room afterward for her fourth cup of coffee of the day. Lingering at the window that afforded a partially obstructed view of the Manhattan skyline, she stood there lost in thought.

A steady job was a double-edged sword. It meant money and security, but she couldn't socialize at all or let anyone close. She was actually lonelier now than in those jobs where she'd only stayed a few weeks or months.

Behind her, someone cleared their throat. Ada whirled around. Her boss was standing behind her, his tall muscular form still immaculate in a crisp suit and perfectly tied tie. In the beginning, she had wondered if he kept a duplicate suit in his office, which was equipped with its own closet, shower, and a long leather couch for the really late nights that turned into early mornings. She soon realized that Mr. Damov just never got messy or sweaty. Tim had nicknamed him the iceman. Since he never showed much emotion, Ada found the nickname fitting.

"I'm sorry I finished the coffee, Mr. Damov," she said, mentally cursing to herself. "Would you like me to make more?"

She didn't know why he liked the coffee in the break room. He had one of those fancy pod machines in his office, but he preferred the drip coffee from the machine the staff used.

"How many times do I have to tell you to call me Sergei?"

"Just one more," she answered, as she always did.

Calling him by his first name seemed too relaxed for the image she was trying to maintain. She did use Sergei in her head, but insisted on using Mr. Damov when addressing him.

"I can make it," he said, shaking his head as she reached for the coffee pot.

His rough, deep voice skittered along her nerves. Ada nodded and got out of the way as she sipped the lukewarm coffee from the previous pot. She didn't know why she was on edge. They had spent plenty of time alone together. But usually someone else was still around in the background: Tim or Niko. Tonight the office was completely deserted, and she felt unaccountably nervous.

"He has a crush on you, you know," he said suddenly.

Ada choked on her coffee. "What?"

Sergei came up behind her and gave her several hard whacks on the back.

"I'm okay, I'm okay," she said holding up her hands.

Her back was stinging from the forceful blows.

"Are you sure?" he asked attentively.

She nodded and smiled awkwardly, itching to step away, but she was already trapped in the corner of the room.

"I meant Tim. He has a crush on you. Before you started to work here, he was out the door at the earliest opportunity. Now I have to order him to go home. He always tries to leave when you leave. And I heard he asked you to dinner."

Startled, Ada stared at her boss. Niko must have told him all that stuff. The craggy-faced older Russian never missed a thing. Niko Zotov was another mixed blessing to working here. He was Damov Industries' head of security. He and his team kept close tabs on Sergei, accompanying him wherever he went.

She had initially thought the four-man security team was a little excessive, but then Tim had told her that about a failed kidnapping attempt a few years ago. Niko had single-handedly foiled the attack, shooting one of the would-be kidnappers in the chest. After that, Sergei had expanded Niko's team to its current number, all ex-military from Russia. Though Tim was English and she was actually Canadian, Sergei preferred men from the motherland when it came to his personal safety.

Sergei was still waiting for an answer. "He did ask, but I don't think it's because of a crush. He's just friendly," Ada lied, a little too aware of how close her boss was standing to her.

Sergei raised a brow. "I think you know that's not true. And he's not the only one. Half the men on this floor flirt with you. You always shut them down. Why is that?"

"Um," Ada said, almost swallowing her tongue.

Sergei never talked about personal matters. It was one of her favorite things about her boss. And it definitely was not half the men. In fact, Tim was the only one she was sure about. The rest of the floor was just friendly. They had welcomed her with open arms. After the first week anyway.

"Hey, more than half the men on this floor are married," she said, frowning.

It was more like three out of four. Sergei just smiled at her sardonically and ignored her comment the way he did all things he didn't think worthy of discussing.

"Maybe you prefer the company of women? Although you also turn them down when they invite you to socialize after work."

It was said with no judgment. Just open curiosity. Ada laughed. "When work ends routinely after nine, all I want to do is go home and sleep."

"So you aren't a lesbian?" he pressed.

"No," Ada said, her smile growing fixed and brittle.

She was starting to get annoyed but tried not to let it show. After all, Sergei was her boss.

"Good," he whispered back.

He leaned closer, and all of a sudden, she was in his arms, his warm lips against hers.

Shocked to her core, Ada froze. Dizzily, she groped for the counter behind her, expecting him to let her go. But he didn't. Instead, his lips grew softer against hers, and his bulk pressed her further into the corner of the break room. A moment of indecision turned into three and then four as her body was flooded with heat.

"*Angel*," he murmured while momentarily breaking the kiss.

Her whole body tensed, and she snapped back to attention. She pushed her boss away with a nervous laugh. "Um, definitely not a lesbian. But also not interested in an affair or a fling with the man who signs my paychecks," she said honestly with a shaky breath.

For a long moment, Sergei didn't move. He straightened up and backed away as if she'd just told him she was a man.

He cleared his throat again and said very formally, "My apologies. I forgot myself for a moment." Then he was gone, leaving Ada staring after him.

That night, sleep was impossible. Tossing and turning, she couldn't stop replaying the scene in the break room, fixating like a broken record on the moment when he called her Angel.

It had been a long time since anyone had called her that.

CHAPTER 2

"What do you mean you're getting married?" Sergei asked in Russian into his cell phone.

He had come into his office early so he could avoid Ada at her desk for as long as possible. He still felt like a complete ass for his behavior the night before. He'd fired assistants for becoming too familiar with him. Twice now, attractive young women had come to work for him with the primary goal of getting him into bed. He'd gotten rid of them without a second thought. And now *he'd* sexually harassed his PA. The best one he'd ever had.

"It's a long story, but it's happening this weekend. Can you make it up to Boston this Saturday?" Calen answered back, his Russian rusty but still good enough to be understood.

Calen had learned the language when they roomed together at the University of Edinburgh. He had insisted on Sergei teaching him if they moved in together, claiming that he wasn't about to live with someone who could be ordering his death behind his back. It was jokes like that, blatant and in your face, that had made them fast friends. Both of them had come to school with 'bodyguards' in tow.

Sergei's father, a Russian oil tycoon from Omsk deeply immersed in the Bratva—the Russian mob—had insisted on the bodyguard. Since saying no had meant not being allowed to leave home for school, Sergei capitulated at first.

Calen had a similar story. His father was a well-known figure in Boston's organized crime network. When they had realized just how much they had in common, he and Calen had banded together. They moved in with each other their first year, and by the time the second year had started, the bodyguards had been sent home.

"Are you serious? I didn't even know you were seeing anyone," Sergei said.

"It's a new relationship, but this girl is special. And I need to lock this down now," Calen said, offering no other explanation.

"I don't get it," Sergei muttered, adjusting his papers as a knock sounded.

Ada popped her head inside, straightening when she saw him at his desk. Tense but trying to cover it, he gestured for her to enter.

"What is your rush?" he continued as she dropped some papers on his desk.

Ada looked a little flushed, but she didn't say anything or make eye contact as she let herself out. Relaxing slightly when the door shut behind her, he focused on his insane friend.

"I'll explain when you get here. You will come right?" Calen asked.

Leaning back in his leather chair, Sergei shook his head. "If you're serious, then yes. I'll cancel my plans."

"I am serious. And thanks. I'll call you with more details later. Liam and Trick have been talking about a bachelor party. They're a little pissed about the short notice. Apparently I'm not giving them enough time to plan."

Sergei smiled. Even with short notice, the Tyler brothers would throw a bash to remember. Liam and Trick had grown up with Calen, and when they were in need of investors for their now-successful hotel chain, Calen had hooked them up with him and some of their other school mates. It had been a profitable relationship. Like him, the Tylers lived by the work hard, play hard motto.

"I have every confidence in Liam and Trick's ability to put something together guaranteed to get us arrested," Sergei replied drily.

Calen groaned. "Don't put stuff like that out there or you'll jinx me. I'll call you later. Or Liam will once he decides what to do. Tell him no strippers."

"Why don't you tell him? He's your second best friend," Sergei growled.

He used to be competitive about Calen's friendship with the Tylers, but after spending a lot of time with Liam and Trick, he was more relaxed about it. Enough to joke about it at least.

"I *did* tell him. But I'm going to need you to tell him, too, 'cause his hearing gets selective when I say things like that. If he does get strippers and Maia finds out about it, she might not marry me," Calen said with uncharacteristic earnestness.

"Maia is the mystery woman? How did you meet her? And how the hell did she get a ring out of you already?"

"Later, I promise. Just make sure there aren't any strippers."

Sergei sighed and gave in, promising to keep Liam and Trick in line.

It wasn't really a hardship. Normally, after being rejected by a woman, he would have welcomed a raunchy bachelor party. But after having his lips on Ada's little pink mouth, the thought of a lap dance made him feel unclean.

Maybe this is growing up, he thought with dissatisfaction. He was almost thirty-four. He was probably overdue to exhibit some sign of maturity.

"All right, thanks a lot брат[1]," Calen said before he hung up.

———

ADA WAS surprised when Sergei buzzed Tim and canceled his plans with Fiona Worth.

"Give her my regrets and send one of my standard apologies," he said, not bothering to specify why he was breaking the date. "And call my pilot and have him file a flight plan to Boston for Thursday evening."

"Right away, Mr. Damov," Tim said, beaming as Sergei clicked off.

"What did he mean by standard apology?" Ada asked, curious despite herself. "Does he send flowers for every broken date?"

"Flowers are for the unwashed masses. Sergei sends jewelry. Bracelets are standard. Sometimes necklaces if they have no charms. No rings. Not ever."

"Ah. Yeah, I can see how a ring would send the wrong message," she said, smiling at her screen as she typed up an email. "Does he have something in Boston that I should know about?"

Occasionally, Sergei forgot to mention a deal brewing, which meant late hours when she found out about it and had to play catch up.

"No, not that I know of, but his best friend is in Boston. Calen McLachlan," Tim said.

"Really?"

It was hard to picture Sergei with a friend. Girlfriends and starlets, yes. But Ada had always pictured Sergei as a lone wolf. He was too aggressive and dominant to suffer the company of other men—unless they were subordinates like Tim.

"Yes," Tim said, leaning over with a cautious glance at Sergei's door. "And he's one of *those* McLachlans," he whispered conspiratorially.

"One of those what?" she asked, looking up from her email.

"Irish mob," Tim whispered, his eyes glinting.

Ada stopped typing completely. Tim must have seen the surprise on her face because he rushed to fill in the blanks. "Oh, he's not a mobster himself. Scuttlebutt says he's totally legit. He owns a string of nightclubs and is supposedly a shrewd investor. Actually, he's got a chunk of Damov Industries stock, enough to be a minority shareholder. But his family is *connected*."

"Wow."

She didn't know what else to say. It made sense though, in a way. Sergei couldn't have normal friends. Someone with a regular job as a banker or a lawyer. He employed those people, but she couldn't see him having dinner or joining one for cocktails. But a mobster's son who ran a nightclub? Yes, that mental image came easily.

"They must not see each other that much," she mused, turning her attention back to her screen.

"Oh, they meet up like once a month or every other month. Mostly here in Manhattan or Vegas," Tim confided, and she nodded.

Sergei spent a lot of time on the road, and Ada usually didn't accompany him. She only joined him for half of his trips, and only in the last few months since Edith, his old assistant, had retired. Her predecessor hadn't liked to travel because she suffered from arthritis.

Since Ada was so much younger and less arthritic, her boss had changed the habit of years and started to travel with her in tow when a deal called for it. But he still left her at home frequently to hold down the fort while he traveled.

Sergei breezed out of the office on his cell phone, handing Tim an empty coffee cup. "He said no strippers, Trick."

Tim rushed to the break room to get him a refill, and Ada held her breath. But Sergei didn't look at her. He didn't acknowledge her at all, and she relaxed incrementally. Mostly. There was still a nagging, unsettled feeling in the pit of her stomach. Ignoring it, she put her head down and finished her email.

Tim came back with the coffee and Sergei swept back into his office without a glance her way. Taking his seat Tim grinned at her the way he always did, and she smiled back...but it was a little weak.

———

ADA CLIMBED up the stairs of the private jet with a heavy heart. A month had passed since Sergei had kissed her. A month since she'd been in his arms. Since then, working for him had become more and more uncomfortable. And it wasn't because of anything he said or did. He acted like nothing had ever happened...and he did it a lot better than she did.

She, on the other hand, could no longer look at him with her usual aloof detachment. Something had changed. Before he had just been her boss. An incredibly demanding one, but still just a boss. Now he was a man. A man who'd kissed her. It was the most intimacy she'd experienced in a long time.

She'd always known Sergei was attractive. He was tall and muscular with deep brown hair and eyes so dark they looked black. His face was more rugged than handsome, but it was perfectly symmetrical with lips hinting at fullness and chiseled cheekbones. His looks rivaled models on magazine covers, the kind that would advertise outdoor gear.

But before the kiss, his sexual appeal had been a distant thing, something she could see without having it touch her—she couldn't afford to let it. Now she was hyperaware of his every move, even when she couldn't see him. He could be in the next room, and she knew where he was standing or when he was about to walk out to leave papers on her desk.

Sleep was a thing of the past.

Niko and his team took their usual seats in the front near the cabin door while the rest of them made their way to the back conference area so they could work. Ada sat in the plush reclining leather chair opposite Sergei with Tim on her left in his usual spot. There was a small bedroom in the back where the boss slept on long trips.

They were on their way to Rome to finalize Sergei's latest acquisition. Damov Industries was buying a small Italian manufacturer of gourmet foods. Sergei had grown fond of their specialty products while vacationing in Italy the previous year, and now he was planning on exporting them worldwide to select high-end grocers.

"Tim, call the hotel and make sure they have given me my preferred suite," Sergei ordered. "And have tomorrow's dinner meeting changed to a lunch. I want to be free for dinner."

In her seat, Ada tensed imperceptibly. Sergei hadn't gone on any dates since his best friend's wedding had interrupted his plans. According to Tim, there were times when Sergei didn't date much, usually when a big deal was in the works. And other than Ivanka and Fiona Worth, there hadn't been any woman since Ada started working for him. But his latest deal was nearing completion, and clearly he was getting ready to resume his normal social life.

Slightly sick to her stomach, Ada turned on her tablet and pretended to work on her latest project—a report on a biofuels startup. Realization set in.

I have to leave sooner than I thought.

CHAPTER 3

Sergei stood up with a satisfied sigh. The meeting had gone well, and everything had been finished ahead of schedule. The contracts were signed, and now he had a whole forty-eight hours free in one of his favorite cities. Too bad Giancarlo was out of town.

Out of the corner of his eye, he watched Ada pack up their things. She had been flawless as usual. Her Italian wasn't half-bad either. He hadn't even known she spoke the language until this trip. Leaning over, she unplugged his tablet's charger, her firm heart-shaped backside tempting him to reach out and touch.

Stifling the urge, Sergei watched Ada as she stood up again and absently wiped her forehead with her sleeve. Other women didn't do that. They would have been afraid of getting makeup on their clothes. But Ada never wore any. At the end of the day, her skin got a little shiny, something the women he dated would never let happen. They would be powdered to a satiny finish at all times. But he liked Ada's natural look more.

She wasn't flashy, but she was beautiful in a quiet, understated way. Her blue eyes contrasted with her dark hair, making them look brighter and bluer. And she always had a natural pink tinge in her cheeks.

"We should celebrate." The words were out of his mouth before he could think better of it. Ada looked up, surprised. But the mistake was already made. "You said you hadn't traveled much outside the states when you started working for me. We should hit the town. Some of the best restaurants in the world are in this city," he added temptingly.

"Uh..."

Shit. She was going to say no. She probably had plans—with Tim. His other assistant's crush had only gotten worse lately, and Sergei had the sneaking suspicion he was finally wearing Ada down.

"Okay," she said finally, then paused for a moment. "Shall I call Tim?"

"I think he has plans," Sergei said. "Let's head back to the hotel and change. Do you have a dress?"

Ada glanced down at her practical wool suit and nodded. "I have one," she said, sounding less sure now.

She'd probably assumed Tim was going to be available to join them.

"Excellent. Let's go," he said, ushering her out before she could change her mind.

ADA PULLED on her little black dress with trepidation. How had this happened? Sergei's invitation had caught her completely off guard. She'd said yes without thinking, assuming she was tagging along while he had dinner with some of his friends, or that Tim would be there. But he'd made it clear in the car that they would be alone when he'd called a restaurant and made reservations for two in passable Italian.

She almost jumped out of her skin when a knock sounded on the door. Old instincts flared to life, and she looked around for a handy weapon. Sergei had said he would send a car for her promptly at eight, and she wasn't expecting anyone else. Snatching up the luggage rack, she walked up to the door in bare feet. Peering cautiously through the peephole, she relaxed with a shaky sigh. She put the luggage rack down and opened the door.

"Hi, Tim. Did you change your mind about joining us?" she asked in a hopeful voice.

Tim was standing there in his casual clothes, dark slacks and a fashionable sweater vest. He was dressed like the quintessential hipster he was outside of office hours. And he was staring a hole through her. He looked at her in her little black dress, his usual earnest cheerfulness nowhere in sight.

"Don't go."

"What?"

"I said don't go," Tim said, pushing his way into the room.

Frowning, Ada stared at him. "Yeah, I heard that part. But why?"

Tim put his hands on her shoulders in a jerky motion. "I just found out about this date. The restaurant called to confirm Sergei's arrival time, and Niko told me it was you he was taking. You can't go. You don't know—you never see."

"It's not a date. And just what don't I see?" she asked, pulling away.

She tried to remind herself that this was her friend, but having his hands on her that way made her feel constricted.

"You don't see the way Sergei looks at you when you're not looking. This won't end well," he said severely.

Completely taken aback, Ada just stared at him. She opened and closed her mouth a few times before she found her voice. "He just wants to celebrate the deal. I actually thought you were coming."

"No, he knew I had plans to meet up with friends. But you should already know this deal is pretty small by his standards. It was more a whim of his than anything else, 'cause he likes the Dolcetto products. He didn't celebrate when he bought that Silicon Valley start-up, and that was a much bigger deal. Why would he celebrate such a small acquisition?" Tim asked, throwing up his hands dramatically. "It's an excuse. He just wants to get you alone. Going out with him is a bad idea. It was okay before because he obviously hadn't done anything. But he has now, hasn't he? You've been tense around him for weeks. He made a pass at you, didn't he?"

Ada didn't know what to say. She didn't want to talk about that kiss. "Not really. Everything's fine."

"*Not really?* What does *not really* mean?"

Another knock saved her from answering. She dived for the door and was surprised to see Niko standing there.

"Ms. Turner, are you ready?" Niko asked, his thick Russian accent chopping up the words.

"Err, uh, yes," Ada said, turning to put on her shoes and grabbing her coat. Once ready, she headed for the door. "Tim, I need to lock up. Have fun with your friends, okay?"

Tim just shook his head and followed her out. Before they got to the elevator, he pulled her aside. "Just be careful. He always gets what he wants, and he wants you. Don't let him charm you. In the end, he'll eat you alive."

He stalked back in the direction of his room before she could think of a reply. Frowning, she joined Niko in the elevator. It was probably her imagination, but she thought he looked a little sorry for her.

A FEW HOURS and almost two bottles of wine later, Ada decided that Tim had blown everything out of proportion. There had been nothing to worry about. The world was beautiful and everything had a fuzzy warm glow around it. Rome was magical. And her boss was actually fun. He'd been perfect company the whole night.

Sergei took her to his favorite restaurant at the top of a small high rise. One entire wall of windows had a spectacular view of the Colosseum, lit up for the night. Ada had to stop herself from running to take a closer look, but the effusive host seated them directly in front of the window.

Sergei watched her expression closely as she stared dreamily at the ancient monument and the Palatine Hill behind it, before proceeding to distract her with a steady stream of small talk. He told her the most fascinating stories about ancient Rome, while pouring generous glasses of a deep red Italian wine. Her anxiety melted away the more she drank, though she still had the wherewithal to deflect his more personal questions.

He must have realized she didn't want to talk about herself, because he soon launched into a series of anecdotes about himself and his friends. Their collective antics in college had her choking on wine, trying not to laugh. She questioned him about his friend Calen's wedding, and he volunteered all the details.

"So he rescued a damsel in distress, and she just happens to be his soul mate?" she asked in disbelief, her jaded, natural-self showing through despite the alcohol.

Or more likely because of it.

"I see it actually. He's crazy about her. And soul mates come around when you least expect them," Sergei said, surprising her.

Ada made a face at him, and he laughed.

He leaned back in his chair with a smile. "I never realized what a pessimist you are."

"And I never realized what a little Mary Sunshine you were," Ada replied with the tiniest slur creeping into her voice.

"You're just so warm at work. Such a people person. I would have thought someone like you would have found the story romantic. Don't you believe in soul mates?"

"It *was* romantic," she admitted. "But also not surprising. Two compatible people were put in a difficult situation and the expected happened."

She wrinkled her nose at a sudden realization—and it wasn't that her face was numb. If Sergei thought of her as warm, then she had gotten too comfortable at work. A professional distance was crucial.

Maybe Uncle Geoffrey was right. She'd been working for Damov Industries too long. Reaching for her wine glass, she lifted it to her lips, only to find it empty.

"May as well kill this bottle," Sergei said, his accent so thick she could barely understand him now.

He poured the rest in her glass. Without pausing to take a breath, she drank it down and put the empty goblet in the middle of her full dessert plate.

Sergei laughed, but then his gaze froze somewhere beyond her. Twisting, she turned around to see Niko. The bodyguard was stationed at a table with a clear line of sight to their table, and he was frowning at them.

When she turned back to Sergei, he looked less jovial. He took her by the arm and guided her up. Ada got to her feet unsteadily, letting out an uncharacteristic giggle as they made their way to the door.

"There's something wrong with the floor," she said as they walked out of the restaurant.

The effects of the alcohol were more obvious now that she was on her feet. Sergei reached out to grab her as she swayed away from him. He took hold of her hand and pulled her closer into his side, which felt very warm compared to the cool night air.

"No, angel, there's something wrong with you. Come here," he murmured.

Drawn in tightly against him, she held on as he ushered her into the waiting car.

SERGEI AVOIDED Niko's dark glance as he guided Ada into the backseat. He shut the door behind him and was surprised by a sudden rush of warmth. His reserved and professional assistant had closed the space between them to cuddle against him like a cat.

"Ada?"

"Hmm," she mumbled sleepily from somewhere just under his chin.

"Nothing," he said quietly, inhaling deeply.

Her hair smelled like jasmine and vanilla. As if his arm had a mind of its own, it drifted down around her to stroke the bare skin of her arm. It was cold, and she had goosebumps. She really should have brought a coat.

If we go home, I need to buy her a fur. Frowning at the turn of his thoughts, Sergei shook his head to clear it. He didn't want to go to Omsk. And he certainly didn't want to take Ada there.

Glancing at her drowsy face, he drew her a little closer as the car sped down the darkened streets. It was going too fast. He was tempted to tell his driver to slow down so he could savor this stolen moment a little longer. But the gods were against him, and they got to the hotel in record time.

It wasn't fast enough for Ada. She had fallen asleep. Sergei didn't have the heart to wake her, so he picked her up and carried her to the door of the private entrance. Niko wisely said nothing until they got to the elevator.

"Shall I take Ms. Turner to her room?" he offered in Russian.

The private elevator didn't go to Ada and Tim's floor. It only went to the penthouse and luxury suites in the high rise hotel. He didn't want to embarrass his assistant by carrying her through the front door.

"There's a spare bedroom in my suite. It will be fine," he finally said, avoiding looking at Niko directly.

He could feel his security chief's disapproval boring a hole on the back of his neck as he walked to his suite, but he shook it off. Niko opened the door, and Sergei entered his rooms with Ada in his arms. He dismissed the security team and laid his very drunk PA on the couch so he could open the double doors to the extra bedroom. When he turned back, she was stirring, struggling to sit up.

ADA DRIFTED AWAKE IN CONFUSION. She was lying on a plush dark blue couch covered in a sumptuous soft fabric. Sitting up, she saw an unfamiliar room. There was a bar with a neat configuration of bottles to her right and an eight-person dining room table on the left.

Where was she?

"Hey," Sergei murmured, coming into view.

He reached for a water bottle from the bar and sat down next to her, his handsome face drifting in and out of focus.

"I'm thirsty," she croaked, her mouth drier than sandpaper.

"I thought you would be," he said, his accent still thicker than usual.

She had to focus very hard to make out his words. Sergei opened the water bottle and handed it to her. He sat down, brushing her hair away from her eyes. Her once neat bun had collapsed and her hair fell below her shoulders in loose waves. She gulped the entire bottle down in one go. A little water escaped her lips and dribbled down her chin and chest.

"Oh god I needed that," she said, absently wiping her chin.

Sergei laughed and moved to help her. Reaching out a little unsteadily, he wiped the water that had fallen on her exposed décolletage.

Surprised by the warmth of his hand on her bare chest, Ada froze and stared down at it. She looked up to see Sergei with a similar look of surprise on his face...but he didn't move his hand. Knowing she needed to put a stop to this, she reached up to move it, but instead she just ended up covering his hand with her own, both just over her heart.

The next thing Ada knew, she was underneath him on the couch, his body pressing hers down into the silky fabric. His lips skated over her face, pressing hot open-mouthed kisses all over her face and lips. Lowering himself, he kissed down the line of her neck while grinding his lower half against her.

Ada gasped aloud as his hard cloth-covered cock pressed home. She could feel the rough material of his suit pants abrade the bare skin of her inner thighs and looked down to see that the skirt of her dress had ridden up to her waist. Sergei's hands moved down the outside of her thighs as he thrust against her again and again.

Ada's quick, shaky breaths turned into a low moan. Her skin was on fire, and she could feel her blood pounding in her veins. Between her legs was a rush of hot wetness that saturated her panties. Every time Sergei rocked, she could feel the inner muscles of her core try to clench down hungrily on nothing.

Startled by the need that had been ignited inside her, she clawed at Sergei's back, her hands digging into the fabric of his button down shirt. Hazily, she wondered where his suit jacket had gone, but then his lips were on hers and she was lifted up in his arms. There was a sensation of being carried and then the world started to fade in and out.

Snatches of awareness came and went like scenes under a strobe light. She remembered landing on the bed, but couldn't remember taking off her dress. Understanding that she was wearing only a pair of cotton bikini panties came in a flash as she stared up into a large skylight directly over the bed.

Sergei was still completely clothed except for his shoes, yet he didn't seem in a hurry to undress as he moved between her open legs. He was whispering something in her ear, but for the life of her she couldn't understand a word of it.

"What?" she said, tearing her lips away from his.

He repeated his words but they were still garbled and incomprehensible, "Я хотел бы переспать с тобой. Ты меня хочешь?[2]"

"I don't understand," she whispered against his warm cheek.

It sounded like he was asking a question, but she couldn't make it out. Sergei groaned and sat up. She sat up and tried to pull him back. Apparently that was answer enough for him.

His clothes magically melted away. For a second, she could feel the barrier of her cotton panties between them and then it was gone after a quiet ripping sound. He came down over her, covering her naked body with his own. His weight pressed her down into the bed, a blanket of hot hard flesh and hair roughened skin. The sensation felt so strange and familiar at the same time.

Above her, Sergei moved her legs apart and slid between them. He hissed as the head of his cock slid against her. Ada could feel his hardness move up and down over her wet, superheated core. The feel of him against her sparked something inside her, a deep craving she could feel in her blood. She moaned again, clutching at him with shaky hands.

"Я люблю тебя, мой ангел [3]," he whispered in her ear as he positioned himself at her entrance.

His lips met hers as he began to work himself inside her. For a moment, her body fought against his invasion, and he said something else—sounding surprised—but she couldn't make it out. Instead, she clung to him tighter, and then he was completely inside, his balls nestled against her, and she was panting, trying to catch her breath. An echo of pain skittered across her consciousness, but it was gone as soon as he started to move.

Ada didn't remember the buildup. When she checked in again, she was pulling Sergei tighter against her, her nails digging into his back as she strained against him. He held her just as tightly, his fingers digging into her arms as he drove forward, relentlessly opening and claiming her.

His cock felt so large inside her tight channel. It was almost too much to take as it moved in and out of her faster and faster. It should have hurt, but there was no pain, only a feeling of completion and pleasure that was growing progressively more intense.

She had never experienced anything like it. For a moment there was a little fear and her body instinctively fought against losing control. But Sergei wouldn't accept anything less than her complete surrender.

He rolled until she was lying across his chest, still joined to him. One fist tightened in her hair while the other pinned her hip in place. Urging her up until he could take her lips, he discarded all attempts at sweetness. The kiss plundered and laid waste, his tongue moving in time to his endless thrusts.

Stretched taut like a violin bow, Ada cried out in relief as the exquisite tension finally broke like a crashing wave, carrying her up off the bed and into the stars above them.

"Ah yes! Oh, God," Sergei shouted, his first English words since he'd touched her.

His cock jerked as he pumped himself into her. It felt like she was trying to absorb him into her body as her inner muscles clamped down on him, her sheath spasming almost painfully. She pushed against him, slamming into him a little too hard as a tight hot wave of pleasure racked her body for an endless moment. It was so intense, it sapped all of her energy, and her body slipped into darkness as it fell back down to earth.

When she woke next, her body had grown cold again. At least the front of her body had. A long, hard body was pressed flush against her back and large arms were wrapped just under her breasts. When she stirred, Sergei moved over her, and then it began all over again.

She lost count of how many times they made love. Asleep one minute, she would be dozing in his arms, then the next minute, they were joined, straining against each other. He pulled her on top of him, her back to his front while he took her from underneath. Other times he was above, and at least once, he was behind, working his shaft in and out of her as she lay facedown on the bed, while he whispered nonsensical words into the shell of her ear.

Each time she tried to hold on to him for as long as she could, flexing muscles she'd never really used before. One orgasm melded into another in a sensual blur of hot soft skin moving against her own. They grappled with each other—two bodies trying their damnedest to merge into one being—with movements that were frenzied and desperate despite the soporific effects of the alcohol that softened every edge into a blur.

Eventually, they collapsed into an exhausted, dreamless sleep, both of them still clinging to each other.

CHAPTER 4

*W*ay too early the next morning, Sergei's eyes flew open. It didn't matter if he'd been up late partying or working on a deal till dawn. At 6am, he snapped awake as if someone had thrown cold water on him. When he'd been a child, someone had, every day until he learned to wake up at that hour on his own. But this wasn't his childhood bedroom in Omsk. He was in a large luxurious bed, and he wasn't alone.

Ada.

She was lying next to him. They had made love last night. Many, many times. He sucked in a breath and realized he was thirsty. And his head hurt a little. They'd both had too much to drink.

I really shouldn't have had those shots of vodka before meeting Ada for dinner, Sergei reflected.

But his body was capable of absorbing a lot of damage thanks to all his past training with Calen and Alex, so the hangover wasn't too bad. For Ada's small frame, it would be much worse. And she wasn't an experienced drinker. He remembered that much from last night.

Slipping quietly out of the warm bed, he went downstairs to the suite's bar for water and to hunt down some aspirin.

A half hour later, Sergei was back in fighting shape. He'd downed a few pills with a liter of water and showered in the second bedroom's bathroom in order to avoid waking Ada. She was going to be suffering enough when she finally woke up. Letting her sleep for as long as possible would give her body more of a chance to absorb the alcohol. With that idea in mind, Sergei's thoughts promptly derailed as he pictured the body in question in greater detail.

God, she was beautiful. And not in the plastic, overdone way typical of the women he usually dated. Those were all so groomed and enhanced that in his mind they all resembled the same woman.

Ada was different. She was normal and natural with average-sized breasts and hips. Her hair was a simple dark brown with no streaks or highlights. And she was hands down the most beautiful woman he'd ever been with. She was definitely the smartest.

On impulse, he called downstairs for room service. If it had been another woman in his bed right now, there was no way he would have even considered sharing breakfast.

He had a set of unspoken rules for his bed partners—calling them girlfriends was too generous. Until Ada, he had only gotten involved with women who understood those rules. They went out with him and shared his bed only so long as they maintained their distance and didn't try to get too involved in his life. Which meant no morning after meals of any kind.

He ordered an assortment of things that would taste fine cold, unsure when Ada would get up. If she wanted something hot, he could order it later. When the coffee arrived, he shotgunned two cups before pouring a generous mug for his still unconscious angel. Even if it got cold, she would probably still appreciate it when she finally woke. She often drank her coffee cold and sweet. Grabbing a bottle of water and some more aspirin, he went upstairs to the master bedroom.

A bit of brown hair peeked up from underneath the crisp white sheets. Ada hadn't moved. She was lying on her stomach, her head buried between two pillows. He smiled at the picture she made, a warm, unfamiliar feeling tightening his chest.

None of his past experiences had ever inspired this strange sense of satisfaction. He actually had an incongruous feeling of pride, like he'd finally slept with someone worthwhile. Whenever he'd had sex with anyone else, all he'd felt was the need to shower and leave as quickly as possible.

With Ada, he wanted to crawl back into bed to hold her until she woke up. He decided to do just that. With a crooked grin, he pulled back the covers to climb in next to her.

With a strangled breath, he froze, the covers twisted in his grasp.

She was covered in bruises. Most were faint, but a few were startlingly dark against the soft cream of her skin. They ran down her entire left side. Finger shaped imprints in blue and green decorated her upper arm. There were more on her ribcage and on her hip.

And it got worse. The white sheets of the bedclothes had some small streaks of red. He'd hurt her so bad he had made her bleed.

Oh God, he thought, sucking in a harsh breath. He dropped the covers and backed away. He didn't even stop to put on his coat before he left the suite, calling Niko to get the jet ready for takeoff.

ADA WOKE up with a splitting headache. Nauseated, she moved her head very slowly, sitting up to look around. Bits and pieces of the night before filtered back slowly, and she breathed deeply and evenly in an attempt not to throw up. Peeking out of one eye, she spotted a bottle of water and a package of painkillers on the nightstand. She reached for it and almost knocked over a full cup of cold coffee.

Sergei. Holy fuck, she'd slept with her boss.

The knowledge of that overshadowed the fact she was experiencing the first and possibly the worst hangover of her life. What was she going to do? How could she have done that?

"*Shit.*"

Thankfully there was no answer. Sergei wasn't there. Cautiously, she rolled over so she could drink the water and swallow the pills. It took the better part of an hour before she felt human enough to get out of bed.

There was no noise coming from the other rooms. She'd thought it was a blessing at first, but now the silence was ominous. When she didn't find a note, she started to feel sick to her stomach for a completely different reason.

Showering on shaky legs, Ada pulled on her dress before she was completely dry, pulling the dress over some faint bruises on her arms. Sergei had apparently gotten a little overzealous last night, she thought, dismissing the marks as soon as she was dressed.

Where was Sergei? If he wasn't here, she had to find him. Or maybe that was the wrong move? He'd had a lot to drink, too, but he was a foot taller and outweighed her by almost a hundred pounds. It wouldn't have affected him as much. Which meant he probably wasn't throwing up in the other bathroom.

So if he wasn't here, then it was because he didn't want to be.

Making her way downstairs in bare feet, she marveled at the size of the suite. She hadn't really seen it that well the night before. The bedroom she'd woken up in was on a second story she hadn't even known was there last night.

Usually when she traveled with her boss, she never saw his suite or set of rooms. He was zealous about protecting his personal time and never worked at home or in his hotel room.

During trips, she would meet the rest of the security team every morning at the car and they would wait for Niko to escort Sergei down from whatever top floor suite he had been given. She was definitely part of the B team in his world.

Except now she'd had sex with him. A lot of sex if her fragmented memory wasn't completely faulty. It wasn't exactly what she'd had planned for her first time.

Her heart sank when she got to the living room. The couch was occupied. But it wasn't Sergei sitting there waiting for her. It was Tim, looking at her like she had just cancelled Christmas. The disappointment on his face was a punch to the gut. That and the fact that he was the one sitting there, all alone.

"Sergei's gone back to New York. He took the jet there this morning. We have the rest of the week off. The jet will come back for us on Saturday," Tim said finally, his tone laced with condemnation.

"Oh," she whispered her stomach roiling.

The headache that had retreated to the back of her head was back at full force, pounding at her temples and behind her eyes.

"I told you this would happen. Why didn't you listen to me?" Tim said, getting up and putting his hands on her upper arms. She flinched, and he looked down to see the bruises she'd noticed in the shower. "God Ada, I'm sorry," he said in a lower voice.

His whole demeanor changed. Instead of angry, he looked upset, the way a friend should if he saw her in such a sorry state.

"It's fine. I bruise easily," she said dismissing the obvious hand prints on her arms. She didn't even feel them. "My dad always said I bruised like a peach," she confessed before she could stop herself.

Realizing she had slipped up by mentioning her father, Ada took a deep breath and immediately regretted it. Tim's cloying cologne filled her nostrils, sending a chain reaction to her brain and stomach. For a second, she stood frozen, eyes squeezed shut, failing to fight the nausea. Whirling around, she ran to the bathroom to be sick.

"Ada, are you okay?" Tim called out from behind the hastily closed door.

Struggling to catch her breath, she ignored him. Flushing to drown him out, she clung to the toilet seat, breaking into a cold sweat.

"Here, sweetheart," Tim said, pressing a cold cloth to her forehead.

She hadn't even heard him come in. He put his arm around her and brought a bottle of water to her lips.

"Keep drinking this if you can keep it down. You'll feel better. Do you need some pain killers?"

"I already took some, but I may have just thrown them up," Ada whispered, shakily bringing the bottle of water up to her lips.

She tried to hide her trembling without success.

"I'll get you some more," Tim said, getting up reluctantly. He was back too soon, his comforting presence grating on her raw exposed nerves. "How much did you drink last night?"

"I don't know. A lot more than I should have. I'm not a big drinker," she said hoarsely.

Before last night, she'd never had more than one glass of wine. She'd been too wrapped up in her studies to party much at school, and since then, it hadn't been safe enough to let her guard down enough to get drunk.

"This is all Sergei's fault," Tim said sharply. "He just can't stop himself from taking whatever he wants, no matter who it hurts."

It was a dramatic change from his usual tone of admiration for their boss. When she'd first started working with him, he'd been Sergei's biggest fan. His half-jealous hero worship had been obvious and oddly sweet. Now he sounded like he wanted to take a bat to Sergei's knees.

"I'm fine. It was...it was just a mistake," she said shakily while secretly hoping it hadn't been.

Maybe Sergei had been called away on an emergency. He had no living relatives, but he had friends. Maybe one of them was in trouble.

"Yes. Yes, it was. One you have four whole days in Italy to forget about. We're going to get you sober, and then we're going to change hotels. Maybe we should even change cities. Venice is amazing. So is Florence. Or we can take the train to Pompeii and get lost in history," he said stroking her hair.

Throat constricted and fighting back tears, Ada nodded. "Maybe we should."

Tim continued to comfort her as she drank the rest of the water and tried to forget what an idiot she was.

ADA HASTILY PACKED HER BAGS, determined to leave the hotel before Tim came back to her room. She'd already left a note for him with the front desk explaining that she needed some time alone and would meet him on Saturday to catch the plane back to New York. The taxi she'd called was waiting to take her to the train station.

Tim had been right about one thing. Getting out of Rome was a good idea.

She climbed on the train to Florence with only two minutes to spare. For as long as she could remember, Venice and Pompeii had been at the top of her must-see list, but she couldn't face those places alone right now.

She didn't want to look back and remember them in association with this feeling.

CHAPTER 5

*O*n Monday morning, Ada grit her teeth and walked to the Manhattan skyscraper that housed Damov Industries on its upper floors.

She had debated missing the plane in Rome. No one would ever know just how close she had come to walking away. But there had been a tiny kernel of hope hidden deep inside her that sleeping with Sergei hadn't been a mistake—that he hadn't been using her. But he hadn't called her or tried to reach her in any way since then.

She told herself it didn't matter. People had casual sex all the time. But it took more strength than she had thought possible to walk inside the building with her head held high. It took considerably more effort to maintain her calm façade when she saw Tim waiting at the elevator for her, a coffee in each hand.

On the plane, she had apologized—a lot—for leaving so abruptly and not answering her phone. He had been so worried and worked up, it felt like she'd had to comfort him the whole way back.

Tim didn't say anything in front of the crowd. He just handed her the coffee and walked into the elevator behind her. It should have made her feel better, but at the moment, nothing was going to do that.

When the elevator got to their floor, she entered and went to her desk, trying to behave as normally as possible. Straining to hear anything behind the closed doors of Sergei's office, she booted up her computer and opened her email. Head down to avoid Tim's gaze, she started to clear the backlog that had accumulated in their time away.

Almost an hour passed before Sergei's door swung open. "Tim, come in here," he said before he went back inside and shut the door.

Tim made a face and grabbed his tablet before he went inside. He was back in less than five minutes, his face flushed and angry. The intercom on her desk went off before he could sit down.

"Ada please come in and bring your notes on the Dolcetto foods purchase."

Sergei's voice broke the thin layer of ice that had encased her as soon as she sat down at her desk. She grabbed her tablet and swept into his office, taking a seat in front of him without a word.

He looked exactly the same as he always did—immaculate in a charcoal grey suit and blue shirt that looked amazing against the contrast of his dark brown hair. Except for a slight shadow under his eyes, he could have been posing for a magazine cover. She tried to find comfort in the fact that he had obviously lost some sleep since she'd seen him last, but when it came right down to it, she had no idea if he had done so over her. For all she knew, he had spent the night before partying with his mobster friend.

He got to business without preamble. "I decided against investing in Adstringo in favor of that small apps developer. I think it's a more sound investment at this time."

It took her a minute to process his words. "Oh, I...I see. I expect it does seem like the safer bet, but I have looked at Adstringo's product very carefully. Their code is sound and their program really works. With the licensing deals we could help them make, they are on the brink of a really big thing."

Sergei leaned back in his chair, pretending to consider her words before dismissing them outright. "I'll take that under advisement. But start getting the paperwork for Ellison Apps together."

"Okay."

What else could she say? What the hell were you supposed to tell the man who'd taken your virginity in a drunken one night stand?

"There's one other thing," he said finally. Chest tight, Ada held her breath and waited for him to continue. "I wanted to let both you and Tim know how appreciative I am of the exemplary work you've both been doing lately. My appreciation will be reflected in your next paycheck. I'm giving you both raises."

It felt like the air had been sucked out of the room. She tried to tell herself it wasn't true, he wasn't trying to pay her off, but he was just sitting there looking at her expectantly.

Was she supposed to *thank* him?

"Oh." It didn't sound like her voice speaking. It was too low and held a hint of a tremor. Ada cleared her throat. "Will that be all?"

He stared at her impassively for a second before answering. "One more thing. Have Tim make reservations for two at Carbone tonight. And have him send yellow roses, not red, to Fiona Worth," he said evenly.

He was looking straight into her eyes, his face cold and remote.

The lack of air in the room became critical. It felt as though a giant rock was compressing her chest. She couldn't speak so she simply nodded. It took everything she had not to run to the door and out of his sight.

Walking as steadily as she could, she made her way back to her desk. It was hard to focus on her surroundings as she sat down with an audible thump. The text on her screen blurred and moved as if she was on drugs.

"*Ada.*"

Tim's voice was so sympathetic it made her want to cry. She squeezed her eyes shut hard for a second before clearing her throat, harder this time.

"Yellow."

"What?"

"He wants you to send Fiona Worth yellow roses, not red ones."

"I can't believe he made you do that! He should never have made you pass on that message," Tim hissed, shaking his head.

"You also need to make reservations for two at Carbone tonight."

"*Fuck.* I'm going to go in there and—"

Ada didn't find out what Tim thought he was going to do. Before he could finish the sentence, the doors to Sergei's office swung open.

"Tim did you call Mz. Worth yet?"

"No, I haven't." Tim sounded furious, and he didn't bother to hide it.

"Good, make the invitation for this weekend and secure two tickets to the Winston charity dinner on Friday in Miami instead," Sergei said, his voice thick and gravelly.

Ada didn't look up. She sat there frozen as Sergei made plans to spend the weekend with another woman.

The silence stretched until the air became thick with tension. Staring blindly at her screen, she pretended to read her email until she gathered enough self-possession to move. With a great effort, she looked up in Sergei's general direction for the length of three heart-beats. She didn't make an effort to focus on his face before turning away.

"*Tim,*" Sergei's voice held a note of warning.

"I'll get right on that," Tim said finally.

"Good," Sergei replied, his tone frigid.

She expected him to go back into his office, but he just stood there as if he was going to wait until Tim carried out his orders.

Taking a deep breath, Ada stood, picking up her coffee cup as she went. She walked out of the room without a backward glance, bypassing the break room until she found herself in the ladies wash-room. She put the mug on the sink's counter and turned on the tap, catching a glimpse of herself in the mirror.

She was as white as a sheet. With shaky hands, she splashed cold water on her face, willing herself to get a grip.

Why did this hurt so much? She'd known this was coming, had seen it clearly.

How could she have expected anything else when she woke up alone that morning in Rome?

I should have left then.

She had really wanted to, but the tiny stupid spark of hope in her chest had still been there. Choosing to believe the lie, she'd gotten back on the Damov company jet. Of course, she hadn't admitted that at the time. It had been easy to convince herself that she was coming back for the right reasons, that she'd wanted to face Sergei and show him that he didn't have the power to hurt her. Well...he did, and he had.

How did I get here?

She hadn't even liked the man a month ago. Not this way. Before that stupid kiss, she'd secretly sneered at the women he dated. She'd felt secure in her superior mental ability and thick protective layer of professional detachment.

Sergei wasn't even her type. He was too handsome, and god knew he was arrogant. She liked nice men like Tim. Under other circumstances, she would be with Tim or someone like him right now.

But Sergei had kissed her, and her foolish, lonely heart had latched onto the only bit of human contact and warmth she'd had in years. Now she thought about him all the time.

Even though he was arrogant, Ada recognized that he had a right to be. Sergei was brilliant and driven in addition to being handsome, in a brutal sort of way. And he had such confidence in her intelligence and her skills that she'd convinced herself he found her special in other ways. But she'd been wrong.

Her eyes flooded with tears, but she refused to let them fall.

No. This wasn't how this was going to go down. Sergei was just a...a *guy*. Fuck the billions he controlled. He wasn't powerful enough to break her. Worse men than him had already tried and failed.

Stiffening her spine, she took a deep breath. This was nothing compared to what she'd already been through. And that man—that stupid, clueless Russian—didn't have the power to touch her. Not the real her. How could he? He didn't know anything about her.

With that reminder came a flood of energy, as if power was literally coursing through her veins. Her fingertips crackled with it, making them tingle as she flexed her hands into fists.

Knowledge—not money—was power. And she was the one who possessed it. Not Tim and not Niko. And definitely not Sergei.

He doesn't even know your real name.

CHAPTER 6

*W*hen she finally stepped out of the washroom, Tim was waiting in the break area. With carefully composed features, she greeted him almost cheerfully as she filled a mug to make tea.

"Ada, I'm so sorry about what just happened in there," he whispered.

No one else on the floor was nearby, but he wasn't taking any chances. Normally he would have been the first person in line for gossip. In fact, when it came to Sergei's love life, he was usually the source. But not this time.

"Sorry about what?" Ada asked. "I'm fine."

She was proud of herself for sounding completely normal. The hurt and confusion she'd displayed just minutes ago was gone, melted away as if it had never been there.

Tim came up and put his arms around her. "You don't have to be brave in front of me. He's a complete asshole. Why don't we take off early for lunch? We can take the rest of the day off. You don't have to deal with this alone."

Backing away, out of his arms, Ada smiled her cool, detached smile

—the one she'd spent years perfecting. "Really, there's no need. I'm okay. I don't need a shoulder to cry on."

Instead of looking relieved, Tim only looked confused. Her performance was flawless. It should be. She'd sacrificed everything she had to get that good.

He stared at her, his eyebrows drawn down heavily over his eyes as she finished fixing her tea. Before he found his tongue, she smiled reassuringly and went back to her desk.

The next time Sergei stepped out of his office, Ada surprised him. She asked him for his signature on some documents the legal department had just dropped off. Her eyes were dry and perfectly clear, with no tremor in her speech or in her movements.

He signed the papers and watched her as she sat back at her desk, smiling serenely. After a minute, he went back to his office and didn't speak to her for the rest of the day.

———

Be careful what you wish for.

Sergei had told himself repeatedly that this was for the best. He had made things clear to Ada the day she got back. Things would return to normal. And they had. His assistant was the same efficient machine she'd been the day he'd hired her—aloof and professional. Completely impersonal. She even smiled at him, though the expression held no warmth.

It was true she'd never smiled at him the way she had at Tim. He was honest enough to admit that he'd been jealous of the affection she'd shown the younger man. But not even Tim got her real smile now. It was all an act, and a damn good one. But that wasn't the worst part.

He'd discovered something truly ugly about himself. It wasn't enough that he'd gotten away with hurting her once. He wanted to see the real emotion behind the mask Ada now wore. Even if it meant reopening the wound he'd inflicted himself. He wanted her to yell and scream at him, to accuse him of using and abusing her, flaying him wide open so he could bleed right alongside her.

More than anything, he wanted to go back to that morning, to beg for forgiveness. The fact that she'd come back had been a hopeful sign. Until he'd done and said all of those things about seeing Fiona.

He had hated saying those things. She had gone pale, her eyes overly bright and her expression frozen. He'd wanted to jump out of his chair and throw himself at her feet so he could beg for forgiveness. But he had to keep his distance. It was the only way to keep from hurting her worse, to save her from the monster that lived inside him.

THIS IS IT. After today, she would never have to see Sergei or set foot in Damov Industries ever again.

Her week had been complete and utter hell, but it was almost over. She just had to get through today.

Unfortunately, Tim was no help. He'd started by walking on eggshells around her, but the more she carried on as if nothing was wrong, the more he seemed determined to make her 'confront her feelings'. It was all she could do not to smack him for making things harder. Still...she would miss him. Even if he was infuriating sometimes.

As for Sergei, he had also gotten worse. He was terse and impatient, spitting out orders like bullets. But sometimes, when he thought she wasn't watching, he would stare at her, his face stiff and his mouth tight. She pretended not to notice.

Her exit strategy—the plan she'd spent all week getting ready—was nearly complete. She just needed Sergei's signature on the contracts, and then she was out of here. But the right time, a moment when he wouldn't be paying attention to what he was signing, hadn't arrived.

Uncle Geoffrey would never approve of her form of revenge. He was too much of an eye for an eye kind of man. Granted, her plan was unorthodox. Making sure the asshole who'd used you made hundreds of millions of dollars wouldn't qualify as appropriate vengeance by anyone else's standards. And if Sergei was the completely one-sided prick he was trying to convince her he was, then it was a miserable plan. But if there really was more to him, then it would bother him.

Once she got him to sign the contracts, he was going to be the proud owner of the amazing company he'd rejected. Adstringo was going to set the standard in data compression for the next decade. The technology they'd developed was already ten times better than the zip program, and the people behind it were still innovating and making progress. From now on, every time Sergei uncompressed a file or made another million from the technology, he would have to think about her.

In just a few weeks' time, when the software was officially launched at the consumer electronics show, all the news media would be crowing about Adstringo. Once they unveiled their new compression algorithm, Sergei wouldn't be able to escape hearing all about it and thinking about her last act as his employee. Not unless he moved to a deserted island.

It wasn't a perfect act of revenge, but it was the best she could do without taking a page out of her honorary Uncle's playbook.

At lunchtime, she went to the ladies bathroom and locked herself in one of the toilet stalls. She had read Geoffrey's last email several times already, but she kept going back to it despite its harsh message. It was, after all, from the only person in the world who knew and loved her.

ANGEL,

I'm glad you're finally taking my advice and are moving on from that place. I know you felt safe there, but it's important for you to stay mobile right now. I've been keeping an eye on Karl, and I don't believe he's stopped looking for you. I also don't think he's any closer to finding you than he has been these last three years, but I could be wrong, and we must remain vigilant.

Your new papers are ready. You'll find the key where the birds carry people in the green.

I'm worried about you, my little Eva. You didn't sound like yourself in your last message. If you need me, use your emergency line. I love you, and I'm proud of you. Always.

GJ

"One day I will find the right words, and they will be simple." - Jack Kerouac

SHUTTING OFF HER PHONE, she rested her forehead on the cool steel of the stall door. She hadn't seen her godfather Geoffrey Johansson since her parents' funeral. Not that he'd been able to come to the funeral service itself. He was still a wanted man in Canada. Praying that he would still find a way to pay his respects, she had waited at the cemetery for him every night.

On the third night of her vigil, Geoffrey appeared. Terrified by the events that had followed her parents shocking deaths, she confessed all of her fears and suspicions to him. Instead of dismissing her fears as paranoia, he listened. Geoffrey had been a legendary conman in his day. He could read people the way other people read directions, and he'd known she was telling the truth.

Uncle Geoffrey wasn't a blood relation. He had been an old friend of her father's. They'd served in the army together and had grown close despite the extreme personality differences between the two.

Her father had been a shy bookish engineering geek. Geoffrey, on the other hand, was a polished smooth talking extrovert, the kind of guy that could sell you anything. But as her father had once said, Geoffrey was the kind of man fond of taking shortcuts.

Her father had turned a blind eye to his friend's inability to play inside the lines, but he had been alarmed when Geoffrey had been forced to leave the country because of the crimes he'd committed. Somehow, long after the dust settled, contact had been reestablished.

When she was born, Geoffrey had been designated an honorary godfather. He wasn't ever able to visit them, but they had gone to visit him two or three times when she was little. And there were phone calls from secure lines and emails from encrypted accounts. Geoffrey, retired now, was patiently living abroad, waiting for the statute of limitations on his crimes to pass.

Through a network of shady connections, Geoffrey had investigated her suspicions. Half-hoping she was wrong, she'd lived on pins and needles until he'd gotten back to her. But he'd come to the same conclusion she had. Karl was the reason her father was dead, and her stepmother Sarah along with him.

Even though Ada had known the truth, she'd prayed that she was wrong. She'd gone to the police, but they had dismissed her claims, and soon Karl's tentacles had encircled her so completely that she'd had no chance for justice and no means of escape. If it wasn't for Geoffrey, she wouldn't have known what do to. He taught her the lessons he'd learned as a fugitive and successful white-collar criminal.

She'd dropped everything and had run for her life, leaving everything behind. Including her name.

Maybe she should be thanking Sergei. If he hadn't done what he did, she might not have decided to leave yet. And she had stayed too long—longer than she'd stayed anywhere else. Who knew when Karl would finally run her to ground? The only reason she was still alive was because she'd stayed one step ahead of him.

Living on the run was exhausting, but she'd tried to make the best of it. Geoffrey had helped her create new identities and backgrounds. Using them, she had gotten a lot of different jobs, and had had experiences she would never have known otherwise. She'd lived entirely different lives, shedding one identity for another every three or four months. A new life was waiting for her now.

With that final thought, Ada kicked open the stall and got back to work. She had to find her opening to get those contracts signed. Without appearing too obvious, she made the rounds, silently wishing all of her coworkers of the last nine months goodbye. The fact she was going to miss so many of them underscored the magnitude of her mistake. She could never let herself get so comfortable again.

Near quitting time, Ada was starting to get anxious. Sergei had been a control freak the entire day as he got ready for his weekend away with Fiona Worth. Despite the fact he didn't mention Fiona by name, she got the distinct impression he was throwing the other woman in her face. He certainly made mention of his weekend plans often enough.

Holding tightly to her composure, she waited for the right opportunity to get him to sign on the dotted line. So it was ironic that, in the end, she owed Fiona Worth for the success of her plan.

It was little more than an hour before Sergei and Tim would leave for the private airfield to catch the company jet to Miami. Tim had repeatedly assured her that everything would be all right. Fiona was supposed to meet them at the plane. But Mrs. Worth had other plans.

Fiona swept into the office ahead of schedule demanding to see Sergei, a deceptively small chic suitcase in hand. A much larger case was in the hand of the security guard she'd badgered into helping her just outside the office.

"You're early," Sergei said harshly when he saw her. He didn't return her cheek kisses when she hurried to greet him. "You were supposed to meet us at the plane."

His displeasure radiated off him in waves, and Fiona became visibly uncomfortable.

"Darling, I haven't seen you in months. I simply couldn't wait. And your office is closer to my apartment. I thought we could ride to the airport together," Fiona said placatingly.

"I'm not done here yet. You'll have to wait for me in the cafeteria," Sergei bit out.

Even Tim raised his brows at the coldness in his voice.

Ada wanted to act normally, but she couldn't help averting her eyes from the sight of Sergei with another woman.

The pain she'd held at bay was back, and it was stronger than ever. It felt as if someone had seized her insides and was twisting them tightly. She could feel his eyes fixed on her, too, despite the other woman's presence.

She was tempted to leave the room for an emergency coffee break when realization dawned. She could use this moment to her advantage...if she got ahold of herself. Taking a deep breath, she looked directly at the couple.

"Hey, boss, before you run out for the weekend, can you sign copies of the Kesey memos for legal?" she asked, rising out of her seat and grabbing the contracts and a clipboard. "You know they want everything in triplicate and then some," she said with a smile as she walked toward them.

This time it was Sergei that froze. Niko, alerted by someone to Fiona's early arrival, walked to Tim's desk to wait as Ada handed the papers to Sergei. Little post-it arrows indicated where he needed to sign. Only the front page was from the memo. The rest was the Adstringo contract.

"Hello, Ms. Worth, it's so lovely to see you again," Ada said with a genuine smile for the other woman.

Fiona gave her a distant nod, the kind appropriate for an underling. Sergei, on the other hand, just stared at Ada. Standing there like a statue, he looked as if he expected lightning to strike him down. With a benign expression, she handed him the papers and produced a pen from her pocket. When he didn't take the pen, Fiona prodded him.

"Sergei, the poor girl's waiting. Sign your memos so you can finish up here."

He still didn't react. It wasn't until Niko cleared his throat loudly that he finally snatched the pen out of her hand and signed.

"Don't forget the second copy," she said politely, pointing to where an arrow post-it indicated.

Staring fixedly at her instead of the paper, he signed on the dotted line, several times. When he handed them back, Ada rewarded him with a dazzling smile.

"Have a nice weekend," she called back casually as she walked back to her desk.

Catching Niko's eye, she sat down. The usually stoic and intimidating Russian looked at her approvingly, as if he was proud of her. She could see the respect in his eyes. Tim gave her a surreptitious thumbs up sign behind his monitor, but she ignored it.

"*Earth to Sergei.*" Fiona was definitely annoyed now.

She'd finally noticed his preoccupation with his young assistant, and she was ready to spit nails.

"*What?*" Sergei snapped.

He sounded more annoyed than Fiona was. Reading his mood, the woman backed down. "Nothing. I was just wondering if there was anything I could do to help you finish up faster."

Ada wanted to smile at Fiona's politic answer. Clearly the woman was smarter than she looked.

"No. I'm...I'm done here. Let's go. Tim, my suitcase," he said as he stalked out of the room.

Shrugging in exasperation, Fiona followed him. Niko took one last look at Ada before he followed. She stared after him with a wistful little smile. She owed him a lot actually. Because of him and his security team, she had gotten more sleep in the last nine months than the two years that preceded it combined. Niko paused at the threshold, sensing something in her gaze. Hastily, she looked away.

"You were amazing," Tim whispered as he grabbed his bag and Sergei's travel case.

"I don't know what you're talking about," Ada replied with a straight face. Impulsively, she jumped up from her seat to give him a fierce hug. Surprised and startled, he dropped the bags to hug her back. Forcing herself to let go, she smiled at him a little weakly. "Have a safe trip."

"Are you sure you're okay? I can go back and tell Sergei I'm not coming. We can spend the weekend eating ice cream and watching really bad romcoms," he offered earnestly.

"Don't be silly. You have to go. Everyone's waiting," she said, slipping the mask back on.

"Are you sure?" Tim asked, reluctant to leave her.

"Yes, go," she said, laughing lightly.

If he didn't leave, she was never going to get the contracts down to legal.

"Okay, but I'm gonna call you tomorrow. Pick up your phone this time," he ordered, wagging his finger at her as he headed for the elevator.

Fortunately, he didn't wait for an answer before he disappeared. Releasing a shaky breath, Ada picked up her contracts. She had a lot to do before she left.

CHAPTER 7

*S*ergei was blind drunk. He'd started drinking on the plane, doing his best to ignore Fiona's grating company. Unable to look at her, he'd poured glass after glass of premium vodka, trying not to listen to her snide comments about Ada.

Fiona knew better than to accuse him outright of having an affair with his assistant, but she couldn't stop herself from needling him. She called Ada a mouse and insinuated a number of nasty things while he got progressively more drunk. He didn't bother to reply; he merely tuned her out.

Sergei simply didn't care enough about Fiona to fight with her. Instead, it was the memory of Ada as they left that he couldn't get out of his head.

Her smile. That smile had been real, and he'd felt it like a knife to the heart. It had taken only a week—*a week*—and she was already over him. Over Rome. Whereas he replayed every moment of that night in his head over and over. Even now, the flood of images didn't stop. So he'd poured himself a vodka. And when he'd finished that one, he poured another.

He vaguely remembered being at the charity dinner. There was some small talk and then more drinking, champagne now since it was flowing freely. But when it didn't do the job fast enough, he switched back to the hard stuff. He had a vague memory of a fine tablecloth that soon became stained with an equally fine dinner—one he'd paid a thousand dollars a plate to eat.

At some point, he knocked into someone, and there was a loud crashing noise followed by flashbulbs. Then Niko was ushering him out with the help of his other bodyguards. They took him to yet another luxurious hotel suite. It looked nothing like the one in Rome, but in his drunken state, the resemblance was all he could think about. Luckily, one of the things it did have in common was a fully stocked bar.

When he resurfaced, he'd lost the entire weekend. It was just like college all over again when he and Calen had celebrated their newfound freedom with an endless stream of alcohol. Bleary eyed, he checked his watch. It was after one in the afternoon...on Monday. He was supposed to be at work back in Manhattan. Instead, he was nursing the hangover from hell in a hotel suite in Miami. But at least Fiona wasn't there. His last memory of her was at the charity dinner. She hadn't been in the car with him to the hotel afterward.

Counting his blessings, he reached for a fresh bottle—Johnny Walker Blue this time. After that, he lost track of time again. Every once in a while, food would appear, usually delivered by Niko or Tim. They would try to talk to him, and sometimes he would pretend to listen, but most of the time it required too much effort, so he didn't bother.

"Wake up, sleeping beauty," a familiar voice said as he was shaken from a deep sleep.

"Hrmgh," he muttered lifting his head.

He was lying face down on the king size bed in the suite's bedroom, and he was completely naked.

"So he's still breathing?" a second voice asked.

It had a familiar rhythm to it, a lyrical cadence he hadn't heard in a while.

"It would seem so," Calen said, forcing one of Sergei's eyelids open with his thumb and index fingers.

"Good thing. I'm not prepared for a funeral. I only brought linen suits, and none of them are black," the second voice said, and it finally clicked.

Sergei opened his eyes and lifted his head out of sheer disbelief. *"Giancarlo?"*

"Buongiorno," Giancarlo Morgese said, bending over to appear in his line of sight for a moment before disappearing again.

Gio had gone to school with them. Of the four of them, he was their group's straight man—a quiet, shy scholar whose good looks and family money brought him more attention than he generally wanted. Calen McLachlan, his best friend, was standing in front of the bed, smirking.

"Here," the bespectacled Italian said, handing him a pile of clean clothes. "Do us a favor and put on some clothes."

He went out again and came back with a cup of steaming coffee.

"Why are you here?" Sergei grumbled, taking the cup from his prone position.

"Gio here saw you on TMZ piss drunk, knocking over a waiter," Calen said. "So we called you. Many, many times. When you didn't pick up, we called Niko. Apparently he was worried enough about you to actually break his Bratva code of silence and tell us where you were holed up."

Dragging the sheet around his waist, Sergei sat up, head pounding. "The thing with the waiter made TMZ?"

"It's not every day a Russian billionaire gets so publicly drunk he knocks over a waiter at a benefit for the pediatric cancer foundation," Gio said, leaning against the wall with his arms crossed. "Do you need a bucket? Trash can?"

"*Shit.* I'd forgotten what charity it was for. I thought it was to support some ballet or opera. Something with music."

"'fraid not. But it's not as bad as it sounds. No actual sick children were present. But someone did get you with a camera phone. Several someones actually," Calen said, dragging an armchair from the corner. He was quiet for a moment before he leaned forward, bracing his forearms on his lap. "Care to tell us what's going on?"

"Not really," Sergei said flatly, looking away as he pulled on some boxers under the draped sheet.

"Come on, this isn't like you. Getting shitfaced in public, going on a weeklong bender. Something's up. If you tell us what it is, maybe we can help," Calen said as Sergei picked up the coffee and drained it in one go.

There was a half-empty bottle of bourbon on the table. He couldn't remember drinking the other half, but that was probably a good thing since he hated bourbon.

Gio did his magician trick again, appearing out of thin air with another cup of coffee and a bottle of water. They waited patiently for him to finish. He was tempted to keep his mouth shut, to send them away and keep drinking until he didn't feel anything anymore. But these were his oldest friends.

"What were you doing trolling TMZ?" he asked Gio, stalling for time.

"Just keeping tabs on what the ex is saying about me now. Forewarned is forearmed," his eminently practical friend said.

Sergei sighed. Giancarlo Morgese was one of the nicest men walking this earth. He had done nothing to deserve being saddled with that crazy bitch ex-wife of his. He deserved better. Hell, he might be the only man Sergei knew who deserved someone like Ada.

Fuck. Thinking about her affected him viscerally. There was a pain in his chest. It was like his heart wanted to crawl out from behind his ribs. Struggling for breath, he finally said, "I fucked up."

"How exactly? Business seems good, considering your most recent acquisition's big splash," Gio said, his thoughts going to work first, as always.

Sergei shrugged. He hadn't expected Dolcetto foods to do well at first given their small introduction to the market, but maybe one of their products had made some celebrity's radar or something. A mention on twitter was sometimes all it took these days between a soft launch and a hard one.

"It's not work. Work is fine," Sergei grumbled.

"It's the girl isn't it?" Calen asked.

Gio raised his brows. "There's a girl?"

It would be news to him. Calen was the only one he'd told about Ada, and he hadn't told him much. Not even her name. Reminding himself that these two men probably knew more about him than anyone else on earth, he got ahold of himself. After having come all this way, they deserved the truth.

"I'm turning into my father," he said quietly, admitting his biggest fear.

That visibly threw them. Calen frowned, and Gio put his hands on his hips. Sergei hadn't mentioned his father once since the old man's funeral. Iosif Damov had died a little after they all graduated from University. All three of his friends had come to support him. Alex had flown them all over in his father's jet, and they had stayed with him in his childhood home in Omsk.

Gio didn't know all the details of his childhood, but he knew enough. Calen was the one person he'd told everything, every last sordid detail, down to where the bodies were buried. He could trust both of them, but he couldn't tell this story sober. He snatched up the half-empty bourbon bottle, opened it, and took a swig.

"Her name is Ada. She works for me."

The two men exchanged worried glances. Calen reached out and pried the bottle from his hand.

"Is Ada your assistant?" Gio asked.

"Yes."

"I was afraid you were going to say that," Calen said. "I don't know how to tell you this, but she doesn't work for you anymore."

Sucking in a harsh breath, Sergei nodded. "So she finally quit?"

He'd been half-expecting it. It was what she should have done right after Rome. Hell, she should have quit after he'd first kissed her in the office. She deserved better than some toxic piece of shit like him. It had only been a matter of time before she realized that and walked away.

"Not exactly," Calen said.

Frowning now, Sergei drank from the water bottle Gio had brought him. "What the hell does that mean?"

56

"She did quit I guess. She's gone. But after she left, your other assistant tried to track her down."

"Course he did. He's in love with her, too," Sergei mumbled, wondering where this was all going.

Calen and Gio exchanged another look at the 'too', but they didn't say anything about it.

"Tim couldn't find her so your man Niko tried next," Calen said.

"*And?*" Sergei was starting to get worried.

His friends were acting too strangely. They kept exchanging knowing looks and both seemed tense. Something must have happened to Ada. *Oh God.* He *was* going to be sick now.

"Well he didn't find her, but he did find something strange," Gio volunteered.

"What the fuck are you not telling me? That she's missing for real? No one can find her? Did he call the police?" he asked, terrified for Ada now.

He hastily reached for his pants.

Gio took the bourbon bottle from Calen and handed it back to him. "Let him have it. He's going to need it."

"Ada Turner isn't missing." Calen leaned forward again. "She doesn't exist."

CHAPTER 8

A freshly showered Sergei collapsed on the couch in the suite's living room where Calen was sitting waiting for him. Gio was making travel arrangements for the three of them, giving him and Calen the opportunity to talk alone.

"Look I don't know what's going on with this girl, what her deal is, or why she lied about her name. We'll figure that out later. What I want to know is why you're here alone in Miami trying to drink yourself to death." He looked pointedly at the bottle Sergei had picked up again after the shower. "And I want to know why you suddenly think you're anything like that piece of shit who fathered you."

Sergei shook his head and immediately regretted it. The headache had receded with the help of the hair of the dog, but he was in danger of becoming drunk again. Calen sat quietly, waited patiently for him to begin.

"I seduced her. I got her drunk, and then I took her to bed."

Though he raised his brows, Calen's expression was nonjudgmental. "*Okay*. Not like you at all. You've never needed anything to get anyone into bed before. But why did that lead to this?" he asked, gesturing to the bottle.

Eyes watering, Sergei swallowed hard. The lump in his throat had grown to the size of his fist, and he was in danger of choking. "I...I hurt her. When I woke up the next morning, she was covered in bruises and...and blood."

The memory swam into focus in his mind, and he came close to letting the tears fall. Wiping hastily with his sleeve, he waited for the condemnation he knew he deserved.

Calen's mouth had dropped open. Whatever he had expected to hear, that wasn't it. "Are you sure? I mean, you've never been rough with anyone before. You were drinking. Did you black out?"

The concern in his voice was like a knife through Sergei's heart. It was sympathy for *him*, and he didn't fucking deserve it.

"*Are you listening to me*? I hurt her. The only woman I've ever really cared about, and the first thing I do—the first time I touch her—and I...I." He stopped, his throat too thick to speak.

"Sergei, I don't know what happened that night, but I do know you. You wouldn't hurt a fly. Not on purpose. And you are *nothing* like your father. Not one bit. Now I want you to start at the beginning. Tell me everything," Calen said, leaning back in his chair.

"I took her to dinner," Sergei started.

"No, I mean at the very beginning. When and where did you meet her?" he asked, taking back the bottle Sergei was still holding.

So Sergei told him everything, starting with watching Ada rebuild the model. He told him about their relationship, how they worked together so well, how brilliant she was. It took a long time. In the background, Gio bustled around, pretending to do God knows what, while overhearing every word.

Calen raised his brows when Sergei confessed to being so nervous about dinner alone with Ada that he had a few stiff drinks before meeting her and then having wine on top of that during the meal. After he described the morning after, how he'd panicked and run, Calen was quiet for a while, a thoughtful expression on his face.

"But she came back to work, right?" his friend eventually asked.

Lying on the couch at this point, Sergei felt like he was in a therapist's office. "I don't know why she came back. I wouldn't have if I were her."

Calen ignored the last part. "And she wasn't there with the cops ready to slap some cuffs on you."

"That proves nothing."

He was her boss, or at least he had been. Ada was gone now, and he might never see her again.

"Look, I don't believe for a second you intentionally hurt this woman. Maybe you held her too tightly and that's why she had bruises. It sounds like things got very intense. When things get that way with Maia, I've been known to leave bruises on her. I felt like shit after the first time and I try to be more careful now, but some women bruise easier than others." Sergei shook his head again, not wanting to be absolved, but Calen continued. Lowering his voice, he said, "And I would never get so personal, but in light of what you told me, maybe you need to ask yourself this question. One I would never have thought to ask given the women we've been involved with in the past. But recent experience leads me to consider the possibility. Is there any chance this girl was a virgin?"

"What?"

Calen looked embarrassed. "Sorry, it's just that you mentioned that there was some blood. It might've been because she was...well, you know."

"No, I—" Sergei started to say before stopping abruptly.

He replayed that moment in his head. He'd been drunk, but he still remembered that precious moment when he'd joined his body to hers clearly. It was burned into his brain. Was it revisionist history or was he imagining that there had been some resistance when he'd pushed inside her? The realization sank in slowly.

Oh God. He must have looked horrified because Calen handed the bourbon back to him as Gio joined them.

"There's still the small matter of this girl not existing," Gio said gently.

"True," Calen said.

Swallowing heavily, Sergei put the bottle down, "I have to find her."

SERGEI WAS MAINLINING coffee as fast as his jet's coffee machine could make it. Calen and Gio were pretending to play poker in the conference area, but in reality they were keeping an eye on him, taking turns to check on him as he made phone call after phone call in the front part of the cabin.

He'd already called Niko twice and Tim once. Niko hadn't had much to say except that he had found some abnormalities in Ada's background check and would get back to him with a full report once Sergei was back in the office. He still hadn't found her.

Tim was nearly incomprehensible. He thought Ada had been kidnapped, and though he hadn't come right out and said it, he blamed Sergei for putting her in danger. And Sergei was worried Tim was right. Once he had exhausted everything he could do from the plane, he joined Gio and Calen in the back.

"Any news?" Giancarlo asked, gesturing to ask if he wanted to be dealt in.

He shook his head. "This is all my fault," he said heavily, staring down at his hands.

Gio cleared his throat. "Sergei, if this girl fabricated her personal history, complete with fake IDs, then maybe she was up to no good."

Bewildered, Sergei just stared at him.

"Usually I hate to agree with our jaded friend here, but he might be right," Calen added sympathetically. "You might want to get your accountants to start a system-wide audit, starting with all of the accounts she might have had access to."

"You think she stole from me?" He couldn't believe it. Shaking his head, he said, "No. If that had been her goal, she wouldn't have stayed as long as she did. She had full access, and she had it months ago. Not to mention the fact that she brought in million-dollar accounts to me on her own. Because of her work, I had the best year I've ever had."

They absorbed that in silence. "Maybe there's a rational explanation, but you can't overlook the possibility she might have had something nefarious in mind. Niko said her fake credentials were pretty good. Not perfect, but good enough if you weren't looking closely. Maybe you need to examine the possibility of industrial espionage. She could have been a plant all along," Gio said.

Sergei put his head in his hands, running them through his hair in frustration. "I just don't see it. I promoted her myself from within, totally based on merit. She didn't even interview to work under me, even though there was an opening."

"That may have been part of the problem. Did you know she was just temping at Damov Industries until you hired her? Niko mentioned it," Calen said.

"No. I thought she'd been a standard hire."

He was confused now. Was he wrong about Ada? No, he couldn't be. There was no way Ada would have known he was coming down to check on Trevor Jones that day, or that he would have hired her after one meeting.

"Well, she wasn't," Calen continued. "She was a long term sub for someone out on maternity leave. Niko thinks that's why her background didn't raise any red flags. If she'd interviewed to work for you directly, then it might not have stood up to the level of scrutiny it would have otherwise gotten. It didn't even get the standard check you do for regular employees."

Sergei was perplexed. "It doesn't make any sense. She was an amazing executive assistant, overqualified in so many ways. If she'd wanted money, she could have found an easier way to make it than working for me. Believe me on that. Maybe she's in witness protection or something."

Gio looked skeptical. "Niko is chasing down every lead. Perhaps she is innocent and she's using an assumed name for some other reason. But you have to check on all of your accounts and anything special coming down the pipeline from your R&D department," he said.

Sergei gave up arguing and made the call to his accounting department, then his head of R&D. In the background, he could hear the other two men speaking in low voices.

"Hey, I'm not jaded. Just practical. Getting burned simply makes you realistic," Gio protested as Sergei made his call.

"You didn't get burned. You got torched, practically cremated," Calen chided him. He said something else, but Sergei blocked out the rest of the conversation, so he didn't hear it or Giancarlo's reply.

What the hell is going on? Where is Ada?

CHAPTER 9

*A*da breathed in a deep sigh of relief when she found the area around the swan boats deserted. The Boston Public Gardens was mostly empty due to the frigid wet weather. There had been a few stragglers in the Common, but out here by the water she got lucky. Hoping the key wasn't on one of the actual boats, she searched the tiny dock where the boats took off.

Checking to make sure there was no one watching, she went up to a green lockbox. Kneeling, she grabbed her tools and worked them into the lock.

She was a little rusty, but she hadn't lost all of her skills. The lock sprang open, and she quickly rifled through the contents. There was gear for the swan boats and their crew and a few odds and ends she didn't recognize. Carefully, she went over each item, searching for something that could be a key.

She'd almost given up and was about to start searching the boats when she felt something at the bottom of the box. A gap. Excited, she took out as many of the contents as she could, enough to pry back what she'd realized was a false bottom. Reaching underneath it, she caught hold of a manila envelope. Making sure there was nothing else, she hurriedly put back all the gear.

Ten minutes later, she ducked into a coffee shop, the envelope hidden underneath her coat. She ordered a hot chocolate and waited to get it before taking a seat in the back. Sighing heavily, she collapsed on an overstuffed armchair in a dark corner where she would be unobserved. Warming her hands on the mug of hot chocolate, she contemplated the envelope in silence.

How many times had she done this? She was losing count. It had been terrifying in the beginning. She'd had a relatively sheltered existence growing up. Her father had done his best to prepare her for the future, but his lessons had revolved around career preparation. He'd wanted her to follow in his footsteps, so her childhood had involved different engineering projects, math proofs, and statistics.

Her father had been a brilliant engineer with a formidable analytical mind. Some of her earliest memories weren't of him or their house. They were of robots, contraptions that he would build in the backyard shed for fun. For years, it had just been the two of them playing with toys, or at least it had seemed that way at the time.

Later she realized just how in depth her education had really gone. She had inherited her father's engineering talent and love of math. Her teachers had predicted great things for her. But she had lived in a bubble. Even starting college hadn't broken its fragile shell.

It wasn't till her dad and stepmom had died that she really felt the outside world. It had rushed in like the ocean's tide, sweeping her up in its violent wake. If it hadn't been for Geoffrey, she would have drowned.

Shaking off her melancholy mood, she opened the envelope. Inside was a key and a piece of paper with a series of numbers. Pen in hand, she pulled out a new copy of the Dharma Bums from her backpack. A simple google search had matched the Jack Kerouac quote from Geoffrey's email signature to that novel. Cracking open the spine, she got to work, using the book to decode the numbers using a simple replacement cipher. When she was done, there was an address to go with her key.

She used to get a rush when she got one of these. For a while, she had looked at it as an opportunity, a chance to lead a new exciting life. Now she was just...tired.

Geoffrey's opinion of the situation was probably spot on, but she couldn't help but wonder if this whole cloak and dagger business was still necessary. Maybe he was being paranoid. Sooner or later Karl would give up looking for her. Maybe he already had. She wanted to stop running, to be able to pick a place and stay there.

Eva would never admit it out loud, but she longed for a home. And for a long time, she'd actually believed the home she'd wanted was in Manhattan working at Damov Industries. Close to Sergei. Not one of her better decisions.

After finishing her hot chocolate, she wiped her mouth, letting the rough texture of the napkin linger on her lips. For a moment, she had a fleeting image of him from that night, Sergei's face above hers before he lowered his head to kiss her.

Forcibly pushing the memory away, she blinked as a rush of hot tears threatened. She was never going to see him again. Reminding herself that that was a good thing, she grabbed her stuff and headed out to the address Geoffrey had sent her.

Later that night, she burned her old IDs in an ashtray at the budget motel she was staying at. Adelinde Turner was gone. Hello Evelyn Alvarez, fresh IDs courtesy of Uncle Geoffrey's paper man. She'd found them at a bus depot locker in a small bag.

And there was something more this time. A short letter with a series of instructions on how to access a new type of digital currency called DaricDollars. It was something similar to Bitcoin, a crypto-currency used to buy all sorts of things—some legitimate, some not.

Geoffrey hadn't given her money since the beginning. They were both pretty sure Karl was having Geoffrey's funds monitored some-how. There was too much of a risk that Karl would be able to track her if her godfather sent her some of his own money. After she'd started earning enough to keep herself going, it hadn't mattered much. But there had been lean times. Very lean.

Fortunately, her last job, and the inordinately long time she'd stayed in it, had ensured that she had real money to start over. There was more than enough to last her quite some time if she watched her spending. The crypto-currency was an unexpected gift. The money was untraceable but also very volatile. Its value fluctuated wildly. She would have to think very carefully about how and when to spend it.

Still heavy-hearted, she got ready for bed. At least this time she could use her real name, or something close to it. Geoffrey had definitely noticed how upset she'd been when she'd told him she was finally going to move on. He must have sensed that she needed something real to hold onto this time.

Using the name Evelyn she would be able to go by Eva again. It wasn't much, but it was something. Now she just needed to decide where to go. Huddling under the thin hotel blanket, she decided that wherever she went, it was going to be someplace warm.

***

"EVERY DEPARTMENT HAS REPORTED IN. Nothing is missing. Not one cent. And as far as we can tell, Ada didn't access any privileged intellectual property outside of the research you specifically asked her for," Tim said.

Ada had been gone a full two weeks, and they were no closer to finding out where she had gone or why she had used a fake name.

"That doesn't mean she didn't use or copy the information she accessed legitimately somehow," Giancarlo pointed out from his position on the leather couch.

He was surrounded by piles of papers, reports, and ledgers from the different departments of Damov Industries. But because he was Gio, the piles were divided into neat square stacks organized along parallel lines around him. Calen had gone home to his new bride, but Gio had volunteered to stay behind and help Sergei with his internal audit.

Sergei thought that was above and beyond the duties of friendship, but Gio honestly loved that sort of thing. He was a paper pusher at heart, not a shark, despite his success at the helm of his family's bank. And the fact that he imagined a femme fatale had gotten her clutches into Sergei *and* his business had roused his protective instincts. Enough for him to stay on in Manhattan while Sergei tried to figure this mess out.

"She was not here to *steal anything,*" Tim argued, not for the first time.

He'd been defensive of Ada and emphatic about her innocence despite the suspicions aroused by her fake credentials. Feeling a tirade coming on, Sergei decided it was time Tim got back to work.

"Have each department double check. And go see if Michael is settling in properly," he said.

"Fine, but we all know why she really left. I don't blame her for making herself hard to find," the younger man muttered on his way out.

Gio sighed. "Has there been a lot of that?" he asked as Sergei collapsed deeper in his chair, face in his hands.

"From pretty much everyone who knew her," Sergei said in a disgusted tone, putting down his hands and leaning back to look up at the ceiling. "What happened in Rome has become public knowledge. Everyone blames me. Hell, I blame myself."

"I'm surprised you didn't fire him for spreading rumors. Even if they were true," Gio murmured.

There was a time when Gio would never have approved of firing someone for such a reason, but he'd hardened somewhat after the divorce. Especially when it came to protecting one's reputation.

"He wasn't the one who spread the story. It was a junior member of Niko's staff. It seems Tim wasn't the only one angry with me for seducing my assistant. But at least Tim knew enough to keep quiet about it, even if it was more to protect Ada's reputation than my own," Sergei said, rubbing his aching temples.

To his relief Gio simply nodded, this time refraining from launching into another lecture about Ada and her likely guilt. He didn't say anything about it, but Sergei knew he didn't approve of getting involved with a subordinate.

Gio's fastidious professionalism balked at the thought, but given Ada's falsified background, he was biased against *her* and not his friend. Convinced Sergei had been seduced by a corporate Mata Hari, he was scouring the records of every major account himself. He was also corresponding with his own computer security personnel from the Morgese bank, charging them to look for any viruses or worms that might be hidden in the computer banks.

"And are you seriously going to keep the replacement your mysterious executive assistant handpicked for you?" Gio asked.

That had been another of Ada's little surprises. They had agreed to find a third assistant to finally replace Edith, but she wasn't supposed to hire anyone without his approval. Instead, Michael Fisher had been at Ada's desk when he'd gotten back.

Michael had been under the impression Ada had left her position voluntarily because she was moving to Europe. He'd been hired through a headhunter, and his references were first rate. Niko had scoured his background with a fine tooth comb, and finding nothing wrong, Sergei had decided to keep him on. And because Ada was Ada, she had found him an excellent assistant. Not one as good as she was, but that would have been impossible.

"She found me the best replacement available. Tim can't function in that role. And Michael's jumped through all of Niko's hoops successfully, so yeah...I'm keeping him on."

A knock sounded, and the man in question entered. He was roughly Tim's age, and technically he had a lot more experience than Ada had claimed to have. In a few years' time, he might be half as good as she was.

"Sir, I got the promotional packet from Adstringo. They wanted to know if you were going to be available for the public offering."

"I'm sorry?" Sergei asked, leaning back in his seat, only half paying attention.

"The limited public offering for Adstringo is set for this coming Wednesday," Michael said.

"And I would care about that why?" he asked, training his full attention on his new executive assistant.

"Sergei, are you all right?" Gio asked, pausing to look up from all of his stacks.

He sounded really concerned.

"Of course I am. Why?" Sergei asked, completely confused.

"Because Adstringo just announced the most revolutionary data compression algorithm on the market. They're calling it the Tardis."

"So?" Sergei asked, rubbing the back of his neck in exasperation.

What the hell was Gio going on about? Why would he care about some bloody computer program right now?

"The Tardis, after the Doctor Who ship. You know...cause it's bigger on the inside?" Gio continued.

He was more of a science fiction geek than the rest of them.

"What the hell are you talking about?"

"It's been all over the news. The software is worth millions. Maybe hundreds of millions."

"And?"

"And you own it," Gio said deadpan, looking at Sergei like he'd gone crazy.

"Since when?"

CHAPTER 10

"It's all right here," Tim said, spreading the contracts over Sergei's desk. "You signed these on the 25th, her last day."

Grabbing the papers and reading the fine print, Sergei shook his head. What the hell was this about? He hadn't bought Adstringo. Except all the financial news media outlets said he had.

"This was supposed to be the Kesey memo I signed for legal. I had decided not to buy Adstringo. I was going for this small app developer instead. Ada tried to talk me out of it. She believed in Adstringo and lobbied hard for me to buy them instead," he said in disbelief.

"Apparently her faith was justified. Adstringo's final product will crush the competition. It can compress data ten times more efficiently than anything else out there. A Gigabyte of data can be compressed into a fraction of that, and it's completely lossless," Tim crowed. "Media companies are already vying for licensing deals."

Unbelievable.

Sergei threw down the contracts back on his desk and grabbed his letter opener. He was tempted to use it on himself.

"So, let me get this straight. Not only is there no sign this girl stole anything at all, but her one act of sabotage will actually net you hundreds of millions of dollars?" Gio asked incredulously.

Tim smiled. "It's brilliant. You're always going to wonder why," he said, a little too smugly. "By the way...I was briefing Michael on some of his new duties and he mentioned something Ada told him over the phone."

"What did she say?" Sergei asked apprehensively, alerted by the glee in Tim's voice.

"She said she was looking for a replacement for *herself* because her partner was being transferred. She never mentioned filling Edith's position at all."

Sergei's stillness was explosive. He seized on the personal information.

What partner?

There had been no one in Ada's life. There had been no emails in her corporate account to suggest a boyfriend, and she had never made any personal calls at all. Not even to family. When he'd asked, she'd said her family was all gone.

"That's what she told him when she followed up with him to tell him he got the job. Which, incidentally, was a week before we went to Rome. After we got back, she simply moved up his start date through the headhunter. Apparently, she had always planned on leaving," Tim finished, a little more soberly.

It was hard to miss the twin notes of longing and hurt in his tone. He and Ada had been friends, and she had left him without a word, too.

Aware that Gio was studying him closely, Sergei dismissed his assistant. "You can leave us now."

His tone was acid despite his attempt to sympathize with the younger man.

Gio waited until Tim was gone before continuing. "How long do you think she was planning it?" he asked, ignoring the issue of the supposed 'partner' for the time being.

Sergei shrugged helplessly. "I don't know anymore. At first I thought that she decided to leave once she got back from Rome."

He felt a disquieting sensation, like the room was spinning around him, but it was just in his head.

"You mean once she realized once and for all that you were rejecting her." Gio's voice was soft.

"I was doing what was best for her," he said, aware of how stupid it sounded out loud.

"From what you said there's no way she could have known that. There's also no way she could have known that if she'd stuck it out a little longer you would have completely broken down and begged for forgiveness," Gio added perceptively.

Sergei closed his eyes, the rush of emotion was so strong. "She would never have forgiven me. I was a complete asshole." He humphed in a derisive laugh. "Not that she didn't find a way to turn that around on me."

"How do you mean?"

"I think that's how she got me to sign the contracts."

He explained about using Fiona to distance himself, how he'd rubbed the relationship with the other woman in Ada's face. Even if he had never intended for it to literally be *in* her face. Gio whistled when he got to the part where Ada used his guilt and discomfort against him to buy the company he'd initially rejected.

Taking off his glasses, Gio leaned back into the leather couch, cleaning the lenses as he reflected. "I don't pretend to know anything about this girl's motivations. God knows I don't have a good track record in that department, but based on all the evidence, I think I get it," he said eventually, putting the glasses back on.

"What do you get?" Sergei asked.

"I get why you're in love with her. Find her," he said, standing up. "And then get ready to grovel for forgiveness. And let's hope there really isn't a partner," he added before heading for the door.

"Where are you going?" Sergei asked.

"Since it doesn't look like there's any fraud here for me to find, I'm going home," Gio replied. "I've been away from the bank long enough. But keep me posted. And if there's anything else I can do, let me know."

Sergei nodded and stood to walk him out. "I can't thank you enough for staying. You really didn't have to."

"You were there for me when my marriage imploded. It's the least I can do," Gio said wryly. "And look on the bright side. There's absolutely no way this could end as badly as that."

Watching his friend walk away, Sergei fervently hoped that was true.

———

HEAT COURSING THROUGH HER VEINS, Eva gasped loudly as she woke up. The room around her was pitch black, but even with the light on there would have been little to see.

She was lying on her small narrow bed, the sheets twisted around her, her heartbeat pounding in her ears. Shakily, she covered her face with her hands.

The dream had been so real. She could still feel his hands on her, moving over her body. The space between her legs was wet, and she was covered in sweat.

Getting up, she went to the tiny kitchenette to pour herself a glass of water. Hands shaking, she drank it quickly, nearly dropping it in the process. Putting it down, she blinked rapidly, but it didn't help. The tears still came, no matter how hard she fought against them. She sank down to the floor, sitting down against the cabinet doors.

It was getting worse. Shouldn't the memories be fading by now? It had been two months for fuck's sake, Eva thought, scrubbing the tears away with her sleeve.

Instead, the dreams were getting more and more intense as time went on. It was like he was in the room with her. She could practically hear his voice. Disgusted with herself, Eva wanted to peel her skin off until the phantom touch was completely gone. She would settle for punching Sergei in the face, beating him till he wasn't pretty anymore.

Maybe she should go out to a bar and pick up a guy. Any guy would do. Some meaningless, anonymous sex might wipe those memories away.

Given how much alcohol she'd had that night, she was surprised she had any memories at all. Instead, she remembered everything with a surreal edge, an alcohol-fueled intensity that stayed with her even when she was awake.

Picking herself up off the floor, Eva went back to the tiny bathroom. For a moment, she stared at her altered reflection. Gone was the mousy brown hair. In its place was a brilliant, hot pink bob. It was still a far cry from her natural blonde, but it comforted her to see it. Though the brown had been as temporary as this new pink hair color, it still felt as if she was closer to being herself. A fake stud decorated her nose. It was held there by a magnet since a piercing was too permanent.

If she needed to make a quick change in her appearance, temporary disguises worked best. The hair color was a rinse, easy to wash out with some persistent shampooing.

Forgetting her hair, she gave herself a stern talking to. There wouldn't be a guy tonight or any other night. It wasn't safe. She couldn't afford to let her guard down like that. The only reason she was still alive was because she always played it safe and took precautions.

If she even suspected she had been recognized, she moved on immediately. She didn't buy anything that required a credit history, and used a Post Office Box as a mailing address. A night out drinking with friends she didn't have wasn't in the cards. And a night of anonymous sex wasn't any more likely.

Not that she really wanted that. It was just the anger talking. After splashing her face with cold water, she braced her hands on the counter, mindlessly watching the water drain away.

Seized by a sudden realization, she tensed. A mental image of what was sitting underneath the sink, flashed in her head like a neon light. She grabbed the box of unused tampons in denial, but it didn't change the fact that the box was still sealed and untouched despite the fact it was the one she'd thrown in the bug out bag she'd packed in Manhattan.

Oh, crap.

The next day, she was back sitting on the floor, flooded with anxiety and more than a little bit of anger. But this time it was for a much better reason. There on the floor beside her were not one, but two used pregnancy tests.

Both were positive.

CHAPTER 11

"This is the best lead we have now," Niko said in Russian.

He always spoke Russian these days when Tim was in the room, regardless of whether or not he was sharing sensitive information about his investigation into Ada's background. The younger man had calmed considerably since the days following her abrupt departure, but he tended to fly off the handle whenever he thought anyone was maligning her.

Tim didn't need to bother with the dramatics. Their initial conclusion that Ada hadn't harmed the company in some way still stood. Her only act of sabotage had led to the acquisition of a highly profitable company. Damov Industries was in the press a lot these days as the public discovered the new software. It was the most buzz his company had ever gotten, its value skyrocketing. And it was all because of Ada.

Sergei looked over the report on her references. None had been genuine, but the two most recent were associated with shell companies that had recently shuttered. The agency who'd initially hired her told them the two most recent were the only ones they had checked. He'd been assured by the head of that agency that at the time he'd been able to verify those references.

Someone had answered when they called the contact number. A member of their staff recalled talking to a man with a foreign accent, either British or Australian. All of their attempts to track down the mystery man had failed so far.

But the fake resume had yielded one surprising result from a three-year-old reference to a defunct small town newspaper. The paper's old contact numbers didn't work, but after some persistence on Niko's part, he tracked down the former editor in chief. The crusty older man was enjoying retirement in Florida, but when he heard who was calling and why, he got in touch. It wasn't every day the head of multi-billion dollar company—one currently in the news—came calling. Sergei talked to the man himself, although it wasn't a promising lead.

"No, I'm sorry. I don't know an Ada Turner," the editor had said, coughing into the phone.

His gravel voice attested to years of heavy smoking.

Sergei's hopes sank. The paper had been obscure, small enough to be a real lead. It had never had a nationwide distribution and no online presence so Ada had to have known it personally to have listed it as a reference. But maybe she had just passed through the town and had picked it up by chance.

"No, sorry, must have misheard your man," the old man said after his coughing fit. "I thought he said Ava. Had a girl working here by that name a year and a half ago."

Tensing slightly, Sergei asked, "What did this girl look like?"

"Oh, she was pretty. Had light brown hair and blue eyes. Real blue, too, almost purple in some lights. Like the color Liz Taylor had. Smart as a whip. Used her as a stringer for a few months, but then she moved on. Shame. I offered her a promotion to permanent staff, but she was probably smart to turn me down. Had to close the doors six months ago. She probably writes a blog somewhere now."

Thrills of recognition coursed up and down Sergei's body. It was her. Ada had been working under another name.

It made sense in a way. She had padded her resume with bits of truth. It had probably been easier than fabricating everything. The time and name were different, but the job had been real.

"Ava you say? I think that I'm looking for the same girl," he said slowly. "She may have changed her name for legal reasons, but the description fits."

"Really?" the old man sounded intrigued. "Is there a story there?"

"Probably not. Besides, aren't you retired?" Sergei asked with a frown.

He didn't want to call a reporter's attention to Ada when he still knew so little about her.

"These days, a newspaperman doesn't retire. He goes online-only."

"Be that as it may, if you come across her old resume or any other information about her, I would prefer you came to me with it instead of updating your blog with this little mystery. I can make it worth your while."

The old man paused for a while. "Hmm. If there's a resume, it would be in my garage. I don't throw anything out. If I find it, would it be worth an interview?"

"Not with me, not right now. But the developers of Adstringo are in demand at the moment. Would that suffice?"

"That works for me. Unless something juicy comes into my hands. If it does, perhaps you'll reconsider the personal interview?"

Smiling at the older man's persistence, Sergei promised to consider it. The next day, he and Niko had received a copy of Ava Wallace's CV. Like the other already in their possession, the most recent references were fake. But one wasn't.

Another position, this time for a librarian, was found under another name. By tracing back those fake references they had found a string of odd jobs their Ada had done under an assortment of aliases.

If they were right, Ada had been a scuba instructor, a sous chef, a hairstylist, and a mechanic's assistant.

After questioning all of her former employers they found that she had been a valuable asset in all those jobs. She had modernized the garage's bookkeeping system and had even learned to do oil changes under the chief mechanic's supervision. At the restaurant she had designed a program that enabled them to keep track of their purchasing more efficiently. The salon where she had cut hair raved about her. Every place they had contacted had been sorry to lose her.

But Ada had never stayed more than a few months in any of those places. Her longest period of employment had been when she worked for him. She had stayed almost three times longer as his assistant than at any other job. He often wondered why, when she had clearly been planning on leaving from the start.

Bringing himself back to the present, he read through Niko's report.

"What am I looking at?" he asked, signaling Tim to leave them.

Tim did so reluctantly, aware he was being excluded.

"It's a copy of the contract opening Felton Enterprises, one of the shell corporations she used as a reference. It was a devil to track down, but I got ahold of it. The signature is fake, as is the founder Simon Felton, but there were clues. The forensic accountants have been at it for weeks, but they think they've finally traced back the company to a real person. A man called Geoffrey Johansson."

"Who is he?"

"A retired white-collar criminal," Niko said.

Sitting up at attention, Sergei gestured him to go on.

"He made a name for himself in the seventies as a commodities trader. A French Canadian educated in the UK. In the late eighties, he was indicted for insider trading and embezzling. He served six years before getting out on parole, after which he promptly disappeared. Rumors placed him all over the place after that. Morocco, the Middle East, South Africa, and Europe. But according to the latest, he's been living abroad somewhere in the Caribbean for the last few years."

"So what age is he exactly?" Sergei asked.

He'd been concerned when he'd heard a man's name. The possibility of another man in Ada's life—one who might know the truth about her—filled him with anger. But this man was probably too old to be a rival.

"Almost seventy," Niko said, and Sergei relaxed. "And from what we can tell, he's behind both shell corporations listed as Ada's references."

"Which means he knows her." The realization twisted his guts. It was a real lead, a way to find her. "Can you get me a meeting?"

"I can try, but if I might suggest another approach, I think you need to surprise this guy. Show up and don't give him time to disappear. Something deep is going on. There are too many identities, too much effort to hide the truth of who Ada is."

Nodding slowly, Sergei agreed. "Yes. You're right. Something else is going on. Something serious. Confirm his location, and when you do, get me there. Don't file a flight plan under my name. Take a page out of his playbook and use a pseudonym."

Niko followed his instructions to the letter with his usual terrifying efficiency. The next day, Sergei was on a chartered boat headed to a small island in the Caribbean.

According to their research, Geoffrey Johansson had lived there quietly, but sumptuously, for the last few years. He had paid the local law enforcement handsomely for the privacy he enjoyed in this out-of-the-way place, but the substantial bribe Sergei had made through Niko ensured that his quarry had no idea he was coming.

Within the hour, he was standing in a shaded salon of a large sprawling hacienda built behind high shielding walls. His unsuspecting host was informed of his presence by one of several servants moving unobtrusively through the mansion via an internal intercom system.

Sergei wanted to smile at their reaction, the surprise betrayed by their hurried movements. Apparently Geoffrey Johansen didn't get many guests. But he didn't smile. He couldn't. Johansen knew Ada, and Sergei wouldn't leave this place until he told him where to find her.

Eventually, the curved mahogany double doors opened to reveal a short but elegantly dressed man in his early seventies. His tan contrasted with a head full of snowy white hair and a matching beard. If he put on an additional twenty or thirty pounds, he would have borne a remarkable resemblance to Richard Attenborough.

Geoffrey gave Sergei a curious welcoming smile with an air of affected surprise, but there was a betraying tightness around his eyes and mouth.

Sergei had no doubt that this man knew exactly why he was there. But every carefully constructed argument—all the persuasive reasoning he was going to use to convince Johansen to tell him where Ada was—flew out the window as soon as he saw him.

"Where is she?"

CHAPTER 12

There was a betraying pause, a hesitation in his step, as Johansen made his way toward him. The smile didn't slip however as he affected an air of polite confusion.

"I'm sorry. I was just informed I had a guest. Quite an illustrious one at that. I was just watching the financial news and your name was all over the broadcast. But I don't understand. Where is she *who?*"

Geoffrey Johansen was an accomplished liar, Sergei decided. He looked and sounded completely genuine. It was easy to see how he had managed to become such a successful corporate con man.

Sergei stared down at his nemesis, too angry and frustrated to calm down. "Where is Ada? Or Ava or Eve or Lina or whatever the hell you call her. I need to find her."

Eyeing him without appearing worried, Johansen made his way to another door at the far end of the salon. Sergei made an effort to control himself, but the air filled with tension.

Johansen ignored it like the professional he was. He led Sergei to a wood-paneled office and sat behind a massive mahogany desk. "Why don't you tell me more about who you're looking for, and maybe I can help you find them," he said affably with a warm paternal air of polite condescension.

He sounded like a favorite uncle trying to talk a crazy person down from a ledge. It had the exact opposite effect.

"Don't even try. I know you set up those shell companies that appeared on her resume. Kudos on the elaborate set up for just a CV by the way. But I know you know her now, which means—" Sergei paused to brace his hands on the desk opposite Johansen. "—that I'm not leaving until you tell me where I can find her."

For a long minute, neither of them moved. When Johansen didn't say anything, Sergei sat down in the chair in front of the desk, trying his hardest to give the impression of an unmovable mountain. The two men stared at each other in silence. But Geoffrey Johansen was a career criminal and one of those didn't give up when someone tried to call his bluff.

Johansen smiled and sat back in his leather armchair. "I really wish I knew what you were talking about, because I would love to help you out," he said, oozing sincerity while simultaneously appearing concerned for his ranting guest.

If the subject had been anything but Ada, Sergei's ability to read his opponents character would have been severely tested. But this wasn't a boardroom, and Johansen's charm only hardened his resolve.

Sergei glared at the friendly looking old man, frowning ferociously. It had been months since he'd seen Ada, and this guy was the only thing standing between them. That and the fact that she probably despised him. He needed to find her to make things right between them. He needed her with him. Period.

"What is she to you? Is she your daughter? Granddaughter? Niece? Why are you helping her? What is she hiding from?" Sergei's hands were opening and closing reflexively. When Johansen simply looked confused, he continued. "Did she tell you how she tricked me into buying Adstringo? How she reprogrammed the office spam filters when Tim downloaded a virus and the entire office got porn-stormed? How she fixed the break room microwave? I mean, who does that? You just throw them out and get a new one. Who fixes a microwave?"

Sergei shook his head helplessly. He missed Ada so much it hurt. It must have shown on his face, because Johansen was looking at him with a softer sympathetic expression that might actually be genuine.

"How well do you even know her? She doesn't look like you. Is that because you're not blood-related? Aren't you worried about her? Is she on the run from the law? Did she get in over her head with something and it got away from her? Was it because of one of your schemes?"

Johansen continued to stare at him, templing his hands under his chin.

Sergei sighed. "Did you even know that she needs glasses? Real ones? It's how I figured out that that unreal blue is her real eye color and not contact lenses. She kept squinting when trying to read things from across the room so I called in an oculist to come in during lunch. Even he couldn't believe she wasn't wearing contacts at first..."

There was still no reaction, but Sergei could sense the other man wavering under the pressure of his honest desperation. Normally he would have eaten his own shoe before baring his soul like he was, but instinct told him it was the only way to get Geoffrey Johansen's help.

"I should have known then that something was up. She was wearing glasses already but couldn't see. They were fakes, but I believed her when she said her prescription must have changed a lot. Said it was from too many hours squinting at computer screens."

Johansen stayed resolutely silent so Sergei continued. "She hums nonsense when she's working. And she can't sing to save her life. She couldn't carry a tune if you paid her. Really she's just *awful*. Niko won't let her sing in the car when she rides up front with him because she ruins the songs."

Johansen didn't bother to ask who Niko was, apparently abandoning the pretense of not knowing what he was talking about. Sergei looked away, thinking about all of the things he missed about Ada.

"When she's eating something she really likes, she closes her eyes and sways from side to side. Not a lot, just a little, and only if she thinks no one is around to watch. And she gets clumsy when she's tired. Tends to drop her pen a lot. Drops her tablet, too—which she jailbroke in the first five minutes of having it. And she debugged a prototype cellular phone from one of our Asian subsidiaries in under two hours."

There was a hint of a smile on Johansen's face now. "Where did she learn to do stuff like that? Is she Batman's illegitimate child? What is her real name?" Sergei whispered the last question, his chest tight.

Johansen smiled sadly but didn't say anything.

"Why can't she be here with you? Don't you miss her?" Sergei was ashamed that his voice cracked a little on the last question, but it finally did the trick.

Geoffrey sighed expansively before relenting. "I do miss her. Every day," he said quietly, rubbing his chin.

He picked up a letter opener in the shape of a miniature sword from the surface of the desk and began toying with it.

Sergei sat up. "Tell me where she is."

"I can't...because I don't know. It's how we set things up."

"Why? What is she hiding from?"

Geoffrey stopped playing with the letter opener to meet his eyes.

"Someone a lot worse than you," he said.

TWO DAYS LATER, despite his earlier resolution, Sergei left Geoffrey Johansen's little island hideaway with no knowledge of Ada's whereabouts.

The older man had convinced him that he truly did not know her whereabouts or what name she was currently using regardless of Sergei's alternating threats, bribes, and pleas. They had talked in circles for hours but to no avail.

Aside from acknowledging that he helped her establish different identities, and that those identities were necessary to protect her, Geoffrey had revealed very little. Sergei hadn't even been able to convince him to get in touch with him if Ada contacted him again.

But Sergei wouldn't let that stop him. He was more determined than ever to find her, especially now that his worst fears had been confirmed.

His anxiety for Ada had tripled after meeting Geoffrey, who refused to disclose the true nature of the threat to her, or even her real name and background. Geoffrey had been vague about his connection to her, except to say that he loved her and was trying to protect her from someone very dangerous.

"If you care about her at all then don't try to find her," Geoffrey had said.

"Why not? Who else is looking for her? Who are you trying to protect her from?" he had asked repeatedly, but he hadn't gotten an answer.

He got the warning and nothing else. His best efforts hadn't been able to crack the wily old con man. Eventually, the sense of urgency to be actively looking for Ada got the better of him, and he decided to leave.

He had to find her before whatever trouble she was running from caught up with her.

Eva gave one last heave before crumpling next to the toilet like a marionette whose strings had been cut. She was a little over three months pregnant, and it had been hell since week six.

She'd had to give up the retail job she'd been at for only a few weeks because of the severe morning sickness, which ironically got worse in the early afternoon and continued well into the evening.

Rising on shaky legs, she rinsed out her mouth and went to sit on her bed. Leaning against the headboard, she hugged a pillow to her stomach, which was already noticeably swelling into a distinct baby bump. It was a little early to start showing for a first pregnancy. She'd hoped to be able to hide her condition for a while longer, but it seemed nature had other plans. On her slight frame, the nascent bump stood out like a neon sign advertising her condition.

She tried to hide it by wearing baggy clothes, but she didn't have many. Most of her clothes were form-fitting, leftovers from her office persona, but until they stopped fastening around her belly, she was going to have to wear them. She was watching her spending very carefully and had even taken the step of finding some local restaurants and cafes that accepted the digital currency Uncle Geoffrey had given her so she could save her actual cash. But money was still a constant concern, especially now that she'd had to stop working.

Her funds would see her through the next few months, but worry about baby-related expenses kept her up at night. She'd started visiting free clinics for prenatal care, but not having a regular doctor oversee her pregnancy made her anxious. Especially given the daily bouts of severe nausea and vomiting that made each day a trial.

The nurse at the free clinic had tried to cheer her up by telling her the Duchess of Cambridge had experienced the same condition before giving birth to the newest heir to the throne. But it had been cold comfort when she'd been forced to curtail all of her daily activities because of the frequent illness.

When Eva thought about the cost of delivering a baby in the states, she broke into a cold sweat. There was no way her little nest egg would withstand it unless she walked into an emergency room after going into labor. Having her baby delivered by an overworked attending intern at an ER was not ideal, but she didn't have a lot of choice in the matter.

Rolling onto her side, she let a few tears squeeze out before forcing them to stop. She wasn't the first unwed single mother in difficult circumstances. And she certainly wasn't the only one without a support system to rely on. However, her current friendless state, coupled with the raging hormones flooding her body, made pregnancy seem more like a Greek tragedy than a beautiful blessing.

But she wasn't entirely friendless. There was still Uncle Geoffrey. She hadn't contacted him since discovering she was pregnant. Squeezing the pillow to her chest, Eva admitted that it was because she was ashamed of herself.

When she had first left home, they had talked at length about the mindset she would have to adopt while living on the run. He'd warned her it would require both discipline and constant self-sacrifice, and that the urge to befriend someone and confide her secrets would be overwhelming at some point. She had promised him she would do everything she could to protect herself, including maintaining a distance to any coworkers or neighbors. The thought of disappointing him so spectacularly had been more than she could handle.

Also, telling him she was pregnant would make the whole thing real and irrevocable. Eva was going to have to confess everything to him. There was no way around it now.

It was possible that her condition would worsen and she wouldn't be able to take care of herself. She needed to formulate a plan. Geoffrey would help her come up with one. Once he'd gotten over the shock that is. Then she would have a course of action, something to hold onto. Having a plan would do a lot to ease her fears.

Breathing in a shaky breath, she got up in search of her latest burner phone. A few minutes later, she'd messaged the encrypted email account Geoffrey had established for their communication. He changed it every time she changed identities to be safe. Her message asked him to call, a step which would probably alarm him since they rarely talked, but she needed to hear his voice.

An hour later, she received instructions for making a secure phone call. The next day, she caught a bus across the nearby border to Mexico and made the call from a public pay phone in a busy open air market.

"Angel, are you okay?"

Geoffrey's worried voice reached out of the phone. Her chest was tight, and she could barely choke out a response.

"Hi," she said hoarsely.

"What's wrong?"

"I messed up. Not about being found. It's something else."

"What is it? I'm terrified over here."

His concern floated over the line, making her feel better and worse at the same time.

"I'm...I'm pregnant."

There was a moment of silence before Geoffrey recovered. "Sergei Damov is the father, isn't he?"

Shocked, Eva froze. That was the last thing she'd expected him to say. Tim was the only man she'd mentioned by name during her time in New York. She had studiously avoided mentioning Sergei in her few emails to her godfather...but apparently he had read between the lines.

"How did you know?" she asked a little breathlessly, holding onto the phone booth to steady herself.

"A lucky guess."

"Oh."

"Are you going to tell him?"

"*What? No!*" Ada's heart raced at the mere suggestion.

Geoffrey sighed across the line, but he was still sympathetic when he asked, "Are you sure that's the best thing? Having a baby while living on the run is going to be next to impossible."

Tearing up, Eva swallowed convulsively.

"Honey, are you okay?"

"Yes," she whispered as the first tears fell. She scrubbed them away with the sleeve of her hoodie. "And it's not impossible. Just difficult. I was hoping we could brainstorm."

"Don't worry about that now. I'll think on things and get back to you with a plan," Geoffrey assured her.

Even though she had expected no less from him, the relief that coursed through her when he said that was so sharp she swayed where she stood. A weathered old woman selling fruit next to the phone booth smiled at her. Eying the baby bump, she brought over an empty crate and gestured for Eva to sit down on it. Gratefully accepting, she sat down amidst the hustle and bustle of the market, clinging to the earpiece a little too tightly.

Geoffrey waited until the exchange was over before asking, "Are you sure you are okay?"

Taking a deep breath, she answered honestly. "Well...I've been having a hard time."

Her voice sounded thin and weak, even to her.

"What's wrong? Is the baby okay?" Geoffrey asked, sounding alarmed.

"Yes, so far. But apparently I have the same morning sickness disease that Princess Kate had."

"Err. Is that bad?"

"You have no idea. I had gotten a job at a shop, but I couldn't stay on my feet all day, so I had to stop working. And I can't keep anything down. I'm supposed to be eating for two and I can't eat a damn thing. Pregnancy is stupid. Just when you're supposed to eat the most you get this horrendous morning sickness which incidentally never happens in the morning and lasts most of the day." Eva sighed, exhausted. "I've started drinking those Ensure shakes they give old people in the hospital because I was losing too much weight. And I haven't been sleeping much, but that at least will change soon. I could drop off right now."

She didn't mention that it was her anxiety and fear keeping her awake.

"Oh...that is bad."

Geoffrey sounded as overwhelmed as she felt, which made sense given the crap ton of shit she'd just unloaded on him.

"Yeah, I know. So your plan shouldn't include me working nonstop till the baby comes like mine used to," she said wryly.

Geoffrey made a soothing clucking sound. "Don't worry. I have the start of an idea. Give me a few days, and I'll send you details. And send me your ideas, too. Together we'll figure something out. Everything will be okay. And I get to be an honorary grandfather!"

He sounded genuinely cheerful at the prospect.

"Yeah, you do. Silver lining." Eva drew her sweatshirt closer around her. The sun was going down, and she was chilly.

"Is it safe where you are?" he asked.

"Not exactly," she answered truthfully. "But it's busy and easy to get lost."

"That will have to do," he said.

"For what?"

"Later. For now, go home and take a warm bath. I need to make some calls. I love you, angel."

"I love you, too," Eva said, smiling sadly before she hung up.

She returned the crate, thanking the old woman using her rusty Spanish before walking back to the bus stop, huddling in her too thin hoodie as the temperature dropped and night fell.

Geoffrey Johansen paced up and down his office lost in thought. He'd been arguing with himself for so long he was starting to wear a hole in the Persian carpet.

His angel sounded so dejected, and from the sound of things, she was in real trouble. He couldn't stop thinking about the potential disaster this could turn into if Karl found Eva in her vulnerable condition.

That's it. His mind made up, he looked for the phone number that he'd been forced to take amidst simultaneous pleas and threats.

Despite the Russian's heavy-handedness, Geoffrey recognized the signs of a man desperately in love. Sergei's confession of everything that had gone down, how he had pushed Eva away with another woman, had actually done a lot to convince him that he was truly regretful.

Geoffrey was fairly certain Sergei would do anything to make it up to his angel. With his resources and small army of bodyguards, not to mention his ingrained Russian secretiveness, there was a good chance he could actually protect her. And Karl knew nothing about the man or his connection to Eva.

He picked up the phone and dialed the number. "Sergei, it's Geoffrey. She called...she needs help."

A week later, Eva was picking her way through the busy Mercado Hidalgo in Tijuana, Mexico. She was so excited, she could almost forget the bad bout of nausea she'd been battling all day. Ignoring the lightheaded feeling that came from not eating enough, she crossed the parking lot while nibbling on a few almonds.

In a few moments, she was going to see her Uncle Geoffrey for the first time in years. Predictably, she was already crying. But tears were frequent now, so she just wiped them with her sleeve distractedly. Worried that it would get as cold as last time, she was wearing her wool coat, despite the fact that it was cut in such a way that it actually accentuated her expanding belly.

Picking her way around a fruit stall, she entered the corner taco shop Geoffrey had chosen for their meeting. She scanned the dim interior for a familiar face, but when she didn't see a head full of white hair, she turned to check outside. She was almost there when her path was blocked by a familiar man-shaped mountain dressed in his habitual black.

"Niko?" she gasped as she took in the forbidding Russian's unsmiling face. *Oh God.*

If Niko was here, then that meant...

Noticing Niko was looking over her head, she spun in a slow half-circle. She tried to focus on the suited man in front of her, but her vision swam in and out of focus before swiftly going dark.

Dropping her pack, she felt herself fall forward in slow motion before being caught and swung up into a familiar embrace. The last thing she remembered before slipping away was Sergei's face looming above hers.

He looked *furious*.

CHAPTER 13

S ergei could feel his grasp on reality slipping away as the object of his insane pursuit took one look at him and passed out cold. He lifted Ada up reflexively, holding her tightly to him. The cooks behind the counter of the taco shop came over and fussed over the unconscious woman in his arms until Niko waved them away.

He hurried to the waiting car. Kidnapping hadn't been his preferred way of dealing with his runaway PA. He had planned on reasoning with her—explaining himself and confessing his love.

Settling her gently in the seat across from him, Sergei sat back as the driver took them to the local private airfield.

With his pulse pounding in his head, he stared at Ada's still form until he was sure her chest was moving up and down. Relaxing slightly, he sank back into the seat. She was breathing. Her hair was pink, but she was breathing.

She was also visibly pregnant. And she hadn't called him for help. She had called Geoffrey. He must know. That had to be the reason he had gotten in touch with Sergei and told him where Ada was going to be.

He tried to be angry at Geoffrey for not warning him about the pregnancy, but he was too grateful to the old man for giving up Ada's location.

From the shock and surprise on her face, it was obvious she'd had no idea that he was going to be there. She had been expecting Geoffrey. At least she had reached out for help to someone. But he was still angry that it hadn't been him. Even if that wasn't totally rational given what he had done.

Impulsively, Sergei dropped to his knees in front of her and reached out tentatively. His large hand settled on the swell of Ada's stomach. It had to be his. If she was already showing, then the timing was right. At least he thought it was.

When did women start looking pregnant?

He kept his hand on her stomach, but the baby didn't move or kick so he sat back in his seat. Buzzing the front seat, he quietly instructed Niko to get an obstetrician to meet them when they landed.

"Already on it. I've also taken the liberty of ordering some medical equipment, including a sonogram machine. And I've instructed your personal shopper to send an assortment of maternity clothes. She's not going to fit into her own things for much longer," Niko answered in an equally low tone. "We'll be at the airfield in a few minutes."

"Okay good."

As usual, his chief of security was two steps ahead of him. A half hour later, they were on his jet on their way to Alex's Greek island home. His friend had volunteered it during a conference call he'd made to his oldest friends right after Geoffrey had called him. He had filled them in on the latest news, and they had collectively decided that it was the best place for them until the threat to Ada had been identified and neutralized.

The location was remote with only a small village on the beach side. The entire island was so small that no stranger could appear without the entire population being aware of it.

The palazzo Alex had built for his bride was large enough to house a whole squadron of security personal, and it was already outfitted with the latest security enhancements. Alex didn't take any chances with his wife and young son's safety, so he'd subtly turned the place into a fortress—one so luxurious and relaxing that his wife hadn't noticed it was effectively a miniature citadel. It was the ideal hiding place for them.

At first Sergei had been relieved that Ada had slept through the transfer to the plane, but the longer she slept, the more he worried that she had been unconscious too long.

"She's just sleeping," Niko said, bending over Ada.

She was lying in the bed of the plane's private back bedroom, so pale and still against the dark blue sheets.

"Are you sure?" Sergei said.

He hadn't been able to stop pacing in front of the bed until Niko had made him move so he could examine Ada.

"Look at the circles under her eyes. She hasn't been sleeping. And despite the pregnancy, I think she's lost weight."

It was said in a matter of fact tone, but Sergei still felt a rush of fear and anger. It was true. Ada was much thinner despite the belly. Her cheekbones were more sharply defined, and she looked as though she hadn't slept in days. God only knew what she had been going through without him. And she would still be facing it alone if Geoffrey hadn't called him.

Tamping down the emotion, he sent Niko away and stretched out his legs on the bed next to his angel. He stayed awake for as long as he could, but the sleepless nights of worry and planning caught up with him, and he dropped off to sleep sitting up.

———

HOURS LATER, a knock on the bedroom door woke him. He opened his eyes to find the spot next to him empty. Scanning the room, he saw Ada sitting on the floor in the corner opposite him, her arms wrapped around her knees.

She was watching him warily, her big blue eyes filled with suspicion and distrust.

"What is it?" he asked in Russian, knowing only Niko would disturb them.

"We're making a final approach to the Athens airport. There will be a helicopter waiting for the final leg to the island," Niko replied from the other side of the door.

"Okay thanks," he answered, not taking his eyes off of Ada.

She didn't say anything as he heard Niko walk away. For a long time, the only sound was the hum of the engine as they continued to stare at each other.

"Why didn't you call me when you found out you were pregnant?" he asked accusingly.

Shit. He hadn't intended to lead with that. As usual, he couldn't maintain a level head around her.

Ada's eyes narrowed, and her lips set in a firm line. "Why the hell would I do that?"

His heart sank. Inhaling deeply, Sergei got ahold of himself. Ada was trying to throw him. She was still angry with him. He deserved her worst. But they were expecting a baby now, and that meant she was going to have to find a way to forgive him. And he was going to have to control his temper.

He shook his head. "I know that baby is mine. You were a virgin that night, and I know you well enough to be sure that you would not jump in bed with someone else right after," he said as calmly as he could.

"Are you sure about that?" Ada asked softly, her voice colder than he'd ever heard it.

He wasn't, but he refused to let his doubt show. "Yes, I am. I also know that Geoffrey Johansen would never have told me where to find you if that baby wasn't mine."

Hurt flashed across Ada's face before she could stop it. She turned pale, her complexion going milky white as her eyes filled with tears. The realization that the only person she trusted had given her up broke down her already weakened defenses. Alarmed, he stood up and pulled her onto the bed.

"It's okay," he soothed, rubbing his hands up and down her back as she curled into a ball, her back to him. "It's going to be okay. Geoffrey didn't betray you. Not that way. But he was really worried about you. And he knows you are safer with me."

Ada tensed under his hands, and he continued on in a rush.

"It may not seem like that right now, but you are. I did everything wrong, and there's a lot of things I need to tell you, but we need to come to an agreement. We need to do what is best for the baby. Right now that means letting me take care of both of you. Geoffrey knows that. It's why he told me where to find you. He's a good judge of character."

Ada hiccuped, wiping the tears away with a little motion with the blanket. "You saw him?"

"A few weeks ago. He's...an interesting man. He wouldn't tell me where you were at first, but he called a few days ago to tell me where to find you. And we both know why."

Ada didn't say anything. She wouldn't even look at him.

"We're landing in Athens, and then we're going to my friend Alex's place," he continued. "He has a big house on a private island just off the coast. You'll be safe there."

That got her attention. She turned to look at him. "How much did Geoffrey tell you?"

Not nearly enough.

"Enough," he lied.

"Really? Then what's my real name?" she challenged. When he stayed silent she responded quietly, "Yeah. That's what I thought."

CHAPTER 14

Sergei was pacing up and down the hallway outside the master bedroom of Alex's fortress. The place was perfect for their needs with one glaring exception. There was no hospital nearby.

Ada had gotten sick twice on the helicopter ride from the mainland. She'd eaten precious little before they'd gotten off the plane, despite the fact he'd had a large selection of breakfast items delivered to them on the tarmac. Unfortunately, Ada had reacted badly to the smell of bacon, and he'd had to send most of the food away so she wouldn't be sick. Instead, she'd nibbled on a croissant and had a little juice to wash it down. But it didn't stay down long.

It was no longer a mystery why she was so thin and pale. He shuddered at the memory of her tiny little body heaving into an airsickness bag during the helicopter flight. She'd been so weak afterward that she hadn't objected when he'd carried her in his arms into the house.

Fortunately, the obstetrician he'd ordered had been waiting for them on arrival. She was examining Ada now.

Rubbing the back of his neck, Sergei decided one doctor wasn't going to be enough. He should probably have a surgeon that specialized in prenatal complications on hand just in case. And maybe a nutritionist and a special chef. He relayed those orders to Niko, who was waiting in a chair outside the bedroom door as well. He rushed away to make it happen.

Though Niko would never say so out loud, Sergei knew that his crusty security chief was very fond of Ada. Everyone was. The entire security team had been quietly freaked out when she got sick on the copter. He couldn't blame them. She looked so frail and vulnerable, so unlike her former indomitable self.

God let it be a temporary phase, he prayed silently. Impatient now, he was about to knock on the door when the doctor came out. After she informed him that Ada had fallen asleep again, he ushered her down the corridor to an upper-level balcony.

"Is that normal?" he asked worriedly. "She slept almost fourteen hours on the plane."

"Pregnant women usually sleep more. She confessed to having been a little stressed out, which given her diagnosis is understandable."

"What diagnosis?" he asked with dread.

"It's called hyperemesis gravidarum, which is doctor speak for severe morning sickness. In her case, she gets sick in the afternoon and early evening. With the proper rest and nutrition, her symptoms should get better. I'm going to prescribe something safe to help with the nausea, and you should follow a special diet. She's been drinking dietary supplements to keep healthy, but she's still underweight, so I would recommend that your chef come up with an assortment of small healthy meals to tempt her to eat more. Try having her eat four or five small meals throughout the day, especially in the morning when the nausea is less severe."

"No problem...Is the baby okay?"

"So far, there doesn't seem to be an issue. Morning sickness is more severe during the period of organ development. It's a protective reaction against possible toxins, things that might adversely affect that process. In most cases, it gets better around week twenty."

"And if it doesn't?" he asked.

"There is a chance it may continue throughout the pregnancy, but it should taper off in severity towards the end."

Sergei did the math. "And she's roughly fourteen weeks right?"

"Wow, yes, that's spot on. I would put her date of conception during the second week of October," she said, smiling at him. "That's very good, so few couples can pinpoint the exact date."

Satisfaction coursed through Sergei as he smiled back at the doctor before dismissing her. He was going to be a father. If it had been anyone else he'd ever dated, he wouldn't be so sanguine, but this was Ada.

Their baby was his ticket back into her life, a way to hold onto her until she forgave him and realized that he was the right man for her. Finally able to relax, he went down to the kitchen to have a talk with his chef.

CHAPTER 15

*E*va woke with a start. *Where am I?*

The room was large and sunny with an entire wall made of glass, beyond which was a sunlit white terrace overlooking the ocean. Gauzy sheer white curtains softened the afternoon light. Inside the room, the crisp white bed linens contrasted beautifully against the deep rosewood furniture.

Oh God.

The memories from the day before flooded back. She was with Sergei. This was his friend Alex's house, and it was on an island. Panic crept in as she realized how neatly she'd been trapped. Sergei had talked about protecting her, but he was also keeping her from getting away if she needed to. She'd been kind of out of it when they got here, but not so much that she hadn't noticed that there were at least a dozen men in dark suits, triple the amount of security Sergei usually had.

She got up and moved toward the balcony, jumping in surprise when the doors slid open automatically. Stepping outside, she inspected the view.

It was crazy beautiful. The house was built on the edge of a rocky bluff overlooking a crystal blue ocean. It was almost disgusting how perfect and pristine everything looked. It was a sharp contrast to her dingy little apartment in Imperial Beach.

A vine-covered arbor provided shade from the bright hot sunlight. She sat in a lounge chair in the shade and stared at the sea until the feeling of being watched made her turn.

Sergei was standing in the doorway. He looked disconcertingly handsome in beige chinos and a white dress shirt he'd left unbuttoned at the throat with the sleeves rolled up.

"Are you hungry?" he asked.

She nodded, and he stepped inside, returning far too quickly for her peace of mind. He sat next to her in an adjoining lounge chair and pretended to stare at the ocean.

"The chef will send something up," he said eventually. "The doctor suggested you try an assortment of things to see what you feel most like eating, five or six small meals a day."

"Nice try. She said four or five, actually," she replied, amused despite herself, although she was careful not to smile.

Sergei didn't share her reluctance. He grinned at her and simply shrugged in defeat. "You're too thin and you're eating for two," he said. "The doctor said it's been a difficult pregnancy so far, and it's not going to get any easier very soon. She's not happy with your weight. I'm not happy, either. You were already too tiny."

"I'm only tiny compared to you. You're ten feet tall. I'm a perfectly respectable five foot three and a half inches."

He smiled. "You're five three without shoes and not a millimeter more, but I'll spot you that half inch if you admit I'm six foot four, not ten feet."

She shrugged. "You seem taller."

And he did. Sergei managed to fill every room with his presence. Shifting uncomfortably, she looked around. "Where is my bag?"

She'd been carrying her bug out bag with her when she went to the meeting. It had all of her essentials: ID, money, clothes, and a few pictures hidden in the lining.

"Niko put it in the closet."

Smiling sardonically, she asked, "Before or after he searched it?"

"After, of course," Sergei replied, unsmiling. They were both quiet for a moment before he spoke again. "I didn't sleep with her."

Startled, Eva looked up at him. She didn't pretend not to know what he was talking about. But she couldn't bring herself to ask if it was true.

Sitting up and turning to face her, Sergei rubbed his face in both hands before continuing. "I was going to come back from Miami to grovel for forgiveness, but you were already gone. I was not involved with Fiona again. I was just using her to push you away. Things...things got out of control that night between the two of us. I saw what I did to you the morning after, the bruises, and I lost it. I didn't want to hurt you again, and I didn't trust myself, so I called Fiona and pretended we were seeing each other again. But I didn't touch her. In fact, I can pretty much guarantee that she'll never want to speak to me again."

"Popular sentiment," Eva mumbled before she could stop herself.

He didn't argue with her. She wrapped her arms around her torso. Her stomach was hurting, but it wasn't because of the pregnancy this time.

She wanted to believe Sergei, but all the hurt and anger from the last three months was still fresh. She wasn't ready to let go of it. And it wasn't like he was professing his undying love. He was just apologizing for being an asshole. And for what? Squeezing her a little too hard? She'd gotten worse bruises playing soccer as a kid.

Eva waited to see if he was going to say more, but Sergei was apparently done apologizing. He just nodded and looked down. The silence was broken by the arrival of the food, delivered by Niko himself. The craggy-faced Russian didn't say anything to her, addressing only Sergei in Russian.

Despite her best efforts at deciphering his words, she still couldn't make anything out. Damn, why had she only focused on the Romance languages in high school?

"So Niko doesn't speak English anymore?" she asked.

"We got out of the habit after you left," Sergei said, wheeling a tray over to her that held an assortment of items.

There were honey-glazed figs on some sort of cookie, baklava, grapes and cherries, cheese, and little empanadas Sergei said were filled with chicken or beef. She picked halfheartedly at the tray until Sergei frowned and she took a few empanadas on a plate. Sniffing cautiously, she nibbled on them steadily until they were gone and Sergei stopped hovering. Thankfully everything stayed down.

"You don't have to watch me eat."

"Sorry," he said, fiddling with his collar. "Is there anything else I can get you?"

"My bag."

He went and got it for her from inside. She rummaged through it, digging out a cheap pair of sunglasses. Hugging her bag, she watched Sergei from behind the protective dark of the lenses as he poured her some orange juice and then sat down.

"Is Niko mad at me?" she asked.

"No," he said, eyes widening. "He's been worried about you. We all have."

"Oh."

She felt small and petty even if she'd only done what was necessary.

"Are you going to tell me what you're running from now?" he asked softly.

She didn't answer. It was better if Sergei stayed out of it. He had no idea what she was facing, and if he ever found out, he wouldn't be safe either.

"At least tell me your name," he said. Eva stayed silent. "I know it's something like Evelyn. All of your pseudonyms hover around that." She must have looked surprised, because he continued, "Yeah, we know about them. And the colorful collection of jobs you did before you came to work for me."

"Oh."

She didn't know what else to say. He'd found out a lot if he'd traced her back to her different pseudonyms. It was difficult to tell the truth, though. She was out of practice. But giving her first name couldn't hurt. And it had been a long time since she'd heard it spoken aloud. She missed hearing it.

"It's...it's Evangeline." A brief wave of panic coursed down her body as she said it out loud. Her heart raced, and blood rushed to her cheeks, but she calmed down when Sergei made a little noise, as though he was pleased. "I usually go by Eva," she added.

"That's lovely. And it makes sense."

She shot him a look, but he didn't explain his comment.

"Do you have a last name?" he asked.

"*No*," she said decisively.

"Okay. What about Geoffrey? I assume that is where you learned to pick a fake name that sounds like your real one. What is he to you?"

She sighed. "He is not a blood relation."

"Is that all I'm getting?" he asked.

"Yes," she said resolutely.

"That's fine...for now."

CHAPTER 16

*D*espite his apology, things weren't getting any easier. It had been a full week since their arrival on the island, and Eva was still keeping him at a distance.

Eva. Evangeline. Angel. He smiled, testing her name out in his mind, marveling that he finally knew what it was. No wonder she had been startled that first time he kissed her. He'd inadvertently used her real name, or something close enough to it. And it was lovely, almost as beautiful as she was. His nickname for her was serendipitous.

The day before, he'd been shocked to his core when Eva came down to lunch after a visit from the hairdresser. He'd been hassling her about her pink hair at breakfast, lecturing to her that the dye was probably toxic and that she should go back to her natural brown.

"The brown's not natural either," she had said absently, frowning at the food as she inspected it.

"What color is your hair then?" he'd asked confused.

She just shrugged and started eating. Frustrated that he wasn't even getting a clear answer about her hair—her *hair* for Christ's sake —he'd ordered a hairdresser to come out to the island immediately to restore Eva's natural color. Whatever it was.

Afterwards, Sergei would never admit to being on pins and

needles over someone's hair, but he'd been anxiously waiting for Eva to finish with the hairdresser and his team for what felt like hours. How long did it take to fix someone's hair? And were three people really necessary to do it? She only had one head.

Sergei told his internal monologue to shut the hell up the second Eva came down to lunch. The hair people had succeeded in rinsing out that awful pink and without it she was transformed. He couldn't have imagined just how beautiful she really was.

Eva was a *blonde*. And it wasn't a normal weak tan or yellow. Her hair was a mix of every shade from pale gold to a rich dark honey wheat. The swirl of colors blended into one another in a rich shiny mass that now fell just below her ears in loose curls that floated around her face.

Honest to god curls. He immediately wanted to run his fingers through them.

Eva's natural hair color accentuated her creamy complexion, which no longer looked as pale as it did when her hair was dark. Her eyes glowed like dark sapphires against the new backdrop, and her cheeks were pinker, although that may have been from the island wind and sun.

His heart gave a hard squeeze. Eva looked exactly like one of his mother's painted angels, the ones depicted on those religious cards she used to carry around. Cards with prayers his mother couldn't even read printed on the back.

When he didn't say anything, Eva began to look uncomfortable.

"You look beautiful," he blurted out. "Perfect. Your natural color suits you perfectly."

"Oh. Thank you," Eva said, blushing slightly.

"Did they give you a permanent?"

"No. They just cut it," she said, making a face at him.

"Was your hair always curly?" he asked, reaching out to touch one of the fat ringlets with a fingertip.

"I used to straighten it. Curls don't look professional," she said, self-consciously patting her head.

Putting his hands in his pockets because he didn't trust himself,

Sergei shook his head emphatically. "They're adorable. Don't straighten your hair anymore," he said, leaning forward despite his intention to give her space.

Eva picked at a curl and frowned.

"Don't you like it?" he asked.

She shrugged. He was really starting to hate not getting an answer. She had always had an answer when she worked for him.

"Are you worried about getting recognized?" he asked quietly.

The look she gave him before quickly glancing away was answer enough. She *was* scared. Without trying to look obvious about it, she scanned the patio where they were having lunch. Spotting three body-guards patrolling, she relaxed in her chair.

Sergei stilled as a realization hit home. He'd seen her do that before. And not just in the last week. She'd done it when she was his assistant. *A lot.*

"That's why you stayed so long, isn't it?"

Brow raised, Eva looked up at him with those big blue eyes. "What?"

"You never stayed longer than three months in your other jobs. But you spent nine working for me. And I just realized it wasn't because of my good looks or charming personality. You liked me for my bodyguards," he said with a self-deprecating smile.

He hoped she would contradict him, but she was quiet a little too long.

"You paid well, too."

EVA HAD NEVER FELT SO conflicted in her entire life. Sergei had been so kind and had gone to great lengths to make her comfortable and safe. When they first arrived, she had been completely prepared to fight him on every issue. He had essentially kidnapped her with Uncle Geoffrey's blessing. And Geoffrey didn't even try to deny it.

She had emailed her godfather the second day on the island, an accusatory letter full of wounded drama about how he had betrayed her to her worst enemy. She sent a second one immediately afterwards apologizing and blaming the pregnancy hormones, admitting that she didn't really feel that way about Sergei.

Geoffrey wrote her back, telling her that he did what he thought best for her and the baby. And he suggested she give Sergei another chance because he really cared about her.

Eva desperately wanted to believe that. Sergei certainly acted like he cared. He was always watching her, trying to anticipate her needs. Even though he pried and subtly interrogated her, he was warm and caring while he did it—not the iceman she was familiar with.

She knew that all of his questions stemmed from his fears for her and their baby. He didn't try to hide it. Despite her resolve to stay angry with him, her heart was softening. Especially after Niko had talked to her on one particularly difficult day.

Sergei had hired a whole team of medical professionals to oversee her pregnancy. He'd been pretty shocked when she told him she hadn't seen the baby yet, given that she was four months along. He'd gone dark and quiet when she told him that the free clinic she'd visited had had a broken sonogram machine. At first she hadn't understood why he was so angry.

"The doctor volunteering at the clinic listened to the baby's heart and said it sounded good," she said, watching Sergei apprehensively.

Her words didn't seem to calm him down at all.

"I'm calling the doctor right now and having her do a sonogram. I mean why did I buy a damn sonogram machine if nobody is using it?" he asked, his decibel level climbing as he finished the question.

Eva backed away with wide eyes. Sergei was yelling now. He never yelled. Not even that time Tim had spilled his espresso all over a brand new box of Cuban cigars his mobster friend had sent him. Afterward, he'd actually said the taste was improved by the coffee.

She hadn't even known there was a sonogram machine in the house. Eventually Sergei finally noticed the way she was moving away from him, and he tamped down his anger and went off to get the doctor. A few minutes later, she was lying down getting cold goo spread on her stomach. Sergei was pacing up and down while the doctor pressed and slid around a wand over the top of her round belly.

"There it is. Looks good. Nice strong heartbeat. Everything is where it's supposed to be. It's a little early to determine the sex, but we might get lucky if the two of you want to try," Dr. Chapman said while Eva studiously avoided looking at the monitor.

———

SERGEI WAS EXCITED about learning what they were having, until he saw the look on Eva's face. She was pale again and wouldn't turn in the direction of the screen.

"Doctor, can you give us a minute?"

"Sure."

The perpetually cheerful doctor left them alone.

Sergei walked over to Eva and took her hand. It was cold as ice. "What's wrong?"

"Nothing," Eva whispered.

Her face was white and set. She wouldn't look at him, so she was surprised when he put his hand on her head and ran his fingers through her hair.

"What are you afraid of? Please tell me. I can help. I really can. I am prepared to hire an entire fucking army of mercenaries to keep you and this baby safe. You just have to tell me what the big mystery is! I'll do anything you want. We can even get married and make ten more babies."

Eva's head snapped up in alarm. *"Ten?"*

"Okay, not ten. But more."

"Can we just focus on this one?" she asked with a frown.

"We could...except you won't even look at it," he protested, running a frustrated hand through his hair.

"Don't call it an it," she said, starting to cry.

Sergei winced. "Oh god. Don't cry. I can't stand it when you cry."

His heart wanted to crawl out of his chest every time she did. Unfortunately, pregnant women cried a lot.

Eva sobbed quietly for a minute before telling the truth. "I lied. The sonogram machine wasn't broken. I told the doctor I didn't want to see the baby because I was going to give it up for adoption."

Sergei's heart threatened to seize up and stop on him. "Is that really what you were planning?"

"No."

"Then what were you going to do? Why wouldn't you look at him? Or her?"

Eva sniffed and wiped her tears on her sleeve. "I was hoping Uncle Geoffrey would come up with something. Some plan so I could keep it," she said, apparently forgetting what she'd said about calling the baby an *it*.

"Is that what you call him? Uncle Geoffrey?"

What would that make him to her? A family friend of some kind. That wasn't going to help much. They'd already gone over all of Johansen's known associates and hadn't come up with a smoking gun.

"Yeah. But worst case scenario, I did have a plan. In case I thought it was too dangerous to stay with the baby," she whispered.

Sergei wasn't sure he wanted to hear what her plan was, but she was finally confiding in him so he just asked, "What was it?"

"I was going to take the baby back to New York and ambush Tim. I was going to leave the baby with him so he would take it to you."

Sergei hadn't cried since he was a small boy, but he was pretty fucking close right now. At least Eva had been planning on reuniting him with his child if she couldn't take care of it. He tried to be okay with that.

"Tim?" he rasped after a minute.

"He's the hole in your security net," Eva said tearfully.

"And easily manipulated when it comes to you," Sergei agreed, stroking her hair.

"There's that." She sniffed, tears finally subsiding. "I'm afraid of looking at it and getting attached because I might still have to run and then I won't get to see my baby again."

Sergei grabbed Eva in a tight hug. "You're not running anymore.

That's over. You are safe now. And you're not going to have to leave me or our baby."

Then he grabbed her and kissed her for dear life.

———

FOR A FRACTION OF A SECOND, Eva kissed him back. But then she remembered everything that had happened, how it had felt to sit in that chair in front of him in his office while he crushed and humiliated her. He had been so cold and cruel, an iceman in fact.

Freezing, Eva blinked before slowly pushing him away. But he wouldn't go far. Sergei stopped kissing her, but he continued to hold her. He kissed the top of her head and rubbed her arms, trying to warm her chilled hands.

She could feel his frustration in more ways than one. Blushing, she turned away from him and his increasingly obvious arousal...although it did make her feel good to know that he still found her attractive when she looked and felt like an elephant.

"Sorry," Sergei murmured, but she had the distinct impression that he didn't mean it.

He was going to say something else when there was a knock at the door and Niko poked his head in. He said something in Russian, and Sergei swore a little.

"Okay. I'll be right there." He turned to Eva and smiled apologetically. "I have to take this call. It's something important about Adstringo," he said before cocking his head at her. "We're going to have to have a long talk about that one of these days, by the way."

He made it sound like she'd saddled him with some sort of money pit instead of a highly profitable company. Feeling better, Eva stuck her tongue out at him, and he pretended to try and grab it before he left.

She was wiping the traces of her tears on her sleeve when a handkerchief appeared in her line of sight. Niko hadn't gone away. Surprised, she took the square of pristine white cloth and wiped her face. When she was done, he was still there.

"Mr. Damov is in love with you."

"What?" she asked, startled.

Niko never had that much to say, but when he did he certainly made it count.

"The boss went crazy after Italy. He got very drunk and smashed a thousand dollar dinner plate on the floor and knocked over a fat socialite and a waiter at that charity dinner. It was all over TMZ. You can look it up online."

Shocked, Eva stared at him. "Really?"

"He got worse after that. He went on a bender that lasted days. We thought he was trying to drink himself to death. I had to get his friends to come down to Miami to get him. But he didn't snap out of it until they told him you were gone," Niko said in his gravelly voice.

Eva gaped at him with her mouth open so long Niko eventually closed her mouth by tapping her under the chin.

"Do you know that's the most you've ever spoken to me? All at once that is," she said.

Niko smiled. It was slightly terrifying but also kind of sweet.

But mostly terrifying, she thought, her lip twitching.

The big bodyguard patted her awkwardly on the back. "It is good to have you back, safe. He was very worried about you, and that was before he knew about the baby. But I think I speak for everyone that it would be best if you were to tell him your secret so we can make plans."

Eva frowned. "So this is part pep talk, part guilt trip."

"Something like that. Think about it. You can trust him."

Niko didn't wait for a reply. He left her alone until the doctor came back to help her clean up.

CHAPTER 17

*S*ergei didn't think someone could be so happy and yet so frustrated at the same time. Finally being with Eva was even better than his most secret fantasies. And they weren't even lovers again.

He hoped that would change soon. He'd taken more cold showers in the last month than his entire life before that. But at least he got to see her every day. And she was funny and sweet but with a sarcastic edge. She was also so freaking smart it would have intimidated a lesser man.

He'd rearranged his work schedule as much as possible, but there were days when he had to fly out for meetings. He kept the travel down to a couple days a month, and worked from Alex's well-appointed office on the island the rest of the time. When that wasn't an option, Tim met him in nearby European cities for the meetings he couldn't avoid.

Sergei was going to have to figure something else out soon. He wasn't going to want to leave Eva after the baby came. In the meantime, he avoided Athens for security reasons, which frustrated Tim. His assistant knew Eva was with him and that she was pregnant, so he kept badgering Sergei constantly to be allowed to come down and visit.

Sergei knew he was being selfish by keeping Eva from seeing Tim. He wanted her to make more friends, to have more anchors to her present life. But she was still cautious about getting to know people.

He could see it clearly now, the way she tried to keep a distance between herself and everyone else. It wasn't her fault that everyone fell in love with her. Eventually they all fell like dominoes. And it happened a lot faster now that she looked like a pregnant angel, her blonde curls framing the fine features of her face.

Just the other day, he overheard one of the new bodyguards waxing rhapsodic on her eyes. Sergei didn't blame the guy, but he had him transferred out of Eva guarding duty anyway. She needed friends, but he didn't need more competition.

Guiltily, he decided to let Tim come visit. *Next* weekend. Or next month. Eva needed to rest up first. She was tired all the time now and was still not sleeping well.

The circles under her eyes were fainter than when he'd first seen her in Mexico, but there were still shadows there sometimes. That, and Niko had reported that the sensor on the balcony doors in the master bedroom often went off after bedtime, sometimes several times a night. He hated that Eva still felt unsafe, but until he knew what it was that she was running from, he didn't know how to help her.

He also hated not being able to touch her. Pregnancy had only made her more attractive to him. Knowing that she was growing round with his child did something to him. It was insanely hot.

When he confided that detail to Calen one night, his friend understood. It turned out that Calen's new wife Maia was also expecting. In fact, she had conceived only a few weeks after Eva.

"I totally get it man," his friend said, his slight Bostonian accent coming out in his enthusiasm. "It's like Maia exudes some sort of crazy pheromone now that she's pregnant. She can barely keep me off her."

"At least you're allowed to touch your woman," Sergei grumbled.

"You'll get there," Calen said optimistically. "It sounds like things are going better. Hey, do you know the sex of the baby yet?"

"Eva decided she wants the sex of the baby to be a surprise," Serge replied casually.

In reality, he had been dying to find out what they were having. But Eva didn't want to know, and he hadn't pushed her. It was enough that he'd gotten her to look at the baby with him. She had even held his hand during the sonogram. Sergei was hopeful that she would come around now to the idea of them as a couple now that she'd seen their baby.

"Do you know what you're having?" he asked.

"A little girl," Calen said proudly. "I hope she looks just like Maia. And I was thinking if yours is a boy then we can marry them off to each other."

Calen sounded more excited than the time his first nightclub opened.

Sergei laughed. "Well, if mine turns out to be a girl, too, we can always marry one of them off to Alex's son," he pointed out.

"Good point. We need to factor in that boy. Did you hear Elynn is pregnant again?"

Sergei snorted. "Not really surprising. Alex is a walking hormone."

"Gio needs to get in on this soon or he's going to be left out in the cold," Calen replied.

"Do you really think he'll ever remarry?" Sergei asked doubtfully while shuffling through a report on Adstringo's latest earnings.

"We're all entitled to at least one miracle."

"That's true, I guess. I got mine, and now he deserves his."

"Is your miracle sharing her deep dark secrets yet?" Calen asked.

"Not yet, but I'm getting close," he said before noticing Eva in the doorway of the office.

"I don't like it man. The fact Niko hasn't figured out what she's hiding means it's some seriously shady shit."

"Yeah, look I'm gonna have to call you back later. Give my love to Maia," he said.

"Okay, but I think it's time for more drastic action man. Get her to spill, and do it now."

"Yeah, yeah. Later man," he said, hanging up.

Eva frowned at him. "Are you marrying off our unborn child? Already?"

Busted. "Been there that long huh?"

"Yes," she said pointedly.

She looked so cute with her bouncy gold curls that it was hard to focus on the fact that she was annoyed—but he got the picture when she crossed her arms and stared him down.

"I promise our child can marry wherever their heart lies," he said generously. "Although if it happens to be to the rich, attractive child of one of my friends, I'll die happy."

Eva rolled her eyes, but she was obviously trying not to smile.

"Did you need anything?" he asked.

"I was just coming to say goodnight," she said, looking down at her feet, which were bare despite the memory foam slippers he'd bought her.

She was wearing white shorts and a peasant top that bared her shoulders. *Damn*, he thought as he started to get aroused.

"Oh okay," he said out loud, wishing he could kiss her good night.

"All right," she said before hesitating and then rushing forward. She gave him a quick peck on the cheek that was over too fast. "Good night," she called behind her as she left him alone.

A few hours later, Sergei decided he had had enough. It was time for things to come to a head. After checking in with Niko, he'd learned the sensor on the balcony door had gone off twice already that night after Eva had supposedly gone to bed.

If she was still so scared she wasn't sleeping, then he was going to do something about it.

EVA SAT bolt upright in bed, heart pounding. In her nightmare, she'd been back in her childhood home on the day her dad died. She'd been trying to warn him that he was in danger, but he couldn't hear her because no matter how hard she yelled, there was no sound coming out of her mouth. She woke up shaking and gasping for air, too out of breath to scream when she realized she was not alone.

She almost jumped out of her skin at the sight of Sergei lying next to her on the bed. The curtains, which had been closed when she'd gone to sleep, were open now. He must have opened them to let in the moonlight so she could see him if she woke up in the night.

Eva wanted to be angry with him for his presumptuousness, but all she felt was an overwhelming relief that he was there and she wasn't alone with her bad dreams.

Sergei's long hard body was close enough for her to feel his heat, but he wasn't touching her. She couldn't tell if he was really asleep. His eyes were closed and his breathing was steady...too steady. Should she poke him in the eye and kick him out of bed?

It was tempting, but when it came right down to it, she didn't want to fight him anymore.

Over the last month, Eva had slowly become convinced that Sergei's feelings for her were genuine. She wanted to take the next step, but she didn't know how—although her pregnancy hormones had more than one suggestion.

But keeping people at a distance was engrained now. Sighing, she decided letting him stay with her tonight would probably be a good way to let Sergei get closer. Literally.

Eva's heart raced for another reason as she inched toward him. Moving stealthily, she moved until her back was against his front. She nestled against him, slowly pulling his arm down over her. Feeling safer and more secure than she had in years she drifted off to sleep, but not before she felt Sergei shift his hand up to caress her cheek and move over her hair.

She slept peacefully for the rest of the night.

CHAPTER 18

The following days fell into a regular pattern for Eva. Sergei worked in the office downstairs during the day, except for occasional visits to the mainland for meetings. He would stop to eat breakfast with her every day when she got up, which was usually a couple hours after him.

Sergei woke up at six a.m. on the dot every morning. She knew because every night, after she went to sleep, he joined her. He would come in about an hour after she'd turned off the lights. She would pretend to be asleep and he would pretend not to be there.

Unless of course she had another nightmare. If she woke up gasping and in tears he would hold her tight until she fell back asleep. And he never said anything about it the next day.

Two or three times a week, Sergei asked her to join him in his office. He would ask her opinion about up and coming business matters, deferring to her in areas where he felt her expertise eclipsed his own. It felt good to contribute and to be valued for her intelligence, although he delegated all of her former tasks to Michael Fisher, who was holding down the fort in Manhattan.

Eva was nervous about the amount of responsibility her replacement was shouldering, but Sergei had assured her that his subordinates were stepping up, and everyone was keeping an eye on everyone else.

When Sergei was working and he didn't need her, Eva kept busy. Every once in a while, Niko came to talk with her, which was only weird once she realized he was giving her security updates like she was the mistress of the house. She also made meal plans with the chef and was consulted by the housekeeper on various domestic matters.

When she was on her own Eva exercised and caught up on her reading. She preferred comedic fiction and thrillers, but since Sergei had bought a ton of baby books and read them religiously, she'd been shamed into adding those to her list. She now knew an uncomfortable amount of detail about what was happening in her body.

"Too bad blissful ignorance is no longer in vogue," she said morosely over lunch one day after putting down *What to Expect When You're Expecting*.

"How can you say that?" Sergei had asked with a hint of a scowl on his handsome face. "It's better to know all the information so we can be prepared for any eventuality."

Eva sighed. "We're having a baby, not planning a war. It's simply not going to be possible to prepare for everything. And quite honestly I'd rather not know that right around now there is something inside me growing hair," she added with a slight shudder.

"Don't say stuff like that so negatively. The baby can hear you now," he chided as he sipped his coffee.

Eva rolled her eyes, but patted her stomach soothingly in a silent apology to her fetus.

"I have a little something for you," Sergei said after a minute.

Eva perked up. She didn't consider herself a materialistic person at all, but Sergei had started surprising her with 'a little something' every few days. His gifts were always personal and thoughtful, completely unlike the things he had Tim send his other women. In fact, there wasn't a single bracelet or item of jewelry in the bunch. Instead, she'd gotten first editions of classic sci-fi books like H.G. Well's *The Time Machine* and *10,000 Leagues Under the Sea* or gourmet chocolates in exotic flavors.

Signaling to one of the ever-present bodyguards, Sergei waited while they brought forward a big box.

"I thought you said it was little," she exclaimed as she tore off the wrapping eagerly.

The side facing her was just directions in Japanese so she turned it over and found more evidence of Sergei's startling insight.

"It's a make your own robot kit," he said when she stayed quiet.

Fighting tears, she nodded.

"Is something wrong?" he asked concerned.

She shook her head.

"I thought you would like to give something like this a try," he continued, watching her face attentively. "You're always fixing things and have such a good way with all things mechanical. But if you don't like it, I can get you something else. Maybe some jewelry or something more romantic?" he asked when she didn't smile.

"No," she said hoarsely, hugging the box. "It's perfect."

***

FOR ONCE, Eva was having a good dream. She was surrounded by a warm soothing ocean, its calm waves caressing her body. Glorying in the sensation, she moved with it, letting it carry her and shift her in its wake. The warm sensation became concentrated between her legs as the waves lapped at her sex in rhythmic strokes.

Awareness came slowly. She fought against it at first, reluctant to let go of the delightful dream. But the pleasurable sensation only increased when she woke up and realized her warm waves were actually lips...and a tongue.

Sergei's head was buried between her legs, a state that would have alarmed her shy inner self if she'd been more awake. But in her drowsiness, it was just amazing.

"Oh god," she moaned as his talented tongue circled her clit before gently sucking it into his mouth.

Her legs closed around his head, pressing him more firmly against her. Clutching at his hair, her back arched as his tongue snaked out to probe her entrance. When she pulled on it, he only laughed, the vibration of his chuckle buzzing her delicate folds.

His hand moved up to gently stroke her clit in time with the movements of his tongue, and she started to whimper—broken unintelligible sounds that would embarrass her later. Her whimpers became cries when he switched the position of his hand and mouth, but he didn't stop the sensual torture until her body tightened, her tight sheath clasping down on his roving fingers.

Shuddering and shaking, her whole body stiffened as a powerful climax rolled over her. The pleasurable spasms hadn't completely faded when Sergei moved up against her. His naked sex rubbed against her wet center, the friction teasing sparks she could see behind her closed eyelids.

"Is this okay?" he whispered into her ear.

She opened her eyes and nodded so enthusiastically he laughed again. But he stopped as she took hold of him and tried to pull him closer. Following her less than subtle directive, he began to press inside her small hot entrance.

"*Fuck*," Sergei growled as his hard shaft was completely enveloped inside her tight passage. "I think you shrank. You feel smaller than the first time."

"No, I think you got bigger," Eva gasped as he moved tentatively inside her.

Smiling, he kissed her forehead before groaning as she flexed hard around him. With a careful shift of his hips, he began to push in and out of her body. Moving her hands to his back Eva dug her fingers into the hard muscle, urging Sergei to increase his rhythm. His every movement was so sublimely good that it almost made her want to cry. She settled for pulling his hair again.

"Hey," he said breathlessly. "That stuff's attached you know."

"Sorry," Eva apologized, not meaning it at all.

"No problem," Sergei growled as he took both her hands in one of his own and held them over her head.

He used the other arm to brace himself as he picked up the pace and thrust faster and faster. Eva let a squeal escape as she wrapped her legs around him and met his surges with her own.

"Shit. Fuck. *Shit*," he swore.

Eva briefly considered swatting his butt for all the bad language, but she couldn't get her hands loose. Instead, she let out a few cries of her own as he shifted her leg higher to change the angle of his entry. He was able to drive more deeply, intensifying the pleasure.

The building climax was so close that she moaned in frustration when Sergei suddenly pulled out of her. He made a soothing noise in his throat as he positioned her on her side. Wrapping his long body around her from behind, he rubbed his length against the silky skin of her backside and down between her thighs. Impatient she pushed her bottom against him, eliciting a little growl from him. Maintaining his hold on her wrists, he entered her in one smooth motion and she cried out in relief. His other hand held her hip, urging her open for his thrusts.

Held tight with her arms over her head she was helpless as he rocked her body, pushing them both across the mattress a little with each stroke. Doing her best to hold him inside her, she tightened on his cock each time he reached the end of her channel, matching his rhythm.

She came convulsively a few heartbeats later, her whole body straining forward, arms pushing against his restraining hands. The feeling of being bound intensified each sensation, and she sobbed, shuddering her release.

A moment later, Sergei followed her with a shout, his hard cock jerking as his seed shot inside her. It was like hot candle wax, burning her up from the inside. His hand let go of her wrists and fisted in her hair as the last spasms shook him.

Once he had completely emptied himself inside her, he collapsed, relaxing his grip and slipping out of her. She waited for her heart to stop racing while he caught his breath.

"If you weren't pregnant before you would be now," Sergei announced. "I think I just came a whole year's worth."

Laughing, Eva rolled to face him. He put a hand on her stomach and reached out to pull her in close, their baby between them.

"I believe you," Eva said with a blush.

She could still feel his seed trickling out of her. Sergei sighed contentedly before nudging her so he could spoon up against her back.

"By the way, unless you want to be pregnant for the next ten or twenty years, you may have to go on the pill, cause now that I've had you bare, I don't think I can have you any other way," he murmured with a proprietary squeeze.

"Well, given how potent you seem to be, getting me pregnant the very first time, I really think I should be on something after the baby comes," Eva agreed wryly.

He ran his hand down her side. "I prefer to think we are just a good, somewhat fertile, combination."

For a few minutes, they lay quietly, enjoying the afterglow before Sergei spoke again. "You and the baby are the most important things in my life," he said seriously, stroking her curls. "I would do anything for you, the both of you."

Eva pressed against him, pulling his arm more tightly around her. "I'm starting to get that. We have to talk, don't we?" she said, growing serious. "I have a lot to tell you."

Sergei's grip on her hip tightened. "Yes," he said before stroking her arm. "But why don't we wait until tomorrow? There are some things I need to tell you, too. It's not fair for me to expect you to spill all of your secrets without sharing my own. And there are some things I haven't told you yet."

"Oh. That sounds...ominous," Eva said with a sinking heart.

"It has nothing to do with our future. But there are some things you need to know about my past."

"Okay. Tomorrow," she said before he kissed her good night.

Soon, Sergei's deep breathing signaled that he had fallen asleep. She, however, was not so fortunate.

CHAPTER 19

*A*fter her restless night, Eva slept until a maid knocked at ten thirty. She woke in an empty bed, the cheerful looking matron bringing her a breakfast tray, complete with Russian samovar, which she set up on the patio outside. But Eva was too nervous to eat much, so she covered the tray and went inside to shower and change.

Sergei had filled her closet with some lovely maternity clothes, most of which she had never worn before because they were too pretty for everyday use. Sighing heavily, she pushed aside some of the more practical outfits to reveal a dreamy looking white chiffon confection.

On impulse, she put it on. It was a stretchy sheath dress with a gauzy overlay that fell in waves over her torso. It didn't look like a maternity dress, but it didn't hide her stomach, either. Instead, it was a designer miracle that somehow managed to make pregnancy look chic. Admiring herself in the mirror, she wondered where Sergei's shopper had found it. Whatever it cost, it was worth every penny.

Slipping on white ballet flats and her sunglasses, she went back outside to the balcony to wait for Sergei.

It didn't take long for him to come find her. She was lying in the widest of the lounge chairs in the shade when he joined her outside.

He paused at the table long enough to peek under the covered tray. Frowning, he made a clucking noise before grabbing a pastry and handing it to her.

"You need to eat more," he said.

"Later," she promised, and he reluctantly put the pastry back down.

"Is there room for me?" he asked, gesturing to the lounge chair.

"It is meant for two," she said, scooting over so he could sit with her.

She frowned at his formal suit. "Do you have a meeting?"

He only wore suits when he went to the mainland for the day.

"No, I...no," he said, looking down at himself. "Do you?" he asked, fingering the fine white material of her dress.

"Yes, I do. With you," she said in a low voice.

He gave her a smile that didn't quite reach his eyes. "I knew this would look great on you when the stylist sent me a picture of it," he said, ignoring her comment.

He ran a hand down her dress, the warmth of it leaving a trail of heat along the front of her body.

"Then thank you for choosing it."

His manner was starting to concern her. Though his words were warm, he was distant, like he didn't want to have this conversation.

Well, she didn't, either. She took a deep breath. Whatever his secret was, it couldn't be that bad. Not as bad as what she had to tell him.

"My father killed my mother," he said suddenly.

"Oh God!" Eva cried out before she could stop herself.

Clapping a hand to her mouth, she turned to apologize, but he was rubbing his face and looking away.

"Sorry," he rasped. "I had a whole speech prepared. I was going to tell you the facts in a completely unemotional and linear way. I didn't mean to blurt it out like that."

Eva crawled into his arms and snaked her arms around his chest. Lifting his hands, he moved to stroke her hair as he held her in silence.

"You don't have to be some unemotional robot," she said, resting her head under his chin. "You don't even have to make sense. I'm here to listen to whatever you have to say, if you want to say anything at all. I don't need to know all the details if you don't want to share them."

"No," he said, tightening his hands on her. "You need to know this because it has some bearing on us. I never really explained why I left you in Italy after I seduced you. And I did seduce you. But it wasn't supposed to happen like that. We both had too much to drink, and I took advantage of you. Truthfully, I'm having a hard time regretting it, because you are mine now and we're going to have a baby, but I do regret drinking so much. If I hadn't been drunk, then maybe I wouldn't have hurt you." He stopped, swallowing convulsively a few times before he got ahold of himself. "You were covered in bruises the next day. And there were some bloodstains. I didn't realize why till much later. I thought I'd hurt you...and there were black and blue marks all over you. Marks *I* made."

The last was said in such tone of condemnation that it shook her into speech.

"I *chose* to have sex with you. If I'd wanted to, I would have stopped you that night. I could have said no. But I didn't want to. And I bruise easily," Eva said trying to comfort him. "Look."

She lifted the hem of her dress to reveal a length of her upper thigh. There was a faint mark from Sergei's grip from the night before.

"*Shit,*" Sergei swore, examining the bruise.

He looked so upset she couldn't stop herself from comforting him.

"It's okay. It doesn't hurt. I just get marked up really easy. It'll be gone in a few days," she said, but Sergei apparently wasn't in the mood for absolution.

"From now on, we only have sex with the lights on, so I can see what I'm doing," he mumbled, rubbing his face the way he always did when he was upset. "My mom was always coming down to meals with bruises. She died when I was eight, but I still remember that."

"I see," Eva said in a low voice.

And she did see now. Whenever he saw bruises on her, he saw his poor mother. Which meant he saw himself as her victimizer.

After a moment, he continued. "My father was a businessman in Omsk. One with ties to the Russian mob, but that was how things ran back there. Everyone was corrupt. Except for my mother. She was born poor in the most miserable place on earth—a town called Verkhoyansk. It used to be one of the places Stalin sent his political enemies. People don't need freezers there. They just store meat in their basements and it freezes just fine. Sometimes the ice under the houses shifts enough to snap them in two."

"You're kidding!"

"It happens more often than you would think. Suicide is common enough there. And wolf attacks. A pack of four hundred wolves attacked the town a few years ago."

"Holy shit! Was it that bad when your mom lived there?"

"Yes," he said, closing his eyes briefly. "She had some colorful stories. I thought she used to make things up so I would appreciate growing up privileged, but I looked into it when I got older, and everything about Verkhoyansk was true. In fact, it was probably worse than she let on."

"Was your father from there, too?" she asked tentatively.

"No. He was from Omsk. His family had money and long tentacles. He met my mother Katya in a tea shop one day when she came to town to stay with a friend. She was looking for a job, but she was uneducated with no connections and couldn't find one. Not a decent one anyway. She was about to give up and go home. She would have been better off. Instead, she went for tea and ran into my father. From that moment, her fate was sealed. You see, she was very beautiful. Almost as beautiful as you," he said, stopping to stroke a stray blonde curl. "She had long red hair and green eyes. My father took one look at her and decided he had to have her. I think he probably just meant to have her as a mistress, but my mother was a very religious woman. She probably told him to go to hell when he asked. Rather than let her go, he decided to marry her."

129

Pressing closer to him, Eva reached down to take his hand while he continued his story.

"Life was pretty good as the spoiled son of a wealthy man in Omsk. I had all the possessions I could possibly want. So did Mama. But I didn't realize just how much she gave up to marry my father. He never let her be educated in any way. She couldn't even read. Even though she was smart and could have learned easily enough. He kept her ignorant on purpose, to keep her subservient. But she wanted to learn to read and go out and make friends."

He exhaled heavily, blowing her curls up as he stared at the ocean.

"He would shame her when she asked to be allowed to do those things. He told her she was too stupid for anything except making babies and that she would just embarrass herself and him. Eventually, Mama stopped trying to go out on her own. And then she stopped trying to accompany him out to social events, too, which suited him just fine, because he could parade his mistresses around town while she stayed cloistered in our house. It may have been a mansion, but it was still a prison for her. Eventually she turned away from him, too, so she wouldn't have to see him for the kind of man he was. Mama took solace in religion and would pray to the angels and the saints constantly. She was still a good mother to me, but she was distant and sad.

"For all of his philandering, my father couldn't stand it when she pulled away," Sergei said, looking down at her. "He was obsessively in love with her, even though it was all twisted up inside. Then he started to hit her," he said, jaw tight.

Under Eva's fingers, his chest and arms were tense. "At first, he didn't care if I saw, but soon he learned to hide his abuse. It would happen behind closed doors or when I was in school. Back then, I didn't wonder why she didn't complain or try to run away, though I've thought about it a lot since," he said and then shook his head. "She probably knew she wouldn't get far. Mama bore everything in silence, immersing herself in religion even more. By the end, I hardly saw her except at mealtimes. And then one day, she just didn't come down to breakfast. Iosif, my father, told me she was sick, too sick to see anyone. Even me. And then he told me she went to visit her family. Finally, he told me she had had an accident when she was driving home. But I knew the truth. He'd killed her."

Eva's heart hurt for the little boy Sergei had been. He must have felt so powerless when he saw one of the two most important people in his life being victimized by the other.

"Are you sure?" she whispered, her head cradled on his chest.

"Yes," he whispered. "Mama couldn't drive. It was one of the many things he wouldn't let her learn how to do. And there was no way he would have let her out of the house to see anyone, let alone go all the way to Verkhoyansk for a visit. That and she had no family left there. Her parents were gone by the time I was five."

"I'm sorry," Eva said, cuddling closer to him. "What happened after that?"

"We buried my mother. Father built a lavish monument to her. He did really love her in his own way, I think...which is sometimes the hardest thing to accept. He never remarried."

"What about you? Did you ever confront him? Did he ever try to hurt you?"

"Me? No, he never hit me. I was supposed to be molded in his image. He provided only the best of everything for me. The best tutors, the best clothes. Even handpicked friends." He stroked her back absently. "I still hated him, though. When I was twelve, I asked to be sent away to school. When he asked me why I wanted to go away, I said 'You know why.' That's the closest I ever came to confronting him. He didn't say anything in response. He just looked at me, and the next week, I was in boarding school. But I still had to come home and pretend everything was normal during the holidays."

"What did you do then?" she asked, feeling sick for him.

"I studied my ass off to avoid him. I got a full scholarship to the University of Edinburgh. He didn't even know I had applied. He expected me to go to school in Moscow, but I put my foot down. It was the only real yelling match we ever had. In the end, I won and moved to Scotland." He smiled distantly. "It felt like being paroled. I didn't bother ever going home for the holidays after that. Instead, I went home with my friends Alex or Gio to their houses, or off back-packing with Calen when he didn't want to go home, either. Calen and I had some stuff in common when it came to family."

"Is your father still in Omsk?" she asked.

"He died just after I finished school. My friends came home with me for a whole month. They stayed for the funeral and helped me get his affairs in order. I sold off most of the properties except the house. It's where my mother is buried. My father was supposed to be entombed with her, but I put him on the other side of the graveyard. He's probably still giving me the finger from down in hell for that," he said, giving her another mirthless smile.

"I donated most of his fortune to charity," Sergei continued. "When I started Damov industries, I only used the legacy my paternal grand-parents had left to me in their will. They died when I was one, and I don't remember them. But their retainers spoke of them well. They were a devoted couple, in many ways, quite unlike their son. I'm not sure where Iosef came from. Just a bad seed, I guess."

It all made sense now. There had always been something about Sergei, something restrained. Even when he had just been her boss he had always been very careful around her, like he had been trying to keep something in check. And he must have always been that way. Ever since he'd been a little boy, growing up in a house full of secrets.

Sergei had built a wall between him and everyone else, afraid to trust people until he had met friends like him. Those walls had continued falling when they met, when he'd kissed her. But it was only natural that he would still be afraid of himself, of what he would be when he let himself feel.

"You are nothing like him," Eva said decisively, tugging on the lapels of his jacket.

"I know that. But sometimes I...I need to remind myself that it's still true. When I saw those bruises I'd left on you in Italy, I ran out of that suite like I was on fire, when I should have stayed and explained. But it was all too much. I thought that if I stayed, you would condemn me, or worse—forgive me. And if you forgave me, I would just end up hurting you again and again until I couldn't stop. I know it was kind of insane, but I've always been afraid that deep down inside I'm a bad seed, too," he finished, dropping his hand down her back and to the side so that he was no longer touching her.

Eva didn't waste a moment. She climbed on top of him so that she was straddling his body. He raised tormented eyes to her face, but underneath her, his body responded the way it always did to her touch.

"Sergei, I don't pretend to know what it was like growing up that way, in a house where such a terrible thing happened. By comparison, I had an idyllic childhood. But later in life, I developed a very sensitive bullshit detector, a sort of sixth sense for evil. Believe me when I say that if there was anything remotely like that in you—any seed of corruption or potential for evil—then I would be out of here. You'd be eating my dust right now. But there's nothing like that in you. You aren't capable of it."

She put her hands on either side of his face and smiled sardonically. "There may be a hint of douchebag here and there, but you make up for it really, really well. But some incipient hint of evil? No," she said emphatically as she stared down at his tight drawn face.

CHAPTER 20

Sergei let out a choking laugh. Only Eva could make him feel better by calling him names. "I'll take douchebag over evil seed."

Eva tugged on his jacket again, "I said a hint of douchebag. I would not have you if you were a full-on asshole. In fact, you are still on probation as far as I'm concerned. If you ever make me feel like you did in your office that time, I will take a baseball bat to your knees. Remember that, okay?"

Sergei lifted his knees suddenly, making Eva slide against him with a soft crash. He put his arms around her, "You never have to worry about that."

"See that I don't," she said authoritatively.

He chuckled again and held her close for a long time. Eventually, the silence stretched into expectation, and Eva sighed and sat up.

"Where's my bug out bag?" she asked.

Letting go of her, Sergei studied her set features. "Back in the closet. Do you want it?"

She nodded, and he went to get it. He returned and handed it to her without a word. Lying back on the lounger, she clutched it to her like she was trying to draw strength from it.

"Man, I wish I wasn't pregnant right now. I could sure use a drink," she murmured.

Sitting down, Sergei put an arm around her and waited. Eventually, she took the bag and turned it inside out. An assortment of items fell out. There was a wallet with her fake IDs, a coin purse, some clothes, a lighter, a taser, a vial of pepper spray, as well as various items of makeup. Feeling around the inside liner, she separated a seam that appeared to be sewn shut. It wasn't—it was held together by a strong double-sided tape. After drawing out two pictures, she showed them to Sergei.

"Niko found these, right?"

Feeling slightly guilty, Sergei nodded. Niko's search of her belongings had been thorough. He'd left no stone unturned when it came to discovering Eva's real identity. One photo was of a large house on a foggy afternoon. It was on a lake and had an attached pier with motorboat next to it. It looked like Washington state, but Niko hadn't been able to pinpoint a location from the photo. There weren't enough landmarks to narrow it down.

The other photo was of a man with the sun behind him, holding hands with a little girl. Only the little girl was recognizable as the man was obscured by shadows. It was clearly Eva as a child. She still had the same blonde curls and pink bud mouth.

"This is my dad," she said, holding the photo between them.

Sergei nodded again. He and Niko had guessed as much. Eva grew quiet as she examined the photo. Something told him she didn't let herself take it out too often.

"He's dead, too," she said.

"I'm sorry," he said quietly. When she didn't add anything, he asked. "Does his death have anything to do with why you're running?"

She nodded.

"Are you running from the people who killed him?"

"Yeah. But it's a person. Singular."

"Who is it?"

She didn't answer right away. Instead, she took a compact that held some powder and fiddled with the lid. He assumed she needed time to work up to the answer, so he was surprised when she forced the lid of the powder apart and took out another photograph.

Sergei sat up, he hadn't known there was a third picture.

"I guess you didn't find this one," she said.

"I don't know how Niko missed it. He should have X-rayed your bag," Sergei said unapologetically, examining the compact when she didn't hand over the picture right away.

It had been pried apart and resealed with a weaker tacky glue. The inner surface of the plastic was concave. It was a good hiding place.

"Niko doesn't think like a woman," she said, finally extending the picture to him.

The photograph was of a family. Eva was maybe ten or eleven, and there was a teenage boy, also blonde, next to her. He was maybe seventeen or eighteen. On either side of the children were a man and woman. Her father had brown hair and was very tall. He had a pleasant looking face, although he looked slightly overwhelmed in the photo. The smiling blonde woman in the photograph was very fashionably dressed and had the air of an expensive socialite.

"He killed them," she said quietly.

"Your whole family?" he asked in consternation.

"No," she said, pointing to the handsome blonde teen. "I mean him. His name is Karl Grayson. This was taken on the day my father married his mother," she said, pointing to the adults in turn. "He's the one. He killed them."

"YOUR *BROTHER* KILLED YOUR PARENTS?

"My stepbrother," she corrected in a sad voice.

Whatever he had been expecting, it hadn't been that. "Why? When? And *why?*"

Eva gave a helpless shrug, "I don't know where to start."

He took her hand in his. "Try the beginning."

Eva exhaled loudly before answering. "My father's name was Wallace Stone."

"Wait, what? The Wallace Stone, of Stonewall Industries?"

"That's him."

"You're Canadian?" he asked, bewildered.

Stonewall Industries had been a highly profitable Canadian company based outside of Vancouver up until a few years ago. *More like three*, he realized, when Wallace Stone died.

"No wonder we couldn't find you or your family. We were focusing on the States."

"Canada wasn't a safe place to hide after my dad was gone. It's easier to get lost in America." Eva sighed.

"Yes, it is," he murmured while his mind swiftly made connections. Everything about Eva was falling into place. "Your dad was a brilliant engineer."

Stonewall Industries was a hybrid. It had been founded to make robotic parts used in manufacturing. It had quickly evolved into a think tank that had generated some key industrial patents in various fields. When the company shuttered, the patent portfolio had been divided up and sold piecemeal for a king's ransom.

Damov Industries had even made a bid for two of the green energy patents. Sergei had been disappointed to learn that they weren't going on the auction block with the rest of the portfolio. He'd been informed that the family was holding onto them.

After his second offer had been rejected, he'd moved on. But beyond that, he had never thought to inquire more about Wallace Stone. It made total sense that Eva was his child. She had inherited his brilliant mind, with its innate understanding of all things technical. But it was more than talent, he realized. It was training. Father had probably made it a point to pass on his knowledge to daughter.

"You're an heiress," he said aloud, suddenly.

Her father's inventions and patents had been worth a fortune.

"No, I'm not. Karl is an heir."

"Oh. He did it for the money," he said in belated realization.

She nodded. "He did have some, but he may have needed more. It's a long story."

"Okay. I'm sorry I keep interrupting. Start here," he said tapping the picture.

Eva smiled at the image, but it was tinged with bitterness. "You know, I think we ended up where we did because of me. Because my dad wanted to give me a mother," she said in a flat voice. "I really don't think he wanted to remarry. We were happy on our own. He didn't date, preferring to get lost in his inventions. If there were women he kept them far away when I was little. He often said he was bad at relationships and he'd been blessed to meet a woman, my mother, who could put up with his distraction. She died when I was two. Car accident."

"I'm sorry. So why did he remarry?"

"I was getting older. Dad was staring down the barrel of puberty with a teenage girl, and he blinked," she said with a rueful shake of her head. "So he went about finding me a new mother in a very experimental way. He made charts with desirable traits, cross-referenced with demographic information about the local female populace, and started dating. In retrospect, he should have had a harder time of it. Dad wasn't exactly gifted in the social graces."

"But he was decent looking and very wealthy," Sergei supplied.

"Exactly. Eventually, he met Sarah. She was a wealthy divorcee from a good family. I'm not sure she was the kind of woman dad was looking for, but he figured the fact that she was already a mother was a bonus. He mentioned it as a plus more than once when they were still dating."

"And was she a good mother?"

"In her way."

"Uh oh. Not exactly what your father intended, was she?"

"Yes and no. The most important thing to Sarah was her position in our small society. Not motherhood. Even though she went through all the motions and was a decent mother to me, before *and* after they married, it wasn't why she married my dad."

"Being rich and important was the point," he supplied.

"Yes, although it feels unkind to say so now. She did try and was never neglectful or anything. She took me bra shopping and bought me my first box of maxi pads when the time came, which was the most important thing to my dad. And in a way, she was good for him," Eva said, stroking her father's image with her finger. "She was a socialite and knew how to throw a proper cocktail party, the kind where people schmooze and make deals. She could speak several languages and would put the best spin on his social ineptness at business dinners and gatherings. I'm not sure Dad would have been half as successful without her pushing him into doing stuff like that. In fact, I know he wouldn't have been.

"I no longer got to spend so much time with Dad, but we adjusted," Eva continued. "Sarah was a force of nature, and to some extent we were just carried along in her wake. She knew exactly why dad had married her, but it was a source of discontent for her. She wanted to pretend that their relationship had been a glorious romance. But my dad was no Romeo," she said with a frown.

"There was this locket," she said tapping the photo. Around Sarah's neck was a blue enamel oval. "It's been in Dad's family for generations. It's somewhat valuable, but mostly because of its history. It belonged to someone in the court of Louis the sixteenth. After the French Revolution, our ancestors moved to the new world and the locket was passed down. The firstborn son would give it to his bride on their wedding day. My mother wore it before she died, and after she was gone Dad saved it for me."

Ahh. "And Sarah wanted it," he guessed.

"Yes. It was very important to her that she wear it. She was the firstborn son's bride after all. That wouldn't have been a big deal, but she wanted Karl to get it when he married. It was their first disagreement. Dad eventually rolled over and gave it to her. However, he did stipulate that I would get it in their will, not Karl. That really bothered Sarah, but she knew when to pick her battles, and she let it go."

He nodded. "What about Karl?"

The suspense was killing him.

Eva shrugged. "Karl was a senior in high school when they got married. He was very popular, the local golden boy."

LUCY LEROUX

Turning to look her in the eyes, he detected a hint of mortification there.

"When they first got married, I worshipped the ground he walked on," she continued, "In fact, I thought getting him for a brother more than made up for the fact that I had to share my father. I used to follow him around everywhere...and he ignored me as was appropriate given our age difference."

Sergei did not love hearing that, but he tried not to let it show. "How did he get along with your father?"

"Well enough in the beginning. At least I think so. I may have been too young to notice every nuance, but everything seemed normal at first. If there was any friction, it was brought about by Sarah. She wanted my father to consider Karl a son."

Sergei was starting to get the picture. "A son *and* heir. One equal in his mind to his biological child."

Eva nodded. "I really don't think Karl cared at first. He was in high school and had all these friends and admirers. Winning over his geek of a stepfather was probably really low on his list of priorities. But Sarah was insistent. She said Karl needed a positive male role model since his father wasn't in the picture, and they both got tired of her nagging that they bond. So they went fishing on the lake and hiking in the woods behind our house. It was all good...for a while."

"And then what happened?"

"I'm honestly not sure. But I have an idea of *when* things first went wrong. It was the spring of Karl's senior year. He used to go off to the woods with his friends sometimes but just as often all alone. I used to follow him, but he would lose me right away. One day, my dad sat me down and told me not to do that anymore. He told me to stay far away from Karl and to avoid being alone with him. He seemed freaked out about something. I didn't understand," she said, smiling wryly. "I thought Karl hung the moon, and I didn't know what dad could have possibly found out to make him dislike him. I'm still not absolutely sure, but whatever it is, it's buried in the woods behind our house."

Startled, Sergei pulled her in close. "Why do you say that?"

"Well...because I didn't listen to my dad, and I kept following Karl

140

out there. One time, I got pretty far. So far I ended up lost for hours. I was scared and hungry, but after dark fell I stumbled on Karl in this clearing. He was burying something. I didn't see what it was, but when he saw me there, he got really mad. He yelled at me, and I started crying, and he told me it was dangerous to go out in the woods so late. Then he took me home. I never followed him again."

"And you never found out what it was?" Sergei asked, afraid for her even though the events she was describing had happened long ago.

"No, but I have a few theories. It was either our neighbor's Husky, Sammy, which disappeared around that time or..."

"Or what?" he asked in dread.

"Or Riley Jans' underwear."

"*What?*"

Eva rolled her shoulders stiffly and wrinkled her nose. "Riley Jans was the prettiest woman in town. She was in her twenties and was engaged to a nice man, but they hadn't moved in together yet. Then there was a series of break-ins at her apartment. Some of her stuff went missing. Word spread around town that she thought someone was following her. But no one ever found out who it was. Eventually, everything died down, probably when she married and moved in with her husband. And things went back to normal. Except for how things were between Karl and Dad."

"So you really think it was one of those two? Dog killer or stalker?"

"It's all I can think of to explain how Dad behaved. Or," she said, throwing up her hands, "I'm way off and it was something else entirely. I honestly don't know which is worse."

Sergei thought the thing about the dog sounded worse...but he wasn't a woman. A woman would feel more vulnerable about a potential stalker. Either way, both possibilities were horrible when he imagined his angel growing up in the same house with the guy.

"After a while, it all blew over. Soon Karl was graduating. Sarah threw a weeklong celebration, and the house was filled with other teenagers. Even Dad seemed to forget he'd ever said anything. And then Karl went away to school. Except for Sarah pushing him around a bit, things turned out pretty much the way Dad wanted. Every once in a while, Karl would come home from school. He even brought girls home sometimes. Sarah hated all of them, but Dad always seemed happy to see them."

Too happy? That would suggest the stalker theory was correct, Sergei thought, suppressing a surge of anger directed at Wallace Stone. Genius he might have been, but no father worth the name would let such a danger near his little girl. Clearly not rocking the boat was more important than his daughter's safety.

"Then what happened?"

Eva shrugged. "Time went on. I started college. I had a chance to go earlier, when I was fourteen, but Dad wanted me to wait so I wouldn't be so much younger than everyone else. So I started at seventeen and things were going great. I studied engineering and economics. I had this idea that I would run Stonewall someday. Dad never said so, but it was what he wanted. But Sarah wasn't so happy at the prospect.

"By then, Stonewall was a real name in business, and Karl had also studied economics as well as international finance and banking. But he had always wanted to be a Wall Street bigwig. It was all he talked about. In fact, he had been working out there for a while, and he rarely came home while I was growing up. His visits in college had been restricted to the major holidays because he'd spent summers interning at Fortune 500 companies. So when he came home for the first time after I'd started college, we hadn't seen each other in person for years."

"And you had changed," Sergei said, filling in the blanks.

He could just picture it. Coming home for a perfunctory family visit only to find that his stepsister had been transformed into a beautiful young woman with angelic good looks. He hated admitting it, but he and this Karl guy had a lot in common. Sergei knew he would have taken one look at Eva and done whatever he had to do to have her. *Almost* anything, he amended silently.

Eva frowned and pulled her knees in close to her body. "All I know for sure is that suddenly Karl cared about being Dad's son. He moved back to Canada and based himself nearby in Port Moody. He came to visit a lot more, and he got involved with the business for the first time. He never said so, but it was like he'd adopted Sarah's idea for him to take over Stonewall as his own. I suspect now that he'd done something stupid, had lost money, and was looking for a windfall."

"How did your dad react to that?"

"At first, it seemed to confuse him. He'd been pretty wrapped in work at the time. I think it was a refuge from all the socializing Sarah forced him to do. But he started paying attention when Karl started spending so much time at home during my college breaks," she said.

At least her father hadn't been a total idiot, Sergei thought. At the very least, Wallace would have been on alert for any changes in his stepson's behavior toward his only child. "How did Karl act with you?"

Eva hesitated. "He was different."

"Different how?"

"He was just different. More...attentive. Interested in my studies and my friends. He wanted to know about my boyfriends. I told him I didn't have any. MIT wasn't exactly a hotbed social scene, although every freshman girl gets her own stalker for a while. It's traditional. But I was a late bloomer and I was very shy in school," she said. Her brow wrinkled. "Karl seemed pleased by that. He said there was plenty of time for that sort of thing later."

I'll just bet he was pleased, Sergei growled internally, although he perked up at the news that she'd gone to MIT. Their kids were going to be geniuses. But there was still the issue of this Karl and his attentions to Eva.

"Did he try anything?"

The question hung in the air.

"No...not exactly," Eva said uncertainly.

That qualification sent a surge of anger through Sergei, but Eva was continuing and, he needed to focus on what she was telling him. Forcing himself to calm down, he gave her his full attention.

"Nothing happened, but Dad didn't like having Karl around anymore. And he didn't like that Sarah was trying to get him to leave more of the daily operations of Stonewall to her son. She wanted to travel and make more trips to New York and other major cities. She said that it would be good for business if they made themselves more available for meetings. Dad argued with her, really argued this time, that Karl would be a better representative for Stonewall in New York than the two of them. Karl knew the people there and was much better at all the wheeling and dealing. Dad had no idea how true that was."

Tears welled up in her eyes as she picked at the corners of the photograph. "It seemed like things were coming to a head somehow. Dad and Sarah were fighting all the time, and Karl was acting weird. Like he was my best friend all of a sudden and it was us against our parents. He didn't say anything against them outright. It was more subtle than that. But something felt *off* somehow."

She wiped a tear away. "I was home for spring break just before I was supposed to graduate. And things were calm. Too calm. Dad came to me and told me he was going to make some changes. He was going to sell Stonewall."

"What?" Sergei asked, surprised.

Eva shrugged. "Dad was a tinkerer at heart. Making money had never been all that important to him. And doing as Sarah suggested, giving up the work to do the social part, it was Dad's worst nightmare. Even me taking over Stonewall wasn't as important to him as making all the conflict go away."

"And if Stonewall went away, so would Karl," Sergei added.

"It may have been naive of him, but that is probably what he thought." She shook her head. "Except Karl was his stepson, and he was never going to disappear. As for the business, Dad planned on keeping some of the new energy patents, the ones with the most potential for growth. He was leaving them to me for when I finished school. He said I could sell them or build my own business around them. His lawyer was already drafting the paperwork. And then...then they died."

Putting his arms around her, Sergei held Eva tightly to him.

"It was a normal enough day," she whispered, her hand fisted in his shirt. "A little colder than usual for that time of year. I had finished up the semester's work early with my supervisor's blessing because I had done well on my final project. Graduating was going to be a formality," she said, breathing in deeply.

"We were making plans for a celebration. Despite all the tension, Sarah was not about to let an opportunity to throw a party go by. Even Dad was looking forward to it. I had breakfast with them and went out to see some friends. I didn't take long. When I got back, the house was empty and everything was quiet. I thought nothing of it until they didn't come home for dinner without calling. I was going to head back to school in a few days, and Dad wouldn't have made plans without checking in to see if I wanted to join them. It got late, but they still didn't call, and I couldn't reach them. I was starting to get worried when Karl showed up."

"Had you called him?"

"No. He said he was dropping by to leave some paperwork on something. Busy work. When he saw that I was worried, he stayed with me and started trying to track them down, too."

A tear slid down Eva's face, and she hastily wiped it away. "When morning arrived and we hadn't found them, I knew something terrible had happened. Later that day...their bodies were found in the lake," she said, swallowing heavily. "The boat we owned was a burnt out shell. They found it in the middle of the water, empty, but still afloat. It looked like something blew up and the rest caught fire." Eva sobbed and covered her face with her hands.

Sergei rubbed his hand up and down her arms, silently trying to impart his sympathy.

"I knew something was wrong when they were found. Sarah hated going out on the boat. Said it messed up her hair, and she found it really boring. And it wasn't a nice day for it. It had been too foggy and cold with no sun. I told the police that they wouldn't have gone on the boat that day, but they didn't take me seriously. They promised an investigation but only because I insisted. Dad was too prominent for them to avoid it. But I could tell that they believed it was an accident."

Sergei agreed silently. In his experience, police dismissed anything that didn't fit their initial assessment of a situation.

145

"I didn't know then that Karl had been the one to suggest they look in the lake. I didn't find that out till much later. At the time, I was too numb to make sense of anything. School didn't matter. My friends came to the funeral, but they didn't know what to say. And when they tried to comfort me, they had to go through Karl. He was there all the time now. He moved back into our family house and took care of everything, including the liquidation of Stonewall."

"The sale was still moving forward?" Sergei asked.

Eva nodded. "Karl said he wanted to honor Dad's last wishes. I thought that was so selfless of him. When the liquidation was over, he would be out of a job. But he said that didn't matter. He said I was the only thing that mattered. Me, and my well-being." Raising a shaky hand, Eva brushed back a stray hair. "Soon it was just me and Karl. He organized everything—the funerals, the memorials, the sale. All of the other things you don't even think about till someone you love is gone. And I let him. He took over everything, and I didn't even stop to question it."

"You were traumatized," Sergei assured her. "It was only natural that you would lean on the only family you had left."

"I've told myself the same thing since...but I should have realized what was going on sooner. Karl had managed to isolate me from everyone, and he did it with my complicity. After a while, once I was thinking more clearly, I started to get suspicious. Everything he said and did was...I don't know. Too perfect. And then the men showed up."

"What men?"

"Dangerous-looking men. Bodyguards, but they weren't like yours. These men were scary looking. And too quiet. None of them looked quite right."

"Criminals?"

"I think so. I didn't know for sure, but they scared me. Karl had introduced them a little at a time. The next thing I knew, I was surrounded. Bodyguards drove me to the store and sat outside the house's library when I read or watched television in the den. I asked Karl why it was necessary to have them around."

"What did he say?"

She gave herself a little self-abasing shake. "He said he agreed that our parents' deaths were suspicious. Dad had been worth a lot of money and had stood to make millions in profits by selling Stonewall. Karl said it wouldn't have been complicated to figure out a way to profit from his death. I was so grateful when he promised to look into things more that I accepted the bodyguards without a big fuss."

"And soon you were a prisoner," Sergei said softly.

Eva nodded. "I didn't even get what was happening for a while. Karl would take meetings and come home and fill me in on all the details. The numbers he threw out were staggering, but I didn't care about the profits from the sale. All I cared about was the investigation. And it was the one thing he didn't want to talk about." She took a deep breath, like the subject was hard to discuss. "Then things between us changed. Karl started acting—"

Eva broke off and twisted her hands in her dress.

"How did he act?" Sergei prompted, even though his chest was tight with apprehension and anger.

"It was subtle. More casual conversation about his day and little touches. He would bring me flowers or some other little present whenever he went out."

Sergei was careful to control his tone. "He was acting like you were a couple."

"Yes. When it registered, I was too weirded out to talk to him about it. Because I had finally figured out that he was trying to distract me from the investigation. And that the bodyguards weren't there for my protection. I felt trapped. I started to suspect that he was keeping me in the dark about a lot of things."

"Like he might have had something to do with your parent's deaths?"

Eva nodded.

"Is that when you ran away?" Sergei asked.

She looked down. "No," she said eventually.

She hesitated, like she was afraid of his judgment.

"It's all right, Angel. Whatever it is, it's okay to tell me," he assured her.

"I...I wanted to forget my suspicions. To bury them and pretend nothing was going on. Even if it meant letting myself fall into a relationship with Karl that wasn't...sisterly. I could just close my eyes and let him have his way. If I did, then it meant my parents hadn't been murdered."

His heart gave a hard lurch at her words. "But you couldn't do that."

She shrugged and looked away. "I might have. If Karl hadn't given me another gift. He came home one day after a big meeting in the mood to celebrate. The deal he'd brokered for one of the patents was done, and it had made a lot of money. The guards disappeared for the night, and he had a special meal catered. It was a...a romantic setting," she said with a little shudder. "And then he gave me a box."

"What was inside?" he asked when she stopped talking.

"It was the locket," she whispered.

"The family heirloom? The one the first born son gives his bride?" Sergei asked, sick to his stomach.

"Yeah. And that's when I knew for sure. Sarah *never* took that thing off except to shower. And even then, she kept it next to the shower in a special holder and then put it back on immediately afterward. It was her ritual. She'd been wearing it that morning at breakfast. But when they returned their things, it hadn't been listed in the inventory. I asked about it. The police assumed it was lost in the lake. But Karl must have taken it when he killed them."

Sergei held her tight as Eva finally let the tears fall.

"I didn't say anything," she said, crying softly. "I wanted to go to the police, but his men were watching me all the time now. The only place I could think of where they gave me some space was the cemetery. Months had passed, and Dad and Sarah's monument was finally up. I started going there all the time. I waited there for the cavalry to arrive."

"You were waiting for Geoffrey."

"Yes. He was an old friend of my father's from back when my dad was an engineer for the army. They parted ways when Geoffrey started breaking the law professionally and not just for fun. But Dad was still loyal to him. Geoffrey had been the one to introduce Dad to Mom back in the day. For that, Dad gave him the benefit of the doubt when he had to leave the country. They got back in contact after a few years and then stayed in touch. We even visited him a few times before Dad got remarried. And even though I knew Geoffrey wouldn't have been able to come to the funeral, he would have to come to visit the monument sometime. Dad had been his best friend."

"How did you know he hadn't come and gone?" he asked.

"Geoffrey wouldn't have done so without getting in touch or leaving me a sign. I didn't have a way to contact him, and I suspected my communications were being monitored because Karl had given me a new phone and computer. He called them upgrades. But Geoffrey would have left me a message somehow. So I waited and waited. For two weeks, I went to the cemetery every day. Karl thought I had slipped into a deep depression, and I let him think that. He even brought in a therapist for me to talk to. Someone he chose."

Obviously, Karl had been willing to go to great lengths to keep Eva under the impression he was taking care of her. Sergei thought about how uncomfortably close Eva had come to losing herself to that man. A weaker person wouldn't have been able to escape the web Karl had created to snare her.

"Eventually, there was a sign. White orchids were left at the monument. Geoffrey cultivates them. I slipped a note inside their wrapper and set up a vigil. I spent hours at the cemetery waiting for him. Long enough for the guards to get bored and wander off to smoke or kill time on their phones. That's when Geoffrey appeared. He had noticed the bodyguards, so he pretended to visit a grave two spaces over in the preceding row."

She put the picture of her family down. "I couldn't go up to him or even hug him. So we sat there on the ground separately, and I started talking. I told him all my fears and suspicions. The guards thought I was talking to my parents again. Geoffrey promised to look into things, into Karl and what he had been doing with the money from

Stonewall. I...in a way, I was hoping he would find nothing. That way I could tell myself I'd imagined the rest. But I knew better. Still, I had no idea what he was going to find."

God, he hated this. He'd been prepared for something horrible, and while the details weren't nearly so dire as he'd imagined, this was worse in a lot of ways. How close had Eva come to closing her eyes to the truth and *letting* Karl seduce her? The idea made him want to hit something.

"Why did he need the money?" Sergei asked, making an effort to keep his voice low and level.

Eva cleared her throat. "It turns out he had been doing some work for some very bad people. Money laundering. He'd spent all that time away making use of his degree in finance, but for the criminal element. He did start out on Wall Street, but apparently he found working for drug cartels paid better."

"*Fuck*," Sergei exclaimed. "And that's where the bodyguards came from?"

"Yes. Working for the cartels had some side benefits, like armed guards and people who specialized in 'accidental' deaths." She sighed, wiping away the tears. "Geoffrey had found all of this stuff out using his connections. He wasn't sure, but there were rumors Karl had made some bad investments, and his customers weren't happy. I wanted to go to the police, but Geoffrey talked me out of it. The people Karl did business for were too dangerous. Geoffrey wanted me to get out of there and promised to help me figure out a way to stay lost."

He was too good an instructor, Sergei thought. But that was probably for the best. For the second time, he silently thanked Geoffrey's interference. He didn't want to think about where they would be without it.

"I was really freaked out, but I decided to do it," Eva said. "Maybe it was cowardly, but I didn't think anyone would believe me about Karl killing our parents. I almost didn't believe it. Plus Karl had been very visible in the aftermath, with the sale and the police investigation. People deferred to him now. And he had let it be known that I was seeing a therapist and was very depressed. The authorities would have been very skeptical, and my suspicions would have been chalked up to grief. So Geoffrey and I came up with a plan. He set up a fake doctor's appointment." She rolled her eyes slightly. "We took a page out of my Dad's book and picked something a man wouldn't question and or even want to know about."

"And what was that?" Sergei asked.

"A visit to the gynecologist."

Sergei couldn't help it. He started to laugh. "Sorry," he said subsiding. "But that was perfect."

"Dad would have thought so too," Eva said with a sad smile. "I went to the appointment and slipped out the back way. The bodyguards weren't expecting it. Geoffrey had a car waiting. I stayed with him at first, but we both knew it wasn't going to be long term. We set up a few safeguards. I took a crash course in living under an assumed name. And we decided I would keep moving for the next few years until we were sure Karl wasn't looking for me."

"Do you know for sure that he tried to find you?"

She nodded. "Geoffrey looked into it. Karl sent people to everyone he thought might know where I was. He had a different story for each of them."

"What story did he try to feed Geoffrey? Did he even know about him?"

"Yes, he knew. Dad didn't bother to keep their friendship a secret, although he never introduced him or Sarah to Geoffrey in person. It took Karl a while to verify where he actually was. I was long gone by then. He told Geoffrey that I'd become unhinged by our parents death and needed psychiatric assistance."

Asshole. "Is Karl still looking now? It's been years."

"I honestly thought he wouldn't bother after a while, but Geoffrey thinks he still is. Maybe Karl's afraid I have evidence of what he did. But I don't have anything. No proof of any kind."

Sergei pressed his lips together and shook his head. From what Eva had just told him, there was more to Karl's search than a desire to silence her. In fact, he probably understood the creep's motivations a little too well. Pushing that negative thought away, he reminded himself that while he was sometimes a fucking idiot, he would never intentionally hurt Eva ever again. He wasn't some deranged psycho. Karl had killed his stepfather and his own mother. There was a huge gaping chasm between his own possessiveness and Karl's obsession.

You're not like him, Sergei told himself sternly. Aloud, he said, "It's more than what he thinks you know. He wants you. He probably thinks he's in love with you and...I wouldn't stop looking for you either," he confessed.

It was the closest he would come to admitting that he was seeing some uncomfortable parallels between him and Karl.

Eva frowned at him. "I don't think it's about me. Not like that. Yes, Karl was getting personal. But I have no doubt in my mind that if he thought I was a threat, if I accused him of murder or embezzlement, then I'd be dead, too."

Taking her face in his hands, Sergei kissed her before saying, "You don't have to worry about Karl or his contacts anymore. I won't let anything happen to you, and I won't let anything happen to our baby."

Eva hugged him tightly, but she didn't say anything to make him think she believed him.

CHAPTER 21

"I can't believe how big you've gotten," Tim said.

It had been a week since she and Sergei had spilled their secrets to one another. Things had been more relaxed between the two of them now that everything was out in the open. And Sergei had stepped up his plan to spoil her completely. One of his 'gifts' was a surprise visit from Tim.

"I know. I feel like a beached whale," Eva said as she stretched out on a lounger on one of the palazzo's many balconies.

They had had brunch together and were basking in the spring sun. Or at least Eva had tried to. After a few minutes of lying in the warm sunshine, Sergei had come out to scold her for not wearing sunscreen. When she didn't rush off to slather herself in SPF 50, he had servants come out with large beach umbrellas to shade her from the strong rays. Sergei had left soon after to catch up on some work in his office.

"You look great. Just very pregnant," Tim said, his eyes passing over her stomach in a fast skittering appraisal.

He had been a little awkward at first. He was still mad about being kept in the dark, but he seemed to be trying to accept her relationship with Sergei. His crush on her appeared to be over. And judging from the looks he kept giving her, her bulging stomach had hastened its quick death.

"And your hair is amazing," he continued, gushing slightly. "I can't believe that's your real hair color," he said as a security guard passed below them in the garden overlooking the beach. He leaned in conspiratorially. "Sergei told me not to ask, but are you sure you can't tell me what is going on? Why the big mystery and fake names?"

Eva sighed. Tim had been behaving pretty well up till now. Sergei had warned her not to discuss the details of her story with him before he'd left them alone. And, of course, he had ordered Tim not to ask. But his social secretary's irrepressible curiosity was too strong for even the most severe of Sergei's directives.

"The less you know, the better."

Sergei had even insisted she not share her real name with him. Not even her first name.

"*Fine*," Tim said with a slight huff. "But you know that just makes me more curious. And I don't like the implication that I can't keep a secret. I didn't tell anyone you spent the night with Sergei," he said indignantly, waving at her baby bump.

"And yet everyone knows, don't they?" she asked sarcastically.

"That's not my fault! It was the new guy who had just started with Niko, Joseph something," Tim said defensively.

"You know I can check that out with Niko right?" she said, continuing to tease him.

"And he will defend my honor." Tim sniffed before laughing it off. He gestured to one of the guards. "Is getting paroled a possibility? You need to do some baby shopping. Or are you going to hide out here for the rest of your sentence? However long that will be."

Eva pursed her lips. "I don't know if that's such a good idea right now. And Sergei will definitely hate it. He has people send whatever we need."

"That's terrible." Tim scowled. "Half the fun of having a baby is the shower. Since that's obviously not going to happen, you have to get some real shopping in. Picking out clothes and baby booties and all that stuff. My sister has had three kids now, and let me tell you, there's a ton of stuff you need to get. And it's fun. You need a little reprieve from all this grim cloak and dagger stuff," he said, gesturing to the now distant bodyguard.

Knowing Sergei, a second one was probably much closer, but he was carefully out of sight.

Eva was skeptical about Tim's reasons, but she did see one argument for doing some baby shopping. She'd been afraid to bond with her fetus. The thought that she would be separated from her baby still lingered at the back of her mind. Because of that, she tried to play down the sensations her pregnancy engendered.

When Sergei would fuss and touch her belly with awe over the baby's kicks, she would paste a smile on her face until he stopped. She felt guilty about it, but she didn't want to worry Sergei by bringing up her mixed feelings. He probably knew of course. He seemed to know everything she was feeling. But at least he was tactful enough not to bring it up.

Maybe shopping would make her feel closer to her baby. Right now they had some baby things, but they had all been chosen by some faceless personal shopper. What if she asked Sergei to let her go on a little shopping excursion to the mainland or one of the bigger islands with Tim? Sergei would probably agree if Niko and his team came along.

"Maybe," Eva said finally. "I'll run it by Sergei and see if he can stomach the idea. He may insist on coming along."

Tim gave a mock shudder, making Eva laugh. They continued to joke and gossip until Sergei came back to join them for dinner.

SERGEI HAD DONE his best to hide his jealousy and irritation with Tim as he and Eva had dinner with him, but once he was gone, his relief was too obvious to hide. It was probably stupid to feel threatened by Eva's friendship with another man, but he didn't care.

I have to start introducing her to other women, he thought as they watched the helicopter carrying Tim back to the mainland disappear from sight. They were on the balcony outside their bedroom. He reached out and pulled his angel to him, letting her feel his hardness against her body.

"Finally. I thought he would never leave," he said, nuzzling her neck before guiding her inside.

Tim had been giving him a hard time at dinner, lobbying hard for a shopping excursion on the mainland. If his assistant was going to be so difficult, Sergei was going to have to curtail his future visits. The last thing he needed was for Eva to become dissatisfied with life on the island.

He watched her as she moved around the room, slipping off her dress and putting on a short silk nightgown in a dark purple shade that set off her blonde curls.

"I don't know why you keep bothering with the nightgowns," he said, reaching out to stroke the silk of her nightie as she drifted by. "They never last longer than five minutes on you."

He'd even ripped a few in his haste to have Eva naked and in his arms.

"I know you like taking them off," she answered tartly as she climbed into bed next to him, curling close into his side.

She rested her head against his bare chest, and Sergei exhaled, his whole body relaxing. He stroked her soft curls before asking how things had been with Tim when he hadn't been around.

"He didn't pressure you into telling him all of your secrets, did he?" he asked, sneaking his hands under her gown.

He managed to sound only mildly resentful instead of jealous.

"No, he didn't," she assured him, closing her eyes as he stroked the satiny skin of her thighs.

"Good," he murmured, moving his lips down to her collarbone as he began to tug her nightgown up.

She stopped him with a hand. "Before you do that, I did want to ask you for a little favor, and I'd prefer to be dressed while I do it."

Sergei drew his head up to look her in the eyes. "Probably not the best strategy. Don't you know I'm much more likely to give you whatever you want if you're not dressed?"

"But if I was naked, you would get naked, and I would forget the question."

Laughing, he nipped at her nose, and she swatted him away. She hated when he did that.

"So what is this favor?"

It better not have anything to do with Tim.

"I was thinking Tim's idea of a shopping excursion might be a good idea. And you can come with us if you want," she offered.

Sergei frowned. "I can have anything we might need flown in. I don't want you to leave the island," he said, his grip on her tightening.

Eva sighed and stroked his tense, muscled arm. "I know you're worried about our safety," she said, gesturing to her belly. "But Karl doesn't know where I am. And except for Niko and his team, none of your staff even knows my real name. Not my full name anyway. We'd take as many security men as you wanted."

"I don't like it."

"I know. But I think getting to pick some of the clothes and toys for the baby might be a good thing."

There was something in her tone that caught his attention. Stroking her silk covered hip, he asked, "Why do you need to go off island to do it? I can always have a bigger selection of things sent. I could have a boat-full delivered, instead of a helicopter."

Eva's face fell slightly. "Oh. Okay. I guess that's fine," she said, settling deeper into his embrace.

Sergei could feel her disappointment. *Crap.* He exhaled roughly before giving in.

"If you *promise* to take Niko and his entire team, then you can go to Crete or Mykonos. Maybe Santorini. Whichever one gets Niko's approval. But you can't go to Athens unless I come."

Eva beamed at him. "Maybe it should just be the two of us. We should both get a say in what we buy for the baby."

Smiling softly, he stroked her cheek. "I think that's a grand plan. But not as good as this one," he teased as he pulled her nightgown off before covering her body with his.

CHAPTER 22

*T*he morning of the shopping excursion was one of the rare days in spring cold enough for Eva to bundle up. Dressed in a black cashmere dress, she pulled on knee high leather boots and a light wool coat from out of her closet.

Sergei walked into the bedroom frowning. "I can't go," he said, frustrated. "There's been a huge dip in the market. It could be the start of a crash. Adstringo is going to take a big hit if I don't get my plan in place to fend off the sharks."

Eva dropped her coat on the bed. She was disappointed about the outing, but more concerned with Sergei's news. Adstringo had been her baby, and she wanted to make sure the company stayed solvent.

"Don't worry about the shopping. I'd rather stay here and help if I can," she said, reaching to put her hands on his shoulders. "*Do you have a plan?*"

"Yes. But it will take hours to put in place. I always set up contingency scenarios with my staff for all of my new acquisitions for situations just like this. Which is why our other public subsidiaries are safe. Mostly. But I've been a little distracted since I've acquired Adstringo," he said, tweaking her curls. "I should have done it already."

"Sure. Blame the pregnant lady," Eva said, giving him a mock frown.

Smiling wryly, he slipped a hand over her belly, stroking softly. "I don't want you to miss your one outing since you arrived. Niko's team is ready to take you to Santorini instead of Athens. And Tim is nearby. He was going to join us for lunch, so I could prove I wasn't actually holding you hostage," he said, bending to kiss above the neckline of her cashmere dress.

"You don't need to prove anything to Tim or me," she said, drawing her hand through his hair. "But I will take you up on your offer. I am starting to get a little stir crazy here, and the nausea finally seems to be gone. But we won't shop for baby things. That's just for us. We'll buy whatever else strikes our fancy."

"All right. There wouldn't be much of a selection on Santorini for baby stuff in any case. It's a shopping mecca for rich tourists, not expectant mothers. But there are a ton of jewelry stores and some interesting galleries. Some clothes, too, of course. Buy anything you like. If I can get out there at all today, then I will call you. Actually, I'll call you anyway."

"I know you will," she said wryly. "Since you can't even stop from calling me when I'm in the next room...even if you've just seen me in the last hour."

Or the last ten minutes.

"I don't do that," he protested with an air of exaggerated inno-cence. "I usually just text," he said, kissing her goodbye.

Rolling her eyes, she grabbed her coat and went out to the helipad to meet up with Niko and his team.

———

"I can't believe he actually let you out of the house without him! I mean, I knew Sergei could be intense, but you don't know how far off the deep end he goes when he's not with you," Tim said, sipping on a complimentary glass of champagne.

She and Tim had already had lunch in one of the cliffside cafes made famous for their gorgeous views of the caldera and the Aegean Sea.

The crescent-shaped island of Santorini was much smaller than she had expected, but that meant she could see the ends of the island from her chair at lunch, as well as the still active, recently-formed volcanic island in the center of the bay. Other older volcanos dotted the vista on the right.

The contrast of the whitewashed buildings with the crystal blue ocean was breathtaking. She had snapped almost fifty pictures of the vista with her smartphone at lunch.

Eva didn't take Sergei's advice about shopping for jewelry. The impulse to watch her spending was too well ingrained. Or at least it had been at first. Her will power had crumbled the second she walked into the art gallery, NikoLa's. It was a shop that specialized in prod-ucts made from semiprecious stones. Before she could stop herself, she had dropped thousands of euros on a series of jadeite and agate vases and bowls.

She regretted it as soon as she stepped out of the store. The need to save every penny was still strong. But when she had tried to turn around to go back and return everything, Tim had talked her out of it, assuring her that nothing would make Sergei happier than to have her buy things for their family home.

Mollified, she had agreed with him, although her head spun slightly from the amount of money she had spent. Now they were in one of Santorini's most exclusive clothing boutiques. Eva hadn't wanted to go in, telling him that the store would not have any mater-nity clothes.

"You're kidding right?" Tim scoffed. "This place will make anything you like in a maternity version. That is how much money Sergei has."

Eva rolled her eyes as she draped a dark-blue silk wrap dress across her front. In the next largest size, the dress would fit across her pregnant belly with only a slight alteration to the hemline. In fact, there were a number of items that would work on her without ordering a separate maternity version. The eager staff had put all of her selections in the dressing room, after assuring her repeatedly that anything she liked that didn't fit could be redone for her.

Her phone buzzed, and she smiled at her screen before putting the new sleek smartphone away. Sergei had assured her that it was encrypted more heavily than the President's.

"What does Sergei say?" Tim asked wryly.

"Is it that obvious it's him?" Eva asked.

He raised a mocking eyebrow. "Seriously? He calls you before and after meetings and texts constantly. And if he's not texting you, that's only cause he's getting updates from Niko," Tim said before abruptly sitting up. "You did know he did that right? It wasn't news to you."

He sounded guilty and a little concerned that he'd told her something she shouldn't know.

"Relax, I already figured that out," Eva said, handing the blue dress to an attentive sales assistant, who rushed away with it. "Niko may be the soul of discretion, but he's a really loud typist. He can't text quietly to save his life," she said, smiling in the direction of the man in question.

Niko was waiting in the front of the store, his rough unsmiling face hidden behind a pair of dark glasses. But, despite the distance, she could see his nose wrinkle. He couldn't hear as well as she could— according to Sergei, his hearing had been damaged by a percussion grenade. But he could read lips.

Eva threw the bodyguard another smile and was pleased to see that Niko almost smiled back. "I'm going to try on the pile of dresses the salesgirl took away before it threatens to spill into a second dressing room," she said.

"Okay, I'll be right here enjoying all the bubbly you are not allowed to drink," Tim said smugly, bringing the champagne flute to his lips as he leaned back in the plush sofa.

He stretched his arm out along the back and crossed one leg over the other in an exaggerated pose of relaxation. Eva threw a nearby hat at him before she went into the dressing room.

The navy dress was hanging on a changing room door at the far end of the room. Putting a hand on her stomach, she was almost at the door when it suddenly opened.

A large man in a black mask moved toward her, grabbing her and putting his hand over her mouth before she could get away.

"Mmmh!" Eva tried to cry out from behind the hand, which was holding a rag to her face.

A chemical smell flooded her nose and she fought harder. Kicking out, she tried to unbalance her assailant. Grabbing at his hand, she clawed at him with her nails, but her hands were weak and the edges of her vision had started to darken.

Batting ineffectually at the restraining hands, she tried to knock over something that would make enough noise to alert the men waiting for her outside. But all too soon, the drug on the rag did its work, and she fell into darkness.

EVA WOKE UP SLOWLY. Her mouth was dry and tasted like metal. Dizzily, she opened her eyes. She was lying on a large bed in an unfamiliar bedroom. There was a loud humming noise in the background, and she sat up, swaying slightly. Her head hurt. Her brain felt like it was pulsing inside her skull.

Putting a hand to her head, she blinked to clear her vision, but the room was dark, and she couldn't see much of anything beyond the bed.

"You're dehydrated," a familiar voice said as a figure stepped out of the shadows. "Here. Drink this."

Standing there, holding out a water bottle, was her stepbrother Karl.

CHAPTER 23

Sergei was on a conference call, delegating orders to his staff at Damov headquarters in Manhattan. Those that were left there anyway.

He'd split his staff and had moved some key personnel, including his new executive assistant Michael Fisher, to a temporary office he'd set up in Rome in the same building as the Morgese bank. The close proximity to the island allowed him to fly in when he needed to meet with clients, with the added benefit of having the staff under Gio's watchful eye whenever he couldn't be there. His good friend had suggested the arrangement a few weeks ago, and it was working out well.

"Do you have the latest figures from accounting?" Sergei asked Michael.

"Yes Sir, just one minute," Michael said, tapping on his tablet to bring up the file.

One of his junior security men threw open the door. He ran inside.

"Mr. Damov, Niko called. They took her! She's gone!"

"HOW DID THIS HAPPEN?" Alex asked, bewildered.

They were in a penthouse suite of a hotel near the store where Eva had disappeared. Alex had flown in from London as soon as Gio had called him. Sergei had been in a meeting with the local authorities in Santorini at the time.

Gio had been in his office at the bank when Sergei had been told of the kidnapping, and he'd insisted on coming to Santorini, bringing the Morgese security team with them. Almost all of Alex's security force, with the exception of Andrea, Elynn's favorite bodyguard, had come with him. They had joined Niko's men in a house to house search in Santorini after sending men to the local airport and nearest marina. Eva had been missing for almost six hours.

"I don't know," Sergei said, rubbing his face. His voice was hoarse and his eyes were red. He was almost vibrating with tension. "Niko was watching the front of the store with one of his guys. There was a back exit, but it only led to the apartments upstairs with no convenient exit. He thinks she was incapacitated and taken to the roof because they didn't hear her cry out. I don't know how they got her down from there. But that whole shopping district is a nest of winding little paths and closely set buildings. They could have gotten her across to another roof easily, but it's hard to imagine that they wouldn't have been seen doing it. There's always a crowd at this time of year," he said, shaking his head.

"Are you sure she didn't run away again?" Alex suggested softly. "Maybe something spooked her, and she's on her way back to the island on her own," he added, hopefully.

"No," Gio answered. "They found a rag with something on it. It wasn't chloroform, but it was equally effective."

Niko came into the room and went to Sergei. They spoke quietly in Russian before the other man went back out again.

"What did he say?" Alex asked.

"He was offering his resignation again," Sergei said with a frustrated exhalation.

"What did you tell him?" Gio asked.

"I told him to shut the fuck up and find my wife and baby," Sergei growled, pacing up and down the room.

"You're not married yet," Gio reminded him gently, but he changed the subject when Sergei glared at him. "You think it's the stepbrother right?"

"Yes, I do. She would never leave me willingly, not at this point. Not so close to her due date. Even if…"

He stared out the window.

"Even if what?" Alex asked.

Sergei took a deep breath. "It's something she said once. Even if she had decided to leave, she wouldn't take the baby. I think she would have waited till after giving birth if something had happened to scare her enough to leave. It tore her up, but the chance the baby might be harmed kept her up at night."

Alex and Gio gave each other worried looks before Gio's phone buzzed. He looked at the screen. "That's Calen's flight information. He'll be here in three hours and he says he's bringing the cavalry. I guess that means the Tylers are coming, too. I'm sending him the address of the hotel," Gio said as he quickly typed a message.

"All right," Alex said, standing up to pace. He always did that too when he was working things out. "Then if it is this Karl guy we need to forget the house to house. He'll want off the island as fast as possible. The police have the airport and the two ports covered so we have to focus on the rest of the coastline. Anywhere a boat could land. They would have had a larger boat waiting off the coast to avoid filing papers with the marina. We need to start bribing fisherman for information."

"I'm sure Niko has started that," Sergei mumbled, stopping to eye the bar longingly.

"Don't even think about it," Gio scolded.

"I'm not going to drink." Sergei frowned, resuming his pacing, avoiding the path Alex was walking.

"I know man. Just keep making calls. Gio and I will make sure everyone's on the lookout for a boat," Alex said.

"It's a fucking island! If that was their escape route, we'll never find her," Sergei said, his voice cracking.

"Yes, we will. And let me tell you how," Gio began in his soothing lyrical voice as he stood up to comfort Sergei. "We're going to follow the money. You said this Karl is a money launderer. Right now I'm directing the fraud experts in my bank to liaise with Interpol and other sources in every hole guys like him hide assets. Everyone leaves a trace somewhere. We'll find him."

"That is probably our best bet," Alex agreed. "But let me take over with the locals. My family has a lot of investments here, and the neighboring islands, as well as Greece proper. I can throw my weight around more effectively."

"Okay. So what the hell do I do?" Sergei asked, throwing up his hands.

"Why don't you call Geoffrey Johansen?" Gio suggested. "He's been keeping tabs on Karl for years. He might know his current whereabouts."

"Oh god," Sergei said, rubbing his face. "Why didn't I think of that?"

"Because right now your heart is threatening to burst out of your chest," Alex said, coming up and putting a hand on his shoulder. "Don't forget, I've been where you are right now. You have to keep a level head. And when you can't, well, that's what we're here for."

Sergei let out a harsh breath. "Thanks, guys."

"THIS WAY MISS," a round face maid said as she led Eva to the deck of the yacht.

Two tattooed men followed close behind her, their bulging biceps on display in the short-sleeved shirts they wore.

When Eva had first woken up, she hadn't realized she was on a boat. But the rolling pitch of the floor underneath the bed, coupled with the low hum of a large motor, soon enlightened her.

Other than offering her a bottle of water, Karl had said nothing at that first meeting. Neither had she. She'd been too freaked out when he'd just stared, unsmiling, at her pregnant stomach. Then he'd left without another word.

The door to the cabin was locked, and aside from some tiny portholes in the bathroom too small for her to crawl through, there was no other opening in the room. She looked everywhere, but there was no hidden door and nothing she could use as a weapon. Despondent, she had cried herself to sleep after drinking three glasses of water from the sink in the bathroom. She hadn't wanted to drink from the water bottle.

A few hours later, a maid woke her. Eva washed her face while the woman waited. Outside the porthole, the light indicated the approach of sunset. When they left the cabin, the muscled men who'd been waiting in the hallway shadowed her every move.

A carpeted staircase led to the deck. The yacht was large, much larger than she'd guessed. There was an elaborately set table centered in the open space, complete with white tablecloth and candelabra. Karl was seated in one of the two chairs, dark glasses covering his eyes as he stared in the direction of the setting sun. She slipped into the empty chair and waited for him to speak.

Karl turned and gave her a long, slow examination, focusing on the changes in her since he'd seen her last.

"How far along are you?" he asked, slipping off his dark glasses.

Eva studied him. He was still handsome, with his cool blonde looks and light blue eyes. But his eyes were a little red and he'd acquired new lines on his face as if he'd been under an enormous strain.

"I'm thirty-six weeks," she whispered eventually.

Karl lifted a glass of wine to his lips to drink before answering. Putting it down, he said, "So it should be soon. I assume the Russian is the father, given how he's been hiding you away."

Eva's heart sank. Her dismay must have shown on her face, because Karl continued with a bitter smile. "Yes, I know all about him. I've been watching him for a while. I even know you worked for him. Your hair was brown then. I didn't like it. Your natural color suits you much better," he said as he motioned for a hovering waiter to refill his glass.

Though her hand trembled slightly, her voice was steady. "Why did you do it?" Eva asked in a low voice.

Karl frowned but he didn't pretend not to know what she was talking about. "I *didn't*," he said, his jaw clenched tightly. "And I can't believe you still think I'm capable of hurting our own parents."

"Then why am I here under armed guard?"

Karl shook his head. "Those men are here for your protection and mine," he said in disbelief. "Our parent's killer is still out there. And then you disappeared." He stopped and glared at her, frustration radiating off him. "Do you have any idea what I've gone through? I thought the killer had gotten you, too. I searched for your body for almost a year, using every connection and bit of influence I had. How do you think I felt when I finally figured out you were still alive?"

His voice rang with hurt indignation. Even his eyes were shiny with unspent tears. For a moment, Eva's conviction wavered. He sounded so damn sincere.

Remember what Geoffrey said. Karl was a good actor. The men surrounding them were not bodyguards.

"If you didn't kill them, why am I here? Why bother to find me? The money was yours. I don't care about it. You can have it all. I just want to leave here and go back to the father of my baby. You said it yourself. He was protecting me just fine. Till your men kidnapped me and brought me here."

Karl sighed and settled back in his chair. He shook his head sadly. "I can't believe you are just sitting there saying such terrible things to me. You broke my heart when you left. *Do you hear me?*"

By the end, he was on his feet shouting. Eva flinched and pushed her chair away from the table. Heart pounding, she took several gasping breaths as her body broke out in a cold sweat. Swaying in her seat, she clutched at the seat's edge to steady herself.

Karl's face softened as he took in her fear and panic. "I'm sorry," he said more softly. "I know this isn't your fault. That crazy old man Geoffrey filled your head with lies when you were at your most vulnerable. Your father should have never let that man anywhere near you. Instead, Wallace encouraged you to think of that criminal as a friend," he condemned, as he sat back in his chair. His tone became entreating. "Don't you know how badly I want to take care of you? You're all the family I have left, and he turned you against me."

Eva swallowed convulsively. What should she do? Keep arguing with him until he snapped and hurt her, or lie? Could she somehow convince him that she believed him? If she won his trust, then maybe he would let his guard down long enough for her to escape.

But if she capitulated now, he would never buy it. Deciding silence was the best option she stared at him, letting her eyes fill with tears. They came easily.

"Look, you need to eat something," he said, giving her stomach a damning glance before slipping into a warmer expression.

He poured her a glass of wine as if in defiance of her pregnancy. "You're still in European waters. A sip is perfectly okay," he said with the semblance of a friendly smile.

Eva pushed the glass away, and Karl's eyes grew cold again. His mouth was tight as he motioned to a waiter. A plate of salad materialized in front of her.

Hiding a tremor, she wiped her sweaty hands on her dress before pulling her chair back to the table. Lifting the fork slowly, she ate mechanically, with little appetite.

She didn't want to eat what he served her, but she wasn't alone in this. Thinking of her baby, she forced each mouthful down until it was gone. When the plate was clean, she asked him the question that had been troubling her since she woke up on the yacht.

"How did you find me?" she asked, meeting Karl's eyes.

His mouth twisted slightly. "You can thank your Russian for that."

Eva shifted uncomfortably in her chair. "What do you mean?"

Karl sat back in his chair and crossed his legs. "I mean, I've been watching your Mister Damov for some time. Ever since he went to visit Geoffrey Johansen. It's ironic that he's the reason you are here, given how hellbent he was on keeping you under wraps. It's not a lead

I expected to pan out actually. I really thought the DaricDollars were going to be key to finding you."

Eva felt sick. "The DaricDollars?"

That was the digital currency Uncle Geoffrey had given her. Was it a fake? But she'd been able to spend some of it.

"Yes," he said. "It wasn't as complicated as I thought to set up a digital currency. I had been contemplating using one for my work. Slapping on a name that Geoffrey would find intriguing was simple. You're the one who told me about his fascination with ancient Persia. You did know the Daric was the name of the coin of the realm. Darius the First named them after himself."

Stricken, Eva had trouble catching her breath, but Karl ignored her distress. *She* had been the one to tell Karl about Geoffrey's passion for ancient Persia over a family dinner years ago.

"Some persuasive advice from one of his old cronies and Geoffrey became a DaricDollars convert. I had people all over San Diego looking for you, but you didn't spend enough of the money for me to find you. But you're here now, and I can finally help you," he said softly.

"You want to help me?" Eva echoed hollowly.

"Yes," Karl said, his eyes filled with pity. "Geoffrey Johansen filled your head with lies about me...and you let him," he said, shaking his head sadly. "You've clearly lost the ability to judge right from wrong. You need me to take care of you, to make sure you don't lose touch with reality again," he said earnestly, reaching over to take her hand.

"What about my baby?" she whispered. "And the baby's father? I *need* him."

She had never said anything remotely like that to Sergei, but it was true. She needed him. She loved him. *And you didn't even tell him.*

Eva could only hope Sergei knew, like he seemed to know every-thing else about her.

Karl's face hardened, and he looked away without replying. He got up and walked to the railing. His hands gripped the bars, his back to her. The longer the silence stretched, the faster her heart beat. Finally, he turned back to her with a warm smile.

"We're having fish for dinner," Karl said brightly. "I know you don't like fish very much, but you'll love how my chef prepares it."

Eva stared at him with her mouth slightly open. What was wrong with him? Was he simply going to pretend he wasn't holding her hostage?

"You have to let me go," she said in a low steady voice. "If you're really so concerned with my well-being, you'll do it. I have a new life that I need to get back to. I'll sign whatever you want. You can have anything you want, all of Stonewall's patents and profits. Just let me leave."

Her voice sounded desperate and pathetic to her own ears, but she didn't care. Unfortunately, neither did Karl. He just gave her another one of those sad pitying looks before proceeding to ignore her as the waiter returned and set an elaborately decorated plate in front of her.

An entire grilled fish, covered in a light green sauce and almonds stared back up at her with its small lifeless eyes. Frowning at it, she breathed in and almost gagged. The fish smell was overpowering. Her stomach rebelled. Nauseated, she pushed it away.

"I can't eat this," she said, trying to draw her head as far away from the smell as possible.

His lips compressing into a thin line, Karl gestured for the waiter to take their plate away. "Bring something else. No seafood."

The waiter rushed away. Karl took her full wineglass.

"Since you're not going to need this," he said, downing the contents of the glass in one move.

He turned back to the setting sun. In the distance, an unknown landmass got smaller and smaller. She knew nothing about yachts, but it seemed like they were going too fast. They were practically flying over the water. And the hum of the engine seemed loud to her, like they were maxing out.

"Where are we going?" Eva asked apprehensively.

And how is Sergei ever going to find me?

Karl smiled at her, but it had an edge to it. "We're going home of course."

171

"Rise and shine!" Karl said brightly, entering the bedroom ahead of a maid pushing a breakfast tray on a wheeled cart.

Days had passed since that disastrous dinner on the deck, and she hadn't seen Karl once since. Instead, she had been locked in her cabin, allowed outside only after meals to get some exercise by walking the decks.

Karl had been noticeably absent during those walks. Once, she had heard him speaking to someone in the distance, but when she asked the guards to speak to him, their stony silence had been so unnerving that she hadn't asked again.

Meals arrived in her room in a timely fashion, but the maids who delivered them had made it clear that they weren't allowed to speak to her, either. The isolation had been more frightening than the thought of spending time with Karl again. Not being allowed to talk to anyone kept her in a constant state of anxiety.

Eva had no idea where they were going. Instead of getting colder, like it should have if they were headed to Canada, the weather grew balmy and tropical. She no longer needed the light coats she found in her closet. Instead, she wore one of two light summer dresses. There were many more in the closet, but none were suitable maternity wear, a detail she found disturbing.

Alone with only her fears, Eva spent her time imagining the worst. Karl clearly resented the fact she was pregnant. The way he had looked at her belly, when he'd looked at it at all, chilled her to the bone. When her meals arrived she waited as long as possible before actually eating it.

The thought that Karl might put something in her food that might hurt the baby terrified her. But if he did, he would endanger her life, too. She was far enough along that she would need medical intervention if he tried to cause a miscarriage. Or at least that's what she tried to tell herself when she finally broke down and ate something.

Fresh food arrived every few days by helicopter whenever they got close enough to certain landmasses. They never stopped anywhere as far as she knew, unless they did it in the dead of night once she had finally managed to fall asleep. But while food and other supplies were replenished, no new clothes appeared in her closet.

Eva pulled the covers over herself when Karl approached the bed, feeling exposed in her thin nightgown.

"Where have you been?" she asked.

"I've been busy making arrangements," he said cheerfully, waving a second maid inside the room.

The woman's arms were full of shopping bags with exclusive names. Smiling at Eva, Karl pulled out box after box from the bags and he set them around her.

"Arrangements for what?" Eva asked bewildered.

"For the baby of course," Karl said rolling his eyes. "I had to interview doctors and buy baby clothes and bottles. I even got you some new dresses. It will take a few months for you to get your figure back afterward, but don't worry about that. There's a gym on the second deck you can use later."

"Later?" Eva echoed.

What happened to going home to Vancouver? He was talking like they were going to be on this boat forever. And why was he suddenly so happy about her pregnancy?

"After the baby comes, of course. Eat quickly and get dressed. There is someone I want you to meet waiting upstairs," he said, sitting down next to her.

Eva shrank away from him, and for a second, the mask slipped. Karl's smile grew brittle, but it stayed in place. Ignoring her tension, he leaned in to place a lingering kiss on her forehead before stroking her cheek.

His touch burned, but it was like the sting of ice instead of warmth. Swallowing hard, she stayed still as he began to toy with her curls.

"I can't eat if you're going to sit there," she said finally, suppressing a shudder as he continued to play with her hair.

"You're right," he said, smiling wryly and getting up.

He pushed the cart closer. Taking a linen tablecloth, he laid it on her lap with a flourish before removing the cover of the tray. There was a plate of eggs next to a diced fruit salad alongside some English crumpets slathered with melted butter.

"Here," Karl said, handing her a glass of orange juice. "It's fresh squeezed with no pulp, just like you like it."

"Thank you," she whispered, taking the glass, causing the sheet to slip.

Reddening, she tugged it back up with her free hand. Karl's sudden and dramatic change of attitude was making her dizzy. Not to mention the way he was standing over her and staring. Forcing a forkful of fruit to her lips, she chewed under his watchful eye.

"It's weird that you're watching me eat," she said softly. Karl's face grew cold. Hurriedly she qualified her words. "I mean while I'm eating alone like this. We should have eaten on the deck...together."

She would have said anything to avoid being isolated again, but her tone didn't sound enthusiastic. However, that didn't seem to matter to Karl.

His frown faded. "I'm sorry I've been so busy, darling. Why don't you eat and join me upstairs when you're done," he said with an indulgent smile.

Darling?

"Okay," she said uncertainly.

Maybe she shouldn't have asked him to resume sharing meals with her. Karl had an odd manic look to him today. His eyes were overly bright and his movements were exaggerated—just a little too quick and abrupt. For the first time, she wondered if he was on drugs.

Growing up, he'd been a star athlete who'd participated in sports all year long. When football ended, he would play basketball, followed by baseball in the spring. Even now he was fit, with a lean muscular build. She would never have guessed that he would abuse anything, but if he'd been laundering money for drug cartels, then anything was possible.

Having never spent time around any drug users, it was hard for her to tell if she was right. But it would explain how he was acting. Although, she reminded herself, there was nothing that could explain what he'd done to their parents. Steeling her resolve, she stayed still when he leaned over to give her a quick kiss on the cheek.

"Try to hurry," he said cheerfully. "You don't want to keep our guest waiting."

He and the maids, who had spent the duration of their conversation changing the clothes in her closet, left her alone to eat.

Though her stomach had been unsettled by the visit, she made herself swallow every bite. Then she showered and changed into a new maternity dress, relieved that at least Karl was starting to accept her pregnancy.

———

"HERE SHE IS, DOCTOR," Karl said with a smile as she entered the room where he and another man were seated.

Giving a silent sigh of relief, Eva moved farther into the yacht's central living room. For a second, she had been worried that their guest was Sergei, tied to a chair with a gun to his head.

175

"Oh, she is just as lovely as you said she was," the stranger said with an effusive smile as he rose to shake her hand.

"Eva, this is Dr. Ritter," Karl said.

"Hello," Eva said quietly as the sweaty man pumped her arm up and down.

Dr. Ritter was only an inch or two taller than her, with a round red face and an abundance of hair on his head and arms. Some of it even peeked through the gap between the buttons of his shirt as they shook hands.

Eva put a hand on her stomach and sat down, keeping the doctor between her and Karl. Hope bubbled in her chest. Maybe this man could help her. Perhaps he could be persuaded to get her out of here. Or at least pass on a message to someone who could. Like Sergei or the CIA.

"Eva, Dr. Ritter is a specialist," Karl said. "I want you to tell him everything you told me. He won't judge you. He's only here to help."

Confused, Eva's gaze shifted back and forth between the two men.

"What are you talking about? Aren't you an obstetrician?" she asked apprehensively.

"No, darling. Dr. Ritter is a psychiatrist. He specializes in situations like yours," Karl said.

"My situation?" she said stupidly.

"Mrs. Grayson, the term for what happened to you is a psychotic break. But I don't want you to let that scare you. It's an intimidating phrase for something that is actually quite common. And it occurs for many different reasons."

Eva's heart sank down to her shoes. "What?" she gasped. What did he call her? "Wait! I'm not married to Karl."

Karl and Dr. Ritter exchanged a glance. Karl's expression was one of long-suffering patience.

"Mrs. Grayson, you were warned this could happen when you and your husband decided to get pregnant and you went off your medication. Of course, he didn't realize something so extreme was possible, that you would imagine a whole other life where he's some sort of villain. I'm here to help you get back to where you were before all this happened. Happily married and expecting your first child with your devoted husband."

The fragile bubble of hope in her chest burst, swiftly replaced by dread. Karl rose and sat next to her on the couch. He took her hand, his eyes filled with genuine warmth and understanding.

"Oh god," she said aloud, squeezing her eyes shut.

CHAPTER 25

"F*uck!*" Sergei shouted as he slammed the phone down on the desk.

He was in the Greek offices of Hanas industries with his three friends. They had taken over the top floor of executive suites in the building, shifting personnel so they could have privacy to organize their search for Eva. Alex had suggested the change once they had determined that there was no way Eva was still on Santorini.

A fisherman had seen a group of men in big coats and scarves carrying a blanket wrapped bundle to a motorboat on the east side of the island, directly from across the area where Eva had been shopping. A midsize cruiser had been anchored in the distance.

After an extensive search by the Hellenic Coast Guard, both of those vessels had been found abandoned. They had been reported stolen from nearby locations in the Mediterranean.

Sergei had just gotten off the phone with Geoffrey Johansen's maid for the third time that day. He hadn't been home when Sergei called the first twenty times. He'd left his Caribbean hideaway a few days before Eva's disappearance without telling his staff where he was going. Sergei had done everything he could to track him down unsuccessfully. Geoffrey hadn't even called home to check in.

"No luck?" Ethan Thomas asked from across the room, where he was surrounded by a pile of papers next to Gio.

"No," Sergei answered shortly.

Calen's cavalry *had* included his childhood friends the Tyler brothers, Liam and Trick. But he'd also brought their sister Maggie's FBI agent husband, Jason White, and his partner Ethan. Both men had taken a leave of absence from their posts to come and help him find Eva. And despite his natural distrust of police officers, a trait instilled by his father, Sergei was grateful for their presence. Even if he wasn't capable of showing it right now.

Jason and Ethan were using their connections to dig up information from Interpol and various other agencies about Karl Grayson. They had found a number of different aliases Grayson had used in the past. By the time Calen and the others landed, a courier had arrived for Ethan with a thick file of background information about Karl.

It turned out the CIA had been keeping an eye on Grayson's activities for years, although they didn't have enough evidence to prosecute him for any crimes. Nor did they have any idea of his current whereabouts. Grayson had dropped off their radar over three months ago. According to Ethan's friend Mason at Interpol, they suspected Grayson had done so because he was planning something big.

Well, he had been, Sergei thought bitterly. It just wasn't what they had been expecting. Whenever he thought about what Eva must be going through, he wanted to put his fist through a wall. He'd come close a few times, but between Calen and Gio, he'd managed to calm down enough to make another phone call or talk to yet another K & R specialist.

In addition to their search, he and the others were busy making contingency plans for a rescue. But until they knew where Eva was, their plans were pure speculation.

Niko knocked briefly before coming into the room. "The uncle has called," he said shortly in Russian. All heads turned to him, but only Calen and he understood Russian. "He has been following Grayson," Niko continued. "He sent GPS coordinates."

"What Uncle? And where is Grayson?"

Niko turned around. The question had come from Ethan. Apparently the special agent understood Russian well enough to decipher Niko's growl.

"Grayson is on a yacht off the coast of Bermuda. He has resources there," Niko said shortly in English for the benefit of the rest of the room.

Gio, Calen, and Alex simultaneously grabbed their cell phones while Sergei sagged in a chair. Eva was on a yacht, waiting to be rescued. Across the room, Alex was making flight plans under Jason's direction.

"We can't fly directly to Bermuda without tipping our hand," Jason was saying. "We'll have to land somewhere else and take a boat in."

Even though the comment hadn't been addressed to him, Sergei nodded. From behind him, the younger Tyler brother, Trick, clapped him on the shoulder.

"Everything's going to be all right," Trick said.

"I know," he replied, trying to sound like he meant it.

SERGEI WAS RELIEVED when Geoffrey met them in a small commuter airport outside of Miami. They had decided to stay away from major airports at Ethan's suggestion, and had flown in using pseudonyms in small batches using chartered planes.

Geoffrey took one look at his face and forced him to sit down in a chair. Without a word, he poured him a generous quantity of liquid from a silver flask into a paper cup.

Sergei drank the strong spirit down in one gulp, unable to taste it enough to figure out what it was. He knew he was a mess. A glance in the mirror showed his eyes were bloodshot and the circles under them were deep black smudges. Every time he tried to sleep, he was startled awake by nightmares he was glad he couldn't remember.

"I'm sorry I didn't call you back," Geoffrey apologized. "I was on the move, trying to track down Karl and his staff. I finally had a bit of luck, some information from one of my people in Bermuda. Karl has been seen on the island, at the home of a retired cartel head."

"Do you have a name?" Ethan asked from behind him.

Geoffrey turned around to the group of waiting men. Calen and Gio were there with Jason and Ethan, but they were still waiting for Alex and the Tyler brothers, who were about to land in a few minutes. Geoffrey assessed the men in front of him with one glance, taking in Ethan and Jason's clothes and bearing.

"Everyone this is Geoffrey—" Sergei began.

"Smith," Geoffrey interjected, offering Ethan and Jason his hand before the others. "I'm an old school chum of Eva's father."

"So you're not her uncle?" Ethan asked, suspicious as always.

"Not by blood," Geoffrey said, giving him a charming, if tired smile.

Ethan started to ask him something else, but Sergei glared at him and Jason cleared his throat. Ethan shut his mouth and backed up a few steps. Geoffrey sat down next to Sergei and took his hand.

There were signs of strain on Geoffrey's face as well, and he was slumped over slightly, his usual neat appearance mussed. And he wasn't the only one. Calen and the FBI agents were almost as disheveled as he was and in need of a change of shirt.

Gio was the sole exception, his linen suit still crisp and neat. That, however, wasn't unusual. He had often teased Gio about his preternatural ability to stay 'starched', and Calen had once accused him of not having any sweat glands.

"Do you have any information on what Grayson is up to in Bermuda?" Sergei asked.

His voice, normally a little gravelly, sounded like sandpaper.

"There is something. He seems to have started gambling again," Geoffrey said.

"Again?" Sergei asked confused.

"Yes," Geoffrey leaned forward. "Poker. That's what got him in trouble with the cartels three years ago. He'd dipped his hand in the till to pay off some of those debts, and his clients got wind of it. Paired with some losses in the stock market, he was in real trouble."

"That's why he needed the money, why he got Wallace and Sarah Stone out of the way," Sergei rasped.

Geoffrey nodded, his face clouding.

"I'm sorry. I forget myself. You must still feel his loss very keenly," Sergei apologized, leaning back in the chair to rest his head on the wall behind it.

"I do, but I didn't get to see him or Eva as often as I would have liked. I just hope we can get her out of this mess. She's just such a little thing. I mean, I know she's brilliant and capable, but this thing with Karl is just too much. Eva is...so innocent sometimes," he said, lowering his voice. "She doesn't know what men can be. Sorry. This is the last thing you want to hear."

"You're not saying anything that is worse than what I've imagined," Sergei said quietly. "And I'm not ignorant of how crazy and stupid men get around Eva. You forget I'm one of them."

Geoffrey smirked. "You are not that bad. If you were, I would never have told you where she was."

"How difficult do you think it would be to get on that yacht?" Sergei asked.

Geoffrey shrugged helplessly and shook his head. "I don't think it's going to be possible without turning it into a bloodbath. It's a floating Fort Knox."

Collectively, the men frowned. Calen sat on Sergei's other side. "Then we're going to need an invitation." The men turned to him. "I have an idea," he continued. "Who do we know that happens to be a world class poker player?"

"You're not serious," Gio said, raising his eyebrows in disbelief. "He can't pull off something like that. Besides, isn't it safe to assume this Karl knows all of Sergei's associates by sight?"

"Not if we give him a haircut," Calen mused. "And we can dye what's left. Some makeup, and he'll be transformed."

"Who are you talking about?" Ethan asked.

"Oh. That's right," Jason said. "You haven't had the pleasure of having your clock cleaned by the Master."

"Don't call him that," Calen said. "He has a big enough head as it is when it comes to his poker playing skills."

"*Who* are you talking about?" Ethan growled.

CHAPTER 26

*E*than frowned as he inspected Geoffrey 'Smith' at work. He didn't know where this guy had learned his craft, but he was good. *Too good.*

"This is never going to work," Liam said, frowning as Geoffrey cut his brother Trick's shoulder length hair into a sharp, contemporary style. They had already dyed it blonde. With a pair of wire-framed glasses over brown color contacts and a little of Geoffrey's make-up magic, the Patrick Tyler who'd been photographed with Sergei was long gone.

"It will be fine," his partner Jason assured Liam. "Maggie's constantly going on and on about how good Trick was in all those plays in high school. And it's not like he's going in alone. Ethan and I will be right there with him."

Ethan nodded his own reassurance.

"And you forget that I killed in the King and I," Trick said. "The non-musical version, of course," he added for Geoffrey's benefit, as the older man fixed a thin layer of latex over his nose.

"This is not the same thing and you know it," Liam bit out.

"He'll be fine. Plus this is our only plausible option right now," Ethan reminded him.

"I know that. But I'm not too happy Jason's going in with him either. I don't see why you can't go in alone," Liam said sullenly giving Ethan a dirty look.

He'd been giving him a lot of those lately. Ethan didn't know what bug had crawled up Liam's ass, but it was starting to get on his nerves.

Jason grinned. "Cause he's a crap poker player and even in pitch black darkness he won't pass for your friend," he said, making both Liam and Ethan scowl. "Besides, this is what we do. Just don't tell your sister or she'll make me sleep on the couch for a week."

"I don't see how I can keep it from Maggie if you get shot," Liam said sarcastically. "And Matthias Raske isn't exactly a friend."

"Well he's obviously not an enemy," Trick observed. "Not if he lent you this floating island."

Liam had surprised them when they landed by announcing that he had 'borrowed' a boat from an acquaintance. As soon as they saw the size of the yacht waiting for them at the marina, they peppered Liam with questions about Matthias Raske, the mysterious billionaire no one had realized he even knew.

"As long as he's as reclusive as you say he is, I don't care if he's your boyfriend," Ethan said, causing Liam to shoot him another dark glance. "Because this won't work if anyone actually recognizes that Trick isn't this Raske guy."

"Matthias rarely socializes and doesn't let anyone take his picture. Not close up anyway," Liam said with a glare.

"And yet dropping his name got us an invitation to a former drug lord's house. What the hell does Raske do for a living?" Ethan asked as he watched Geoffrey putting on the finishing touches to Trick's disguise.

"Relax. He made his money the old-fashioned way," Liam said, pouring himself a drink from the well-stocked bar. "He inherited it."

Ethan rolled his eyes and then caught himself, suddenly remembering the company he was keeping. Gio, Calen, Sergei, and Alex all came from family money and they were all here watching the preparations.

"I'm more concerned with how he uses his money," he sniffed, "but that's a question for another day. Today we just need an in with Grayson so we can get an invitation to *his* yacht."

"Speaking of yachts, you said this one is the mysterious Matthias' *second-best* yacht?" Alex asked, doing a price-calculating circuit around the saloon.

The *Sha naqba īmuru* was one of the most luxurious boats any of them had ever seen. It made Alex's yacht, the recently rechristened *Elynn*, which Ethan had been on once for a party, look like the fishing boat from Jaws. The furniture of the *Sha*, as they called it for short, was luxurious without being ostentatious, and it had enough cabins for all of them.

"His other boat is what is referred to these days as a super yacht," Liam answered. "He lives on it most of the time, but he keeps this one in these waters year round so it's lucky he was willing to help out by lending it to us, even if he couldn't come personally. It shouldn't raise any red flags with the locals."

"Raske has a yacht *and* a super yacht?" Gio said disapprovingly, looking around the spacious saloon.

Despite his sizable personal wealth, Gio was practical, and the only one of the billionaires he knew that Ethan felt really comfortable around. The thought of anyone wasting money on more than one yacht was probably enough to get Gio's fiscally conservative shorts in a bunch.

"Matthias has a lot of things," Liam mumbled, still frowning at his brother as Geoffrey brushed the stray hairs off Trick's shirt collar.

The effect of the makeup was subtle but transformative. Trick looked completely different. From a distance he could pass for Matthias Raske. Jason was going in as one of Matthias' entourage and Ethan was going as his bodyguard.

"All right, I think this is it. Does he pass muster?" Geoffrey asked Liam.

Liam shrugged. "I guess. As long as you haven't actually met Matthias."

Geoffrey nodded. "This adhesive is pretty good in warm weather, but if you sweat too much then you should make an excuse and touch up somewhere out of sight. There's some more glue under the false stone of that pinky ring. If they find it, pretend it's Vaseline or lip balm but don't actually put it on your lips," he warned.

"I'm not going to ask where you learned how to do all of this," Ethan said as he leaned over to examine Geoffrey's handiwork.

The old man snorted slightly. "Yes, well thank you for your reassurance," he said as he stepped back to take pictures of the finished product so he could recreate it later as necessary.

Ethan ignored the sarcasm. "Just remember the plan, Patrick. Win big early and then lose a chunk at the end of the night after you have a few drinks. If Grayson thinks you can't hold your liquor, he should be tempted enough to invite you onto his boat for a private game. If he's following his current pattern, that is," he instructed.

"Yes, I *know*," Trick said drily, having heard those particular instructions a few dozen times already.

By pumping a few of their contacts in low places, the group had learned that Grayson was not only gambling again, but he was also entertaining a select group of people on his yacht. Though they were pretty sure Grayson wasn't gambling with cartel money this time around, they were hoping to induce him into deep play, deep enough to get close to him. However, none of their sources had heard anything about Eva Stone.

"All right, I'm ready," Trick said, going up to Sergei and presenting himself.

Sergei stood up and sighed. He looked like shit and for the first time since he'd met him Ethan felt genuinely sorry for the guy.

"Thank you for doing this. I don't want to add too much pressure, but I'm counting on you," Sergei said quietly.

"I won't let you down," Trick promised, slipping on his exclusive Savile Row coat.

He may have needed the makeup to impersonate Matthias Raske, but he already had the wardrobe.

"We'll be back in a few hours," Jason said as the three of them headed out.

THE ONLY WAY Sergei could stand the long wait was to have a few drinks, but he limited himself to two as the other guys tried to distract him with poker and blackjack. For a while, he let them think they were succeeding, but as the evening wore on, it got harder and harder to pretend.

Sergei hated taking a back seat in their effort to get Eva back. He wanted to get in the yacht's speedboat and ride to the rescue himself, but he knew that was the last thing he should do.

There was no way Karl Grayson didn't know his face. For a moment, he wished he'd taken a page out of Matthias Raske's book and had avoided or threatened every paparazzo who'd ever pointed a camera in his direction. But when he said as much to Liam, the other man just rolled his eyes.

"That's not how he does it," Liam said before taking a big swig from his highball glass full of scotch. "He pays them off, and when that doesn't work, he just buys the paper or website."

"If he's such a recluse, then how did you meet him?" Sergei asked.

"Um," Liam said, his mouth a little open.

Calen's head whipped around, but Liam didn't continue. Sergei was about to press him when they heard an engine. His heart in this throat, he ran out to the deck to help tie up the boat. The others joined him on the deck as Jason looked up, giving him a huge shit-eating grin and a big thumbs up.

"Trick was perfect. He really should have been a goddamned actor. Maggie was right," Jason said with a laugh as the three men boarded. "We're in."

Sergei heaved a sigh of relief before he turned to thank Trick. He almost smiled when he saw the younger man waving and blowing kisses to an imaginary crowd before taking a bow.

"Thank you, thank you," Trick was murmuring to his invisible adoring fans. "No, of course you can have an autograph..."

Frowning, Sergei raised a questioning brow to Jason, who cleared his throat. "Yeah, so it was easier for him to pretend to be drunk at the end, after a few drinks. But it's mostly the high you get from a successful first op."

"It really worked? Grayson actually invited you to his yacht?" Sergei asked as he sat on a bench on the deck.

He still wasn't completely convinced their gambit had worked so easily.

"Apparently this Raske character is mythical, even among the criminal element. They know he has more money than God, money Grayson wants to 'invest' for him. Trick pulled off acting like he was a smug over-privileged blue blood with just the right amount of stick up his butt," Ethan said, folding his arms and leaning against the railing. "Then he shifted into a careless sloppy ass the more he drank. The temptation was too much for Grayson. We're supposed to go over for a friendly poker game tomorrow so Karl can try and win back the money he lost in the first few rounds."

Sergei nodded before he ran an impatient hand through his hair. "So what's he like?"

Jason and Ethan exchanged a glance, but it was Trick who answered, after he stopped bowing to his imaginary audience.

"You know, it was kinda weird. Except for being a little manic, he seemed so normal," he said, his arms falling to his sides.

Ethan frowned. "It's hard to judge someone when they're on their best behavior in a single evening. We got what we wanted. Hopefully tomorrow we'll be able to confirm he has Evangeline Stone and then we can formulate an extraction plan."

"Did he say anything about her or something that could be about her?" Sergei asked, the dread in his voice clear.

The question was hard for him to say aloud, but he had to know the answer.

"No," Trick said with a sympathetic frown. "But don't worry. Tomorrow we might be able to see her," he said, sitting on the bench to pat him on the back.

"Unless he has her locked in a dungeon below deck," Sergei said, voicing his worst fear.

Or second worst, he thought. There was one other thing that was tearing him apart. Something he needed to talk to Trick about before he went to the Grayson's yacht, the *Angel's Folly*, tomorrow.

No one said anything until Geoffrey spoke up, "Whatever else he's capable of, I really don't think Karl would ever hurt Eva," he said.

Sergei closed his eyes and nodded.

"Look, this is not productive," Gio said. "We need to get some sleep so we can be sharp for tomorrow. Everybody to bed."

Liam gave Gio an exasperated look, but he agreed. "Fine," he said as he downed another scotch and walked away.

The next day, before the men were going to leave for the *Angel's Folly*, Sergei worked himself up to tell Trick something he desperately needed to say, even if it was killing him by inches.

"Trick, I need to talk to you," he said after Geoffrey had finished recreating his masterpiece from the day before. "Alone," he added as Liam got up, too.

Trick nodded. "Okay."

He was far more serious than yesterday. The realization that he was the lynchpin in Eva's rescue plan was settling in as Jason and Ethan drilled him on his fake background and various what-if scenarios.

Together, they went out on the deck. Making sure there was no one else nearby, Sergei leaned in and put a hand on his friend's shoulder. "Look, I know that a note is too risky, but if you do see Eva and by some miracle can talk to her alone, there's something I need you to tell her," Sergei said.

"I promise I'll tell her you love her," Trick said, his face uncharacteristically grave.

"No, that's not it. Listen..."

CHAPTER 27

"If you bring that up one more fucking time, I swear I will push you overboard. I'll wait till you're least expecting it —when no one else is around, you fucking asshole," Eva hissed.

She sounded absolutely venomous, like a real crazy bitch, but she didn't care. Dr. Ritter was a piece of shit, and she'd had it with him.

At first she'd thought the doctor represented a chance at rescue. She'd gone into their sessions apprehensive, but hopeful of somehow convincing him to help her. That pipe dream had evaporated like smoke all too quickly. Ritter wasn't on her side, and the idea that she could win him over was impossible.

She'd been stupid to even consider it. By the end of the first session, she knew what his true purpose here was.

He *knew* she hadn't had some sort of psychotic break. Ritter was just here to convince her she had. His arrival had started a campaign by Karl and everyone else on board to convince her that she was crazy. That somehow the life she knew had never happened and that her life had always been with Karl. But the doctor wasn't as good an actor as he thought he was. He knew the truth about her. She saw how he turned a blind eye to armed guards and the way she was locked in her room every night.

Then a few days ago, Ritter suggested medication. The first time he'd offered her a pill, she'd surprised him by knocking it out of his hand. Up until that point, she'd been quiet and nervous, so when she'd refused, he'd been surprised enough to let it go. But that didn't stop him from trying again. He had been hired to get results, so he kept pushing and pushing.

"Mrs. Grayson, I assure you these will have no adverse effect on your baby. Your husband would never allow anything to endanger your child," he'd said, looking at her with feigned concern.

"Fuck you," Eva had spat, causing his eyes to open wide.

"Then I'm afraid I have little choice but to ask Mr. Grayson to administer these some other way," he had said, looking at her with annoyed condescension.

That had been the final straw. She had opened her mouth and let out an earsplitting scream before grabbing a picture frame and swinging it at the doctor. Stunned, he had fallen to the floor to avoid the blow, which shattered the glass in the picture frame as it hit the heavy mahogany coffee table.

Karl had rushed in first, just ahead of the bodyguards.

"Darling, the doctor is just trying to do what's best for you," he'd said when she accused the both of them of trying to poison her and her baby.

Karl had seemed shocked at her outburst. Her tenuous situation had made her timid and quiet in his presence, and everyone else's except the doctor.

Well, *fuck that.*

Heedless of the presence of the armed guards, she'd grabbed the nearest object—an expensive crystal ashtray—and hurled it at Karl's head. He'd ducked, but the shattering sound was explosive in the silence.

"Go ahead!" she'd taunted the ring of guards. "Shoot me now. Cause if this cocksucker," she'd said, pointing at the doctor, "pushes one more fucking pill at me, I'll gut the worthless piece of shit like a fish!" she'd yelled, grabbing one of the shards of glass from the picture frame, not caring that it cut her hand.

One of the guards had laughed aloud before Karl's glare shut him up.

"No pills!" Karl had promised, his hands out entreatingly as he turned his attention back to her. "I swear."

Her eyes had filled with tears. "Swear on our parent's graves," she said bitterly, and his face had fallen, his arms dropping to his sides.

For one wild second, she'd considered rushing at him with the piece of glass, but she'd let go of it and dropped it on the ground instead, turning her back on the entire group and walking out to the bow alone. It had been the first time a bodyguard hadn't followed her.

A few minutes later, Karl found her out there. Neither of them said anything. He'd just sat next to her, his eyes on the horizon until it got too cold, and he'd asked her to go inside to her room. But the doctor wasn't sent away. Instead, other forms of pressure had started.

Rather than seeing Karl after the servants had brought her meals, he was the one who served them. He would take her out of her room to walk the deck, the guards nowhere in sight. She still had to go to sessions with Dr. Ritter, but otherwise Karl was the only other real presence in her life.

She knew what they were up to. But there was nothing she could do about it. Every day, Karl would do something sweet and kind, referring to a fictional past by mixing it with real details of their childhood. He was trying to confuse her. And Eva was certain that if she wasn't already pregnant, he would have already drugged her up in an effort to wipe away her real memories. Ritter was teaching him how.

And now she had to sit here and listen to the doctor bullshit his way through another session. She ignored his psychobabble with her arms crossed and her eyes closed.

"Mrs. Grayson, if you don't start taking your treatment more seriously, I'm going to have to overrule Mr. Grayson's decision on medication once you've given birth..."

The pompous little shit trailed off, letting his threat sink in.

She didn't know why he even bothered. She knew the moment she had the baby, the good doctor would pump her so full of drugs she wouldn't be able to see straight. Eyeing him through slits, she seriously contemplated carrying out her threat while he droned on.

"Now, Mr. Grayson really wanted you to join him for dinner tonight, but I'm afraid I can't recommend it since you continue to resist therapy," Ritter said, but Eva continued to ignore him until their session was over.

Dinner. That was another thing she had to endure. Karl had started socializing on the boat, inviting people over for meetings and the occasional dinner. She had fully expected to be locked in her room for those events, but that hadn't happened. Instead, she had been introduced to his cohorts as Mrs. Karl Grayson.

In those situations, she had to maintain a stoic silence. Karl had known his circle of thieves and criminals offered no possibilities for her. They were a dangerous-looking, jaded lot. Even the few women who had come aboard looked like they would walk all over your back if it could get them something they wanted. And all of them had been told lies about her.

Eva had had to sit there through meals and cocktail parties while she and her belly were examined like insects under a microscope. She didn't really think she would be locked in her room tonight, no matter what the doctor recommended. Karl always wanted her close so he could pretend they were a happy couple.

If Ritter managed to convince him, then she didn't care. It would be a relief. She hated those evenings, the way Karl would touch her, his genuine affection on display for all to see.

He hadn't pressured her for sex, but she suspected the only thing holding him back was the fact she was carrying another man's baby. Or he was working up to it. Either way, it felt like she was living on borrowed time. The only reason she slept at all was because her pregnancy made her so exhausted.

Later that evening, she was woken from a nap by a maid instead of Karl. It was the first time that had happened since Dr. Ritter had arrived with all of his wonderful advice. After changing, she followed the servant up to the saloon where Karl was waiting with three men.

One of the men, a burly bodyguard type with dark hair, stood in the corner, eyeing the guards patrolling the deck from behind mirrored sunglasses. His head tracked them as they moved from one end of the deck to the other. The other two men were both blonde and expensively dressed. They didn't seem like Karl's usual set.

"Darling, come meet Matthias Raske and his associate Jason Edwards," Karl said as she waddled toward the group of men.

She didn't bother to smile as the men said hello, while Karl pulled her close to lovingly nuzzle the top of her head. Eyes closing briefly, she nodded as the men greeted her before sitting down, her hands on her stomach.

"I had no idea you were married," the man called Raske said as he examined her from head to toe, his eyes lingering on her swollen stomach.

"Oh, yes," Karl said. "For years now. Eva and I are childhood sweethearts," he said, putting his arm around her. "We're expecting our first child," he said proudly before launching into a discussion about poker.

Eva tuned out the conversation, focusing on the setting sun instead. Every once in a while, one of the men said something to her, politely trying to include her in the conversation. She gave them one word answers to their inquiries on her health and pregnancy before letting herself drift off again.

"Poor darling, I think you're too tired for company. Why don't you have dinner in the cabin and turn in early?" Karl asked, his smile a little tight.

"Probably a good idea. Sorry," Eva muttered.

Karl didn't usually care about what kind of impression she made. These men must be very important.

"No!" Raske said. "It's fine with me if she's a little...sleepy. You don't have to banish her from dinner. It's not every day I get to share a meal with such lovely company. I absolutely insist she join us," he said jovially with a warm, friendly grin.

Karl looked at him a little startled, but he smiled indulgently when Raske finished the drink in his hand with a big swig. Apparently, their guest was a bit drunk. But Eva was not up to another night of play-acting.

"It's all right. I really am exhausted," she said, patting her belly for emphasis. "I think a quick meal and a warm bath are just what I need. If you'll excuse me, I'm going to go to the powder room and then my cabin."

She stood up, smiling stiffly and nodding at the men before heading down the hall to the restroom. Letting her shoulders relax, she bent to splash water on her face, lingering in the stall before she was taken downstairs and locked in her cabin. After waiting a few minutes, she opened the door to step back into the hallway when it swung wide and Matthias Raske stepped inside, covering her mouth with his hand.

Startled, she paused for a second before starting to scream.

"Shh!!! Don't scream. Sergei sent me," he whispered urgently.

A garbled '*What*' escaped from behind his hand.

"Sorry," he said, removing it. "My name's not Raske. I'm Sergei's friend, Patrick Tyler. The men with me are FBI agents; they're friends. They're here to help."

Oh God. Recognition dawned. She did know who this man was. "Is one of them married to your sister?"

"Yes!" he said excitedly. "Jason is. The other one is his partner Ethan. We're trying to figure out how to get you out of here."

Eva grabbed his hand. "When?" she asked desperately. "How?"

"I'm not sure yet. Ethan is getting a head count of the bodyguards and figuring out this boat's security features. But it will be soon, I promise!" he said, putting his hand on her shoulders as her eyes started to water and she put her hand to her mouth.

Patrick pulled her in for a hug, before drawing back and holding her at arm's length. "I don't have much time, but Sergei wanted me to give you a message if I managed to get you alone."

She grabbed his arm, her heart in her throat. "What is it?"

Patrick looked uncomfortable. "He said to tell you he loves you and no matter what he always will. No matter...no matter what you have to do to keep yourself and the baby safe..." He swallowed hard before continuing. "Until we get you out of here, whatever you have to do to keep Grayson happy he—he wants you do it. You know...if you have to. Do you understand what I'm telling you?"

Eva's welled tears finally escaped and ran down her cheeks. A small sob escaped as she nodded.

"Oh god, don't cry," Patrick said, whipping out a handkerchief to blot her face, but it was too late.

The floodgates had opened.

He hugged her again, whispering soothing inarticulate sounds as she tried to calm down. He wiped her tears and whispered, "I have to go. If anyone sees you, just say it was a mood swing that got you going." He kissed her on the forehead. "I'm going to see you again real soon, and when I do, it means we're getting you out of here. It may involve you faking labor by the way. Now, nod so I know you understand me."

Wiping her tears on his handkerchief, she took a deep breath and nodded before handing it to him.

"I can't have this," she said tearfully.

"Oh, right," he said grimacing and taking it back.

He gave her one last smile and slipped out of the bathroom, leaving her to collect herself. Relief and hope made her dizzy as she scrubbed her face clean of tears before heading to her cabin. Thankfully, this time the bodyguards let her make her own way below deck.

CHAPTER 28

Sergei rushed to the saloon when he heard men arguing. He'd been in his cabin, trying to get some sleep at Gio's urging, when the sound of a motor alerted him. His friend had pointed out that they had no idea how long poker was going to take. Trick's marathon games could last till morning. But it was just after midnight, and the men were already back.

Worried something had gone wrong, he practically ran into the room to find Ethan and Jason arguing with Trick. And they had an audience. Gio and Calen were already there. Jason stopped talking as soon as they saw him.

"What happened? Was your cover blown? Did you see her?" he asked, stopping short and holding his stomach.

It felt like the creature from Alien was about to burst out of it.

"Yes, and she's okay," Trick said, shooting the agents a dirty look.

"*Trick*," Ethan said warningly.

"She *is*," he insisted. "But things are...complicated. Sit down," he said before turning to Jason and Ethan. "Why don't the two of you start researching what you were talking about on the way back?"

"Okay, fine, but don't add your spin. Just stick to the facts," Ethan hissed, putting his hand over his eyes before he and Jason left the room.

Trick sat down on the ottoman in front of Sergei. Liam and Calen sat on either side of him while Gio stood at the end of the couch.

"Just tell me," Sergei said, holding up his hands.

"She really *is* okay. We saw her. And you were totally right, she's so beautiful, even though she's out to here," he said, gesturing in front of him. "And considering the circumstances she looks fine, healthy. Some dark circles under her eyes, but he's not beating her or starving her or anything like that. And the fact that she was able to walk around the *Folly* instead of being locked in some room below deck, it says a lot."

"Then what the hell were you all arguing about?" he asked, his chest heavy with dread.

Trick looked at the ceiling and took a deep breath. "Okay, so the thing is Grayson introduced her as his wife."

It felt like the air had been sucked out of the room. *"They're married?"*

"No!" Trick ran a nervous hand through his hair, seemingly surprised when his hand didn't make it past his ears. "He *said* she was his wife, but he also said she was his childhood sweetheart and that they were expecting *their* first baby. Her body language was all defensive whenever he lied about them and how happy they were. She only sat with us for a little while before she excused herself, pleading fatigue. I was able to sneak off and talk to her alone before she went to her room. I gave her your message."

"You did? What did she say?" Sergei rasped.

"Not too much because she started crying. But I told her we were going to get her out of there. I...I promised her. And we need to do it soon. She's going to go into labor any day now."

Sergei nodded. "Is there anything else? Why are Ethan and Jason so upset?"

Was there a squadron of armed guards between him and Eva?

Trick squirmed. "Well, yeah. There's one more thing. I didn't think you needed to know because it doesn't change anything, but they said you should be told."

When he didn't elaborate, Sergei felt like he was going to explode. He started to get up, but Calen put a restraining hand on his back.

"Just tell him!" Calen insisted.

"Okay, okay!" Trick said, rubbing his hands on his slacks as he sucked in a deep breath. "See there's this doctor. A shrink. He joined us for poker. From what he said, he was hired to oversee Eva's treatment."

"Treatment for what?" Sergei was more confused than alarmed.

"For her psychotic break," Trick said, his mouth twisting in distaste.

"Her what?" Sergei couldn't make sense of what he was hearing.

Trick looked like he was trying to pass a kidney stone. "So the story they're trying to pass is that Eva had a psychotic break because of her pregnancy hormones. This quack Ritter said it was actually quite common, which is bullshit. But he seems to be there to convince her that she had one. He actually complained that Grayson nixed the idea of medication until after the baby was born."

"That fucking asshole!" Gio said. "I swear I'm going to wring that that *mafankulo's* lying shit-filled neck!"

Heads turned to Gio in surprise. It had been a long time since any of them had heard him even raise his voice, let alone swear.

"Which one? Grayson or the shrink?" Calen asked, rubbing his temple.

"Either. Both," Gio said, the disgust in his voice clear.

He went to the bar and poured himself a large drink.

Sick to his stomach, Sergei stood up to pace.

"We have a plan," Trick said, turning to watch Sergei. "We're supposed to go back to discuss a lucrative investment opportunity Grayson mentioned after I let him win a stack. If Eva pretends to go into labor, we can call the paramedics, which will be our own men."

"What if Greyson has his own staff ready for that?" Sergei asked.

He did. Why wouldn't Eva's captor?

"He doesn't seem to. The shrink said they didn't anyway when

Grayson stepped away to the can, but he may not be in on all of Grayson's plans. It's a risk we have to take. If someone else has been lined up, there's always plan B."

"Not that again," Sergei said. "She's *pregnant* for fuck's sake."

Plan B had been discussed and debated to death. Eva was supposed to *jump* overboard where a team of mercenaries, ex-seals, would be waiting with extra gear for her. They would then have to swim, pregnant woman in tow, till they were out of sight of the yacht, where a boat would be waiting.

All of that supposed Eva could somehow get overboard without being seen. Alex had even consulted with medical specialists to find out what the exact risks would be to a developing fetus. There had been little consensus but the possible complications they outlined had been enough for Sergei to reject the idea out of hand.

Jason and Ethan came back into the room. "We got the perfect men to pose as paramedics. Two guys I served with are security specialists in a private firm now. One even went to medical school for a few years before he enlisted," Ethan said, heading for the bar. "And I rounded up some good candidates for plan B."

"We are not doing plan B!" Sergei ground out.

"It's only if we don't have a choice," Jason said, holding out a palm. "A worst case scenario. It won't come to that, believe me."

Sergei threw up his hands. "Fine! Just make sure you have a legion of men in the water and whoever else you think you need. Doesn't matter what it costs."

"These guys don't come cheap, but they're worth it," Ethan assured him. "Now here's what I have planned for once we get there," he said, pulling out a sketch of the boat. "He has at least four men, and they patrol here, here, and here…"

CHAPTER 29

*E*va had to fight her way out of sleep, pushing the remnants of her dream away like a swimmer struggling to the surface of a dark pool of water. The nightgown she was wearing stuck to her body, and the sheets were twisted around her waist.

The dream had been so unsettling. She had been back on the island, reliving meals and conversations she'd had with Sergei, but in the twisted landscape of her mind, Karl had taken his place. In her dream, she had known with certainty that it was Sergei, but every time she'd looked over at him, she'd seen Karl's face.

Shifting to her side, she put a tremulous hand on her stomach. The baby was moving like crazy, kicking and shifting inside of her like it, too, was panicked.

"Is the baby kicking?"

Startled Eva sat up. Karl was sitting in an armchair at the foot of the bed.

"What are you doing here?" she asked anxiously, covering herself with the sheet.

Karl gave her a wounded look before getting up and sitting next to her on the bed.

"I was worried about you. We hit a spot of bad weather, and I came to check on you. Don't you feel the boat rocking more than usual?"

"I must have been preoccupied," she murmured, trying to edge away from him without letting the sheet slip down.

The last thing she needed was for him to have an unobstructed view of her chest. In the last stage of her pregnancy, her usually small breasts had swelled to pin-up proportions, and Karl didn't bother to hide his stares. It was bad enough that she felt like she was going to tip over all the time. Living on a boat certainly didn't help her balance.

"Darling, there's something I've been wanting to talk to you about," Karl said as he took her hand. "I think it's time we moved back into the same room."

"We've never shared a room!" she hissed, shoving his hand away.

Karl sighed. "Not that again, sweetheart. You need to accept the fact that we are married now. Sleeping in separate rooms is only reinforcing your delusion. It's not healthy," he stroked her hair lovingly before pressing a soft kiss to her forehead.

He put a hand on her stomach. "Once our baby arrives, you and I are in for some late nights. It's going to be a lot of work that we need to do together. Which is why I've asked that your things be taken to the stateroom."

Eva shot out of the bed, throwing the sheet around herself.

"*No*. You can't keep pretending we're together and this baby is yours!" she gasped, holding her hands in front of her stomach.

His face growing cold, Karl got up and stalked toward her. He backed her into the corner and slapped an open hand on the wall over her head, hard. Flinching, she quailed and tried to shrink further into the corner.

"You're the one that needs to stop pretending. This is your life now, so you better get used to it," he hissed before his face softened. "I don't want to argue anymore," he said, pulling her out of the corner and guiding her to the bed.

He sat her down at the edge and kneeled in front of her. "I promise you, things are going to be absolutely perfect once the baby arrives."

Because you're going to drug me up, she thought bitterly, trying to shut him out. But Karl made that impossible. Kissing her hands, he moved up her body, stroking her stomach before running his hand over her breasts. Eva closed her eyes and turned her head away as Karl's fingers traced the outline of her nipples over the fabric of her nightgown.

"Please don't do this," she whispered, tears welling behind her tightly closed lids.

She wanted to hit him, or at least push him away, but he was so much bigger than her. If he decided to force himself on her now, she couldn't fight him off. If she tried, would he hurt the baby?

The hand on her breast moved up to cup her face. "Eva look at me," Karl said.

Reluctantly, she opened her eyes to see his earnest face looking up at her.

"You need to believe me when I say that there is nothing more important to me than you and this baby," he promised in an eerie echo of Sergei's words as he ran his other hand over her thigh. "And we are going to be happy together, but you need to give me a chance. You will try to do that, won't you?" he asked in a low voice, his intense blue eyes on hers as he traced the seam of her closed legs up to their apex with his fingers.

Suppressing a shiver, Eva squeezed her legs more tightly together, but that didn't deter Karl. Moving slowly, he massaged the top of her mound, trying to coax her legs apart while her eyes filled with tears. Sergei's message echoed in her head, but she couldn't bring herself to give Karl what he wanted.

Stomach roiling, she pushed him away. "I don't feel well."

As if to punctuate her words, the boat listed hard to one side. Clutching her stomach, she closed her eyes, truly feeling sick now.

Disappointment swept over Karl's features before they cleared. He paused to press a soft kiss to her lips.

"You're right, this isn't the best time. But tonight we start trying again, okay? We don't need to jump into a physical relationship right away, but no more distance. I'm going to send the servants in for your things in a few minutes. Now I better go get things ready for tonight. We're expecting guests for dinner again. I hope you don't mind."

Heart in her throat, she swallowed hard before saying, "Of course not. Who will be joining us?"

"Raske and his crew. I wouldn't have asked him, but if he decides to invest with me, it would be a very lucrative account."

Trying not to look too eager, she nodded. "I understand," she said in a low voice.

Karl smiled at her. "Good," he said, turning to leave. "Dress warmly. The bad weather is supposed to last until tomorrow."

Once he was gone, Eva sighed with relief. Her stomach still hurt, but it was for a whole other reason now. Rubbing her stomach, she tried to silently comfort her unborn child.

"Hold on just a little longer baby," she whispered. "Daddy's coming."

CHAPTER 30

*E*va was so nervous about endangering the plan for her impending rescue that she'd stayed out of sight by pretending to nap until dinner time. Wiping her sweaty hands on her dress, she made her way to the living room, her stomach still jumping with anxiety.

"There you are, darling," Karl said, waving her inside the room when she paused at the entrance.

"Hello, everyone," she said, her voice thready and small.

Jason and Patrick stood to greet her while the dark haired one whose name she didn't remember took up his position as sentry. She sat down after shaking hands, wondering what to do next.

In his role as Matthias, Patrick launched into a steady stream of small talk about the islands and famous poker players. Grateful that Karl was diverted she willed her heart to stop beating so quickly.

"Are you all right, Mrs. Grayson?" Jason asked.

Clearing her throat, she nodded. "Yes, it's just the baby is very active right now. And this weather isn't helping. I don't like being out on the boat in it," she said honestly.

The yacht, large as it was, rolled a little too much for her taste on the choppy water. Closing her eyes briefly, she breathed through her nose in an effort to compose herself.

"Well, the two of you are welcome at my bungalow on Barbuda if you want to be more comfortable. It's very private and secluded. The perfect spot for a little romantic getaway before the baby comes," Patrick offered.

"Thank you, Matthias, but that's not necessary," Karl said a little stiffly before changing the subject.

Picking up on Karl's reluctance, Patrick let it go, chatting amiably before suggesting Karl open the bottle of wine he brought.

"It's a particularly fine Richebourg Grand Cru," he said with a little wave.

"Fine is an understatement," Karl said expansively, rising and going to get a corkscrew from the bar. "This is one of the most expensive bottles around," he called behind him.

As soon as his back was turned, Patrick leaned forward. "After dinner, on my signal, fake labor," he whispered.

Nodding with a small motion of her head, Eva shifted in her seat. Her stomach really hurt now.

"Oh darling, you don't look so good," Karl observed as he sat back down with the corkscrew. "I think Dr. Ritter should take a look at you."

"I'm *fine*," she assured him resolutely.

There was no way she was letting that man examine her. The moment passed, and she lapsed into silence as the men resumed talking. The pain in her stomach turned into a steady pressure, but it was minor compared to the ache in her back, which had been troubling her since Karl had left her this morning. Doing her best to ignore it, she sipped on a glass of mineral water, surreptitiously rubbing the small of her back when no one was looking.

Distracted, she was nearly scared out of her skin when a loud crashing sound filled the air.

"Well, I thought the weather was supposed to clear up by this evening, but the wind has really picked up, hasn't it?" Jason said, turning around to the open door.

"Yes, I think that was one of the deck chairs," Karl said, rising to look behind them. "You may have to spend the night if it gets any worse."

Heart sinking to her shoes, Eva put a shaky hand on her stomach.

"It's just a squall," Patrick said. "It'll clear up in a bit. Why don't we have some dinner and worry about it later."

He sounded so blasé that Eva was reassured. Rising with some effort, she stood when a maid entered the room to announce dinner. She had taken a few steps when she felt a twisting popping sensation before a rush of liquid ran down her legs.

Gasping, she put her hand over her belly.

"Your water broke!" Jason exclaimed, alarmed.

All the men crowded around her. "But it's too early. Your due date isn't for almost two weeks," Karl said, looking at her with dismay.

"It's fine. Call the coast guard or the paramedics. I have a concierge medical service on call if you like," Patrick offered, seemingly calm. "They can take her to the hospital on the island."

The pain in her back intensified, and Eva sank to her knees. "I think it's too late," she groaned as Karl and Jason knelt beside her. "The baby's coming."

"WHAT DO WE DO?" Trick hissed at Ethan and Jason.

Their whole plan had fallen apart when Eva went into labor for real. She was in the stateroom with Karl, being examined by Dr. Ritter. In the distance, they could hear her cry out, a long terrible sound of pain. Collectively, the men flinched.

Karl had wanted to send the helicopter for a physician he had lined up to deliver the baby, but the wind had been too strong for that. The water was also too rough to safely transport Eva to the nearest island in the speedboat. Not that there was time. Judging from her screams, her contractions were too close together.

"Should we call the *Sha?*" he asked. "Sergei has an entire medical team waiting there for when he gets Eva back."

"Not unless you want this to turn into a bloodbath," Ethan hissed. "There are not four guards tonight, there are six, and they all have enough firepower to blast a hole into hell."

"What about the divers that are supposed to be in position underneath us?"

"I doubt they're there. It's too early. Extraction was supposed to happen much later after we got Grayson liquored up," Jason muttered. "And if conditions get much worse, they won't be able to get out here at all."

"*Shit.*"

Dr. Ritter and Karl stumbled into the room. Karl looked distinctly green.

"What's wrong?" Trick asked.

"Eva threatened to slit Dr. Ritter's throat and mine if I let him deliver her baby. I'm going to call the obstetrician I hired and have him brought in by boat. I don't care if I have to get a yacht this size to bring him," he said before wandering off to the bridge.

Dr. Ritter poured himself a big drink from the bar, liquor sloshing out of his glass with the movement of the boat. He gave the trio of men an unctuous smile.

"Her misplaced hostility aside, I'm rather relieved I won't have to deliver Mrs. Grayson's baby. Haven't done it since my medical school days, and that was under supervision," he said as he sipped his glass.

"Really?" Jason asked. "Jesus, Ethan's got more experience than that. And he went to med school," he said under his breath.

"Are you serious?" Trick asked, turning to give Ethan a surprised glance.

Ethan rolled his shoulders uncomfortably. "Only for a semester. Shut up, Jason," he muttered, turning to make sure the doctor hadn't heard him.

"Suck it up, you may have to do this again," Jason said to his partner before leaning over to Trick. "He's delivered two. Once in the army in a little village outside Bangladesh and once in a cab in downtown Boston," he whispered.

"That last one hardly counts," Ethan said grimacing. "The baby was half out already. I just yanked it the rest of the way. And the first time I called one of my buddies from med school and he talked me through it."

"But you *did* get through it," Jason muttered.

A distant scream made them all wince before Karl came back inside, looking upset.

"The medical team is going to be delayed until they find a boat big enough to be secure in this weather," he said sitting down.

Trick exchanged a worried glance with the other two men. "That's it. Get in there," he told Ethan. Turning on the Matthias persona, he straightened his sleeves. "Don't panic. My bodyguard is trained for this sort of thing," he said casually. "Get in there and help the young lady out Ethan," he said with a little gesture of his hand. "Jason get him the medkit from the speedboat."

Jason ran out and got the bag, a small duffel with a medical caduceus emblazoned on the side. He handed it to the reluctant bodyguard. With a damning glance at Trick, Ethan left the room, his exit punctuated by Eva's distant scream.

"Jesus, I better get in there," Karl said, standing back up.

"Are you sure?" Trick asked, feigning surprise. "I wouldn't. There's just some things one can't *unsee*, if you know what I mean," he said, sitting down across from Karl.

"She did threaten to cut off your testicles for making her give birth on a boat instead of a hospital," Ritter called out from the bar.

Karl frowned. "Yes, well, maybe I'll give her a little bit of time to cool off," he said, sitting back down again.

CHAPTER 31

"One more push, Eva," Ethan ordered. "And you need to try to do it quietly unless you want Karl running in here."

Stifling a scream, Eva bore down. There was a rush of liquid and the pressure inside her peaked and then rushed out of her as the baby arrived.

"Shit," Ethan cursed as he gathered a slippery mass and wrapped it in a towel.

"Why isn't the baby crying?" Eva asked worriedly, too tired to raise her head.

Ethan did something she couldn't see and the baby gave a small cry before subsiding. "I think he's okay. He's breathing evenly and on his own. Here he is," he said, before laying the bundle on her stomach.

"Oh my god," Eva whispered as she saw her son's perfect little face. He was the most beautiful thing she'd ever seen. "He looks just like Sergei," she said.

"Yeah, he kinda does, except red and squishy," Ethan said with a wry grin, but he didn't sound very happy.

"What's wrong?" she asked.

Ethan paced in front of the bed a little before taking a towel and moving it between her legs.

"You're bleeding much more than I would like. There's been some tearing and I think you might need sutures. The first aid kit only has bandages. We'll have to wait for the medical team Karl called to get here."

"The one he called? What about your team?"

"They were going to try and overtake them but Karl had specific personnel handpicked and waiting. If his people don't show up now, he's going to be tipped off. In any case, I don't think we're going to be able to move you."

"*What?*" Eva gasped. "Oh god. You have to!"

Ethan winced. "It's not safe until we stop this bleeding. You might need a transfusion."

Desperate now, Eva grabbed his arm. "Then just take the baby."

It was Ethan's turn to be horrified. "What?"

"Please. Tell Karl the baby didn't make it. Hide him. Please, he's being quiet. Make an excuse and leave now. Take him to Sergei," she said tearfully.

"Christ. If we're caught..."

"I know, but you have to try. If you don't, Karl will have two hostages. And if he has the baby, then I'll have to do whatever he says..."

"Fucking shit," Ethan swore under his breath. He looked at the sleeping bundle in her arms. "Let me check and see if the coast is clear. If it is there may be a way. Wrap him in a second towel to make sure he's warm enough and leave a flap over his face. If the outside air hits him he'll definitely start screaming."

Ethan went out and Eva wrapped her son in the second towel, kissing his little face before covering it with the towel loosely. In a few minutes, Ethan came back.

"I must be out of my fucking mind," he said. "But I've got a small window right now. Half the guards are waiting with Karl because the boat with the medical team is a few minutes out and the rest are drinking," he said, emptying the first aid kit onto the bed. He opened the nearest porthole and threw the contents overboard. "Give me the baby," he said.

Nearly blind with tears, Eva handed the bundle over. "I'll see you soon little guy, I promise."

"And I promise you we will get you out of here," Ethan said as he placed the baby in the duffel and zipped it shut.

He silently slipped out of the room and didn't return.

THE DEVASTATING NEWS that Ethan delivered threw the saloon into a stunned silence. The medical team had just arrived, and Karl had been about to direct them to the stateroom when Ethan came back in, his shirt rolled up to the elbows, blood staining the pristine white cloth ominously.

Even though Trick knew the baby wasn't his, Karl's reaction was painful to see. It was almost as if Karl believed the lie that Eva was his wife and they'd just suffered a huge loss. The guy looked gutted, but once Ethan told him that Eva needed urgent medical attention, he snapped back into action, showing his medical team into the stateroom. He stayed inside to comfort her and Ethan suggested they leave.

"Shouldn't we stay and make sure she's going to be okay? Sergei will have our balls if we don't know at least make sure," Trick whispered urgently.

Sergei was going to be destroyed by this. Not only had they failed to rescue the woman he loved, but their baby was gone forever, and he hadn't been there with her.

"No. We need to get the hell out of here," Ethan hissed between gritted teeth before ushering them to the speedboat.

"Jason, get us the fuck out of here as fast as you can," Ethan said in a low voice as they climbed aboard. "No questions," he said as he untied them from the yacht.

Jason pulled away without a word while Trick went to sit down, confused as hell.

"Don't sit there you ass!" Ethan hissed as he started to lower himself on the nearest bench.

Jason sped them away from the Angel's Folly. As soon as they were far enough Ethan ran to the bench Trick had been about to sit on and he removed the false top. He pulled out the medical bag and started frantically pulling down the partially zipped closure. Reaching inside, he drew out a towel wrapped bundle. A bundle that started crying as soon as he lifted it into the night air.

CHAPTER 32

*S*ergei was pacing the deck of the *Sha* with a large scotch in hand. He wasn't really drinking it, but holding it gave him something to focus on.

Something had gone wrong. The divers from plan B had checked in to say that their window had closed without a signal from their men on board the *Folly*. It had been hours with no word from Trick or the others, despite the fact the speedboat had a satellite phone. He wanted to call them, but he couldn't risk it. If his timing was off, he could endanger everything he loved.

Calen was sitting on a lounge chair on the deck nearby, keeping a silent vigil with him. His best friend knew better than to try and talk to him right now. Calen just stayed close, trying to hide the fact he was surreptitiously checking his watch every other minute. He was actually doing a lot better than Liam, who was somewhere below deck steadily getting drunk.

Sergei was worried about Trick and Jason, too, but Eva was his priority. He knew it was sexist to worry about her more than the other two, but he could see her so clearly in his mind's eye, so small and vulnerable in her pregnancy.

He had no idea what she had gone through during her captivity—

what she had had to do to keep herself and their baby safe while in the hands of an unstable criminal. Sergei could only pray that she would let him help her work past it, because no matter what had happened, it didn't change how he felt about her and their future.

God, please let her be okay. And if she's not, leave me a place to start from to make her well again.

If he was honest with himself, he wasn't sure there would be such a place for him. During sleep, his worst fears took over. In that nightmare landscape, he lost Eva over and over again.

It was the same every time, a mysteriously not pregnant Eva was rescued only to tell him that she loved Karl before she walked away from him forever.

He knew that wasn't going to happen, but the dream stayed with him nevertheless. Somehow torturing himself with the idea that Eva would leave him by choice kept him from thinking about all the things that could happen to her that were outside of her power and his.

Only one thing was certain. If he got Eva back, he was never going to let her out of his sight again. In fact, there were going to be times in the future when she would want to strangle him for the way he was going to obsess over her safety. But as long as he got the opportunity to surround her with love as well as protection, maybe she would overlook the aggravation he was sure to cause her.

Calen suddenly stood. "Did you hear that?"

Sergei rushed to the rail. In the distance, he could just make out the speedboat. Behind him was the sound of footsteps, but he couldn't tear his gaze from the fast approaching boat. He clutched the rail reflexively as the people in the back of the boat came into view.

Eva wasn't with them. It was only the three men. Trick was clutching a duffel bag and Ethan...Ethan was covered in blood.

"Oh God," he whispered brokenly.

Eva was dead. She was dead, and his life was over. Grayson had killed her.

He felt a hand on his shoulder, but it couldn't break through the sudden numbness that had enveloped him. A crowd had gathered behind him, but no one said a word as Ethan tied up the boat and Jason killed the engine.

Trick climbed aboard first. He had let go of the bag but was still clutching a bundle of towels. Oh, god. Maybe he'd been stabbed too and was holding the rags to his wound.

Trick stopped in front of him. His mouth opened and shut a few times as he held the towels in front of him. But Sergei couldn't take his eyes off Ethan's bloody shirt.

"Is she..." He couldn't finish.

Trick shook his head. "I...I don't think so. Oh god Sergei she went into labor early."

The sky above spun around his head with dizzying speed.

"I delivered the baby," Ethan said suddenly. "I had to. That's how I got this way," he said gesturing to his shirt. "The medical team Grayson assembled was too far out. We had to leave her in their care...she was bleeding and needed their attention."

Sergei just stood there frozen. What were they saying? It didn't make sense.

Ethan leaned closer to him. "Eva begged me to take the baby out of there," he said. "She didn't want Grayson to have two hostages. She said if he got his hands on the baby, then she'd have to do whatever he said..."

"The baby?" Sergei asked blankly.

Wasn't the baby gone? How could there be that much blood all over Ethan if the baby made it?

Trick pushed the bundle of towels into his arms. He held on automatically as Jason pushed him inside the saloon onto a couch.

"I don't understand," he said hoarsely.

Then the towels in his arm moved. Frowning, he drew back the cloth. A pair of sleepy blue eyes blinked up at him.

"*Oh,*" he breathed.

Alex showed him how to feed and change his son for the first time. He even had to show Sergei how to bathe a newborn, because Ethan hadn't had time to clean the little boy up before he had gotten him off the *Angel's Folly*.

Without Eva.

He didn't know how everything had gone so wrong. Eva wasn't due for almost two weeks. She was supposed to be here now. They were supposed to do this together.

"Sir, would you like me to take the baby and put him down for a nap?" one of the pediatric nurses asked him.

He had hired her months ago, and she had been brought on board a few days ago just in case Eva needed her when she was rescued. But Sergei didn't feel like congratulating himself for his foresight.

"No," he said shortly, and the woman tactfully excused herself.

There wasn't anything anyone could say or do that would make him let go of his son right now. Or possibly for the next year—whenever it was babies learned to walk. If the worst happened, his son would have to leave his arms on his own power...or not at all.

"Are you ever going to put him down?" Calen asked.

Sergei swung around to look at his friend. Everything he was feeling was there in that one tortured look, as if his eyes were bleeding.

"Okay, stupid question."

Alex had fallen asleep on the couch near the door. Gio was 'resting his eyes' in the chair next to him. They were all waiting to hear back from the surveillance team.

Though the divers from plan B hadn't been able to act, they had planted some high tech listening devices on the hull of the boat before retreating. But they had to be nearby to hear anything from the surveillance feeds, which was why there was now a substantial delay as word had to be relayed from a small boat in between them and the *Folly*.

"Thank you for staying. I know you must be worried about Maia. If she goes into labor, you have to go. Promise me you won't wait," he told Calen in a low voice.

Calen looked uncomfortable, but he nodded. If he missed the birth of his daughter, he would never forgive himself. Ethan came back into the room. He had showered and changed, but whenever he closed his eyes, Sergei could still see him covered in Eva's blood.

"We heard something. They managed to stabilize her and stop the bleeding. She's going to be okay," he whispered in a loud voice.

Sergei sat down carefully on the couch, worried he would drop the baby in his relief. He gave the powers above a silent thank you, rocking the baby back and forth with his eyes closed.

"That's good news," Calen said, wiping his face. "Are they taking her to a hospital?"

"Not as far as we know. All the guys got was that she had been stabilized. But as a precaution, we're moving personnel around. Every ER within a helicopter ride is under surveillance. If they move her, then we'll know, and we will be there. And if not, we'll take a dive team back in a few weeks once she's recovered and retry plan B," he said carefully. "I promised her we would get her out of there."

He sounded angry, but it wasn't directed at them. Ethan had been wound up tight since they had to leave Eva behind.

Sergei nodded, reminding himself not to squeeze the baby too tight. "Did she...did she have a message for me?" he asked hoarsely.

Ethan frowned. "Not exactly. Things were so crazy and scary. But in addition to ordering me to bring the baby to you she also said he looked like you."

"Really?" Sergei asked surprised. He looked down at the sleeping infant. "No. He's too cute. I think he looks like Eva."

"No. That little guy could be your clone," Gio said, surprising him by speaking. "Except for his eyes."

Alex was still snoring softly next to him but Gio was wide awake now. Sergei shook his head. "I don't see it. And Eva's eyes are blue, too, although they're darker, almost violet."

"Well babies' eyes usually change from blue to something else in the first few months, but it can take almost a year. They might even go from blue to bluer, but chances are they'll turn brown like yours,"

Calen said knowledgeably. Gio looked at him in surprise. "I've been reading," he added with a shrug.

"What the hell am I supposed to do now?" Sergei asked, swallowing hard.

His throat was killing him and he wasn't even sure why. He hadn't raised his voice since the baby arrived.

Ethan sighed. "I don't know, but I really don't think Grayson would harm a woman who just gave birth. From all appearances, he appears to sincerely care about her." His lips firmed. "He may even love her," he added reluctantly.

"That's what worries me," Sergei confessed.

CHAPTER 33

*E*va woke to bright sunlight. Her limbs were like leaded weights, and her eyes were like sandpaper behind her lids. She did a silent inventory of her body before even attempting to open her eyes. Everything below her waist felt numb, but she was afraid to move in case that changed.

"I know you're awake," Karl said in a low voice.

Reluctantly cracking open her eyelids, she saw a man-shaped blur stretched out next to her. Blinking, she focused on Karl's face above hers. He was watching her pensively. He didn't look very good. His usual preppy clothes were rumpled, as if he'd slept in them, and there were dark circles under his eyes.

"I'm just checking," she said finally in a hoarse voice as she looked down at herself.

She was wearing a pristine white nightgown. Someone had changed her.

"Checking what?" he asked.

"That everything still works," she said, shifting away from him slightly.

"Eva don't move. The doctor had to sedate you so he could stitch you up properly, but the numbing agent will wear off soon. You had some sort of hemorrhage. They were able to fix you up without surgery, and for now they even left some packing in you. Gauze and sterile sponges—but you need to stay still. Very still or you'll start bleeding again, and you can't afford to lose any more blood. I'm afraid you're going to be on bedrest for the foreseeable future. The doctor is going to come back at noon to give you another shot, but in the meantime, you can't move."

Sinking back down, she moved his restraining hand away weakly. "I want to be alone," she said.

Karl sucked in a breath. "Not just yet...Eva, I'm so sorry about the baby. I can't imagine how you must be feeling right now, but if it's anything like I feel, you're just devastated."

Her heart nearly stopped. Did that mean Ethan really made it out with the baby? Or had he been caught? Was Karl faking his sympathy? Or was her baby really gone? Uncertain what to say, she stayed quiet.

He reached out his hand to stroke her hair, and she closed her eyes and turned her head away. "Eva, I will make this up to you, I promise. I'm going to take you someplace wonderful, and once you're all better we can start over. From the very beginning. We can go out on real dates and do everything the way we should have. The way *I* should have from the start."

Exhausted and beginning to feel the aches and pains from last night, Eva tried to shut him out. She didn't want to start over with him, and she didn't want to hear any of his promises.

"Please look at me," Karl pleaded while stroking her back. "I've gotten rid of Dr. Ritter," he added after a pause.

Surprised, she turned around. Encouraged, Karl stroked her face lovingly before running his fingers over her hair, which was still a matted mess.

"I know you didn't like him. And we don't need a therapist as long as we both agree to commit to starting over. That's not asking too much, is it?" he asked earnestly, his handsome face creased with distress.

"What if it is?" she asked quietly.

Face tight, Karl sat up. For a long moment, he was silent. "I know you may not believe this, but all I want is a chance to make you happy."

"Then let me go home," she whispered.

Karl passed a hand over his face. "Eva, when are you going to understand? You *are* home."

She stiffened as he pressed a gentle kiss to her lips.

He stood. "One day you're going to forget how you feel today...once we start our own family," he promised before he left her alone.

Tears slipped out of a corner of her eye before she rubbed them away with the heel of her hand.

What was she going to do now? Would Sergei be able to find her again if Karl moved them? How had he tracked her in the first place? And now she was trapped in this bed, unable to see him or their baby.

I should have forgiven him sooner.

She should have told him she loved him. Now she might never get the chance. Heart racing, she swallowed, her already sore throat tightening painfully. She had to get out of here now before the doctor came with his sedative and Karl got them so lost she never found her way home again.

A desperate idea came to her.

Too desperate.

I can't, she thought hopelessly. There was every chance that she could die. Even right now, they could be too far from a hospital. But...the longer she waited, the farther they would get. What if Karl was instructing his captain to take them to Antarctica or Australia right now?

Breathing hard, she struggled to sit up. Knives of pain lanced her abdomen as damaged and torn muscles stretched with her movement. Whatever they had injected her with had definitely worn off. Panting and trembling, she shifted one leg over the side of the bed and then the other.

Oh god, oh god.

Slowly, she stood up on legs so shaky they nearly refused to support her. Mechanically, she took one step after another, intentionally widening her stance with each movement of her legs. When nothing happened she lowered a hand and started probing and tearing at herself. She was surprised when she was able to fish out a bloody sponge from the recess of her body. Nausea rose as the excruciating pain from the damage she was inflicting racked her body.

Shaking and sweating, Eva kept walking to the door. Dark spots appeared in her vision as her body threatened to shut down in an effort to stop the agony. But she kept taking jerky steps forward, even as twin trails of blood ran down her legs underneath the white nightgown.

Reaching down between her legs, she gathered some blood on her hands before passing them over the pale beige grain of the wooden door. With trembling hands, she smeared it above the doorknob before passing it over the brass handle. Then she let go of it.

Vision already darkening at the edges, she sank down to the floor, taking care not to block the door.

When she was found lying in a pool of her own blood, she was going to need to be taken to the hospital right away.

She just hoped it was in time.

CHAPTER 34

"What are you going to call him?"

Sergei looked up to see Calen standing in the doorway of the saloon. Gio and Alex were sitting at the bar, deep in conversation. His son, now almost two days old, was still 'the baby' to everyone on board.

"I don't know yet. Can't name him without Eva. She'd probably take a bat to my knees if I tried," he said, refusing to acknowledge the possibility she wouldn't come home.

They hadn't heard anything about Eva for hours, and he was struggling to stay calm. Lack of sleep normally made him short-tempered, and he'd been running on empty for days now. He was exhausted, but part of him was spoiling for a fight. He wanted to hit someone, anyone. The only thing keeping him in check was the baby in his arms.

"She's going to be all right. And from everything you've told me about her, she can take care of herself," Calen said comfortingly. "In fact, she'll probably rescue herself, you know. Once she's rested up after having this little guy," he added, pausing to kiss the sleeping baby's head. He inhaled deeply. "They smell really great, don't they?"

"Yes," Sergei said. "They do. But they're too small and fragile. I keep worrying that if I put him down, he's going to stop breathing or something."

He sat down on the couch cradling the baby in his lap. His son was wearing a onesie that had been sent by Calen's wife, Maia. It said 'Diaper loading, please wait' with a progress bar underneath it.

The baby slept on as he transferred him from one arm to the other. He frowned. "Shouldn't he cry more?"

Calen shrugged. "I'm sure he will once he gets over how tired being born made him."

"Hell yeah, he will. In fact, I'm going to remind you that you said that," Alex added as he and Gio joined them in the sitting area. "We've been trying to brainstorm ideas. I was thinking we could try and flip someone on Grayson's staff. Maybe a nurse or one of his doctors. We already know Ritter's for sale. Why don't we just buy him?"

"You missed the latest. Dr. Ritter is already out of the picture according to the last surveillance," Calen said. "But it's not a bad idea. Jason and Ethan are already working on profiles of the rest of the medical team and even some of the security guards. Maybe one of them could be bought. Preferably more than one."

Sergei shook his head. "It's not enough. I've had another idea."

"What is it?" Alex asked.

"I'm going to give Grayson whatever he wants," Sergei said simply.

Calen frowned. "He already has what he wants," he said gently.

"I know that, but I'm going to offer him something else, something he can't turn down," Sergei said, rocking the baby as the little one shifted in his sleep. "I'm prepared to sign over Damov Industries to him if he lets Eva go unharmed."

A stunned silence fell over the men.

"But that's your whole life," Gio said.

He looked poleaxed, and Sergei didn't blame him. The Morgese bank was Gio's one and only passion outside of his friends. Sergei used to feel the same way about Damov Industries.

He shook his head and covered the back of his son's small head with his much larger hand. "Not anymore." He looked at all of the men in turn. "I can start over again. As long as Eva's okay, it doesn't matter."

"I don't think that's going to work," Alex said. "I mean Grayson's a criminal. He's a money launderer, not to mention the fact he kidnapped someone. He's not going to be able to accept your offer. The CIA or Interpol would be here to slap cuffs on him the second he showed up to sign the contracts."

"Then he can have the money. However much of it I have that's liquid right now," Sergei said with a sigh, too tired to argue.

His personal net worth was over a billion. Grayson would have to think long and hard before turning that down. He was about to say as much to the others when there was a commotion at the saloon door. Ethan and Jason burst into the room followed by some of the security specialists they'd contracted.

"Get on the helicopter," Ethan ordered him.

"What happened?" Calen asked alarmed.

"We're not sure, but our man at Andrew's Memorial Hospital just called. Eva is in surgery," Jason filled in. "Grayson took her there himself, and he's still there."

Sergei was too overcome to speak. His muscles screamed with protest as he stood up. They were suddenly locked so tight he almost fell over in the effort.

"What happened?" he asked, finally finding his voice as he struggled to move.

"We're not sure. The helicopter took her there a little over an hour ago. Whatever it was, it must have happened really fast," Ethan said, checking his sidearm as he went for the door.

"Give him to me," Alex told Sergei, taking the baby from him.

His arms felt strangely empty as he ran after the FBI agents. A rush of violence swept through him. He needed to have his arms free in order to strangle Grayson.

"We'll follow in the speedboat," Gio called after him as Sergei climbed onto the four-seat helicopter with Ethan and Jason.

"Don't bring the baby until Grayson is gone," Sergei ordered Alex as he closed the door behind them.

He started praying as the helicopter took off.

CHAPTER 35

By the time they got to the hospital, Eva was out of surgery, but she hadn't recovered consciousness yet. They had put her in a private recovery suite, and Karl Grayson was in there with her. Grayson's pilot and bodyguard had melted away when Sergei's security personnel flooded the ICU.

Their men now blocked the door to Eva's room, guns drawn. Ethan stepped in front of them, checking on the situation through the small window in the door. But Grayson gave no indication that he was even aware he was surrounded, despite all the noise they had made.

Sergei waited impatiently for the surgeon who had operated on Eva to give him his report.

"Why did you operate on Eva?" he questioned when the man was finally brought before him.

Looking nervously at all the weapons, the doctor fingered his nametag. "We treated her for blood loss. She had suffered a minor hemorrhage during delivery, and there was some new tearing damage from earlier today that needed to be repaired. She also needed a transfusion," he said, finally turning toward him. He swallowed heavily as he met Sergei's burning eyes. "She's going to be fine."

"How did the new tearing happen?" Sergei asked horrified.

The doctor shrugged apologetically. "Her husband didn't say."

"That man is her kidnapper, not her husband," he said sharply. "Thus the guns," he finished bitingly with a gesture at the men who stood around the room, weapons drawn.

"Oh, of course. Sorry," the doctor said nodding before Ethan stepped up to them and he could escape.

"Grayson isn't moving, and he doesn't appear to be armed. I'm going in," Ethan said, checking his vest and weapon.

"No, you're not," Sergei said shaking his head. "I'm going."

"You can't. You're not law—" Ethan started.

"*Fuck that*," he hissed, cutting him off with a sweep of his arm. "That man has come this close to destroying everything I love," he said, holding his fingers a hairsbreadth apart. "Now I'm going in there to get him away from my wife, so just stay the fuck out of my way."

He turned on his heel and strode for the door, but Jason moved to block him. "We don't know for sure that he's not armed."

"He's not. He wouldn't risk having a shootout with Eva lying there. Now move," Sergei said, bodily shoving Jason out of the way.

"You can't know that for sure," Ethan hissed quietly behind him.

"I can. He wouldn't...because I wouldn't," Sergei argued before turning back to the door.

No one else tried to stop him as he opened it and slipped inside.

KARL GRAYSON DIDN'T MOVE when he entered the room. He just sat there, holding Eva's hand as she lay there in the hospital bed, her eyes closed.

She was paler than he'd ever seen her. Her usually rosy cheeks were white and drawn, and her lips were nearly colorless. She looked so frail and defenseless that Sergei quickly forgot his exhaustion. Instead, a cold anger filled him, propelling him further into the room. But Grayson didn't even look up when Sergei moved to face him across the bed.

230

His arch enemy was younger than he thought. And better looking, Sergei admitted to himself grudgingly. Grayson was handsome, despite the haggard appearance lack of sleep had given him. He was tall with broad shoulders and a lean wiry build. His blonde hair was a different shade from Eva's, but if you didn't know better, he could easily pass for her brother. His suit was an expensive lightweight wool, but it was wrinkled and marred with dark stains that were probably blood.

Eva's blood.

"She would rather die than be with me," Karl said slowly, his eyes never leaving Eva's face.

"Can you blame her?" Sergei asked coldly.

"No, I guess not," Grayson replied, stroking Eva's still hand with his thumb.

That small touch sent a surge of rage through Sergei. "Do yourself a favor and get your fucking hands off my wife," he bit out.

Grayson finally looked at him. "You're not married. She would have said," he contradicted, meeting his eyes steadily.

"We will be married soon enough," Sergei said. "Once you're rotting in a jail cell."

Giving himself a little shake, Grayson ignored his comment. He looked Sergei up and down, studying him for a long moment.

"So you're him," Grayson said finally, inhaling deeply. "The famous Sergei. I've seen your picture on the news and the gossip sites. Usually with some slutty socialite on your arm," he sneered slightly, twisting his lips in distaste. "I honestly can't imagine why Eva would fall for someone like you."

"Likewise...but then she never did fall for you, did she? That was just in your head," Sergei said, not bothering to pull any punches.

"Maybe it was. In the end," Grayson admitted, his shoulders falling slightly. "But in the beginning, we did have something. A chance," he added, a touch of defiance in his tone.

"Maybe you did," Sergei admitted. "But you pissed that away when you killed her father and your own mother. And that was just to start."

Grayson closed his eyes briefly before turning back to look at

Eva's still form. "Did she tell you that?" he asked flatly. "Did she really say I killed them?"

"Yes. Are you honestly going to pretend you didn't?"

Grayson let go of Eva's hand to rub his hands over his face. "No, actually," he replied, hunching over in his chair. "I didn't want to hurt them...but they are dead because of me. Because I said the wrong thing to the wrong person."

"Don't bother to try and deny your involvement," Sergei scoffed. "I already know about the debts to the cartels you worked for. We've verified how much money you owed. We know you killed Wallace Stone to cover those losses."

"That's not how it happened," Karl said, closing his eyes briefly. "I'd lost some money, but not enough for the cartel to want me dead. It was only a temporary setback. I had enough of a track record for doing good work. Enough to earn some leeway. And I was already well on my way to making the money back when my mother asked me to come home."

"Because she wanted you to take over Stonewall," Sergei filled in. "Tell me, was it her idea to bump off Wallace Stone, and she just got caught up in the crossfire accidentally? Or did you decide you were better off without both of them so you wouldn't have to split the money?" Sergei asked, crossing his arms as he stared the younger man down.

"No, of course not!" Grayson said. "My mother loved Wallace. And I didn't want either of them dead. I'd come home to *help* because my mother asked me to."

"Why did she need your help?"

Grayson sat up. "Wallace had a heart attack while Eva was away at school," he said, leaning forward. "It was minor, and he got out of the hospital in less than two days. But Wallace didn't want to worry Eva, so he never told her. And my mother agreed that it would be best to keep it confidential, because it would be bad for business if it got out. She asked me to help, so I went home and took over the day to day at Stonewall."

"What about the cartel?" Sergei asked, still not buying it.

"I made sure I met all of my obligations. I took care of some things remotely, put others on hold. My associates were okay with it so long as I checked in, but I won't lie. It was bad timing."

"So what? After you got there you decided to raid Stonewall's coffers to make up the difference with the cartel and Wallace caught you?"

"No. Like I said, I was taking care of the cartel in my own time. As for Stonewall, I didn't care that Wallace wanted it all to go to Eva. I was just there temporarily, no matter what my mother wanted. She wasn't exactly privy to the details of my real profession, so I didn't bother to argue with her when she would push for me taking over Stonewall. It was just easier," he said with a sigh of frustration.

"So what happened?"

"Eva came home for the holidays," Grayson said. He shook his head, his eyes faraway. "God, she was such a little nerd growing up. When she was little, I just thought of her as Wallace 2.0. And then she came home from college, and she had grown up into this amazing woman."

"So it was always about Eva," Sergei scoffed. "She swore up and down that it was about the money."

"I told you, I didn't need the money. But I was frustrated with Wallace and all of his bullshit. He didn't want me around his precious little girl. He could see how much she liked me, how close we were getting, and he freaked out."

"Can you blame him?" he asked, his nostrils flaring in disgust. "Tell me, what was buried in the woods?"

Grayson looked confused before his face cleared in recognition. "God, I can't believe that old bastard told Eva about that stupid dog. It was an accident for fuck's sake. It ran into the road. But that sanctimonious prick Wallace always blamed me, just because I'd had a few beers that night at a party."

Sergei studied him. Grayson appeared completely genuine, but he could just be a good actor.

"If all that is true, why are Wallace Stone and your mother dead?"

"I told you, I was frustrated with Wallace. He told me flat out he didn't want me courting his daughter. That asshole married my mother, but somehow I wasn't good enough for Eva," Grayson said, shifting angrily before subsiding. "And then I heard from one of my associates. He wanted me to handle some transactions for him, things I needed to deal with in person. So I went to visit him. He had a gathering, a meeting of sorts. One with lots of alcohol and blow. It was just how those nights always ended," he said, casually waving away the drug reference. "I was used to that sort of excess. I can handle it. But that night, I was upset, and I ended up whispering in the wrong ear. I told someone I shouldn't have been talking to about all my problems."

Sergei stayed silent, considering Grayson's confession. If all of this was true, then Karl had gotten swept up in something he couldn't control. But the asshole had taken Eva, so as far as he was concerned, the guy deserved whatever came next.

"I didn't even realize what I had done at first," Grayson continued in a distant voice. "I was almost in the clear with the cartel. I was busy working on that while pulling double duty at Stonewall. When our parents died, I didn't even suspect that it was because of what I'd said, that I was the one responsible. Not until I got a package delivered by private courier."

"Let me guess. It was the locket, the Stone family heirloom, wasn't it?"

"Yeah, that's right," Grayson said in surprise, but he let it go to continue his story. "I got a call shortly afterward. Someone I had done business with in the past got in touch," he said, continuing to choose his words carefully as he took Eva's hand again, looking at her guiltily. "This associate wanted to apologize. My mother wasn't supposed to be dead, too. But she got in the way. He said he had simply intended to do me a favor, but now he owed me."

"What's this man's name?"

"I can't tell you that. My mother was collateral damage, but if I told you his name, he wouldn't hesitate to kill me. He's crazy, a total psycho. I didn't know that at the time. I had heard whispers, but I thought his reputation was exaggerated. I was wrong."

"Do you honestly expect anyone will believe you if you won't name this mystery murderer?" Sergei asked in disbelief.

Grayson shrugged. "Doesn't matter anymore," he said despondently. "I'm not getting out of a prison sentence. Whether I live through it or not depends on me keeping my mouth shut."

Sergei stared at him for a while. "None of that changes what you did to Eva. You could have kept all of Stonewall's assets for yourself and forgotten about her," he said.

"Could *you?*" Grayson scoffed. "I loved her...I still do. But Geoffrey thought I was a murderer, so Eva did, too. Even after I realized she wasn't dead, that she ran away from me, all I wanted was to bring her home so I could change her mind," he whispered.

"But you couldn't tell her the truth, because that alone was enough for her to turn on you. So what, you were going to brainwash her into loving you?"

"I lost everything," Grayson said tonelessly. "And after all that I was just supposed to sit back and let her go?"

"*Yes.*" Sergei's tone was acid.

Grayson looked down at Eva's hand. It didn't move when he finally let go of it. "For what it's worth, I'm sorry about the baby," he said. "I didn't want her to lose it."

"Our son is still alive," Sergei couldn't resist adding.

Grayson's head jerked back. Understanding lit his eyes. "The bodyguard," he said.

"Was with me," Sergei confirmed.

"And Raske?"

"That wasn't Raske. We just borrowed his name. And his boat."

Grayson closed his eyes and smirked. "You rich guys all stick together, don't you?"

Sergei didn't answer.

"Is she really in love with you?" Grayson asked in a low voice.

"Yes," Sergei said uncompromisingly.

His voice was deceptively confident. He actually wasn't sure. Eva had never mentioned the word love. But he had faith that if she didn't love him already, she would soon. At least he hoped so.

Someone cleared their throat loudly. He looked up to see Ethan and Jason just inside the doorway, their guns trained on Grayson. Karl looked up at them and then back at Eva.

"I want to be here when she wakes up," he said anxiously.

"Forget it," Sergei scowled as the agents moved toward Grayson.

"Wait," he said, holding up his hands. "I need to explain to her what really happened with our parents. She has to know that I didn't mean for them to die," he protested as Ethan hauled him to his feet.

Sergei sighed and looked away briefly. "I'll tell her what you said," he conceded. "But that's no guarantee she'll believe it."

Jason kept his gun pointed at Karl while Ethan cuffed him. They hauled him away, and Sergei was finally alone with Eva. He moved into the only chair in the room, the one Karl had been sitting in. Taking Eva's hand in one of his, he used the other to take out his cell.

"Niko, I need you to find the best trauma surgeon money can buy and get him to Andrews right away. Get the second and third best as well. I want an expert team assembled as soon as possible."

He hung up and then texted Alex. Eva was going to want to see their son as soon as she woke up.

CHAPTER 36

*I*t was the pain that assured Eva she was still alive. Whatever the next life might have in store, it probably wouldn't hurt as much as she did now. Which meant she had lived through her desperate ploy to escape. Whether or not she had actually succeeded in getting off the *Angel's Folly* remained to be seen.

She cracked open her eyelids and almost wept in relief. Sergei was asleep slouching in a chair next to her, a small bundle in a blue baby blanket nestled against his chest. It was the most beautiful sight she had ever seen.

And he wasn't alone. There were three other chairs around her hospital bed. Each had a ridiculously good looking man in it. If these were Sergei's friends, then it was true about what they said: the beautiful people traveled in packs. Two of the men were also asleep, but the one next to Sergei was awake.

"Hey there," he said, sitting up. He gave her with a wide smile, and for a second, he reminded her of Sergei. But there was no real resemblance other than their smiles and perhaps their tall muscular builds. The stranger's hair was a lighter brownish red and it was longer than Sergei's, with more of a wave to it.

"Hi."

Her voice came out as little more than a raspy whisper. Her mouth was dry, and her throat felt like sandpaper. The friendly stranger got up and poured her a glass of water from a pitcher on the bedside table. She tried to take it from him, but an IV she hadn't noticed attached to her arm snagged on something, and she flinched.

"Let me help," the man said, concerned, and he held the glass to her lips.

She drank a little and then waved him away with a tiny motion of her hand.

"Thank you," she whispered.

One of the other men stirred, and he blinked sleepy eyes at her before smiling.

"Bongiorno," he said.

His hair was darker, blacker than Sergei's, but his eyes were a unique hazel that was mostly gold in color.

"Hi?"

She didn't mean to make it sound like a question.

"I'm Calen, and this is Gio," the first man said.

"I figured he was Gio, but you were a coin toss. You could have been Alex or Liam," she said, starting to sound like a human again.

"I'm going to get the doctor," Gio said before giving her a little half bow in parting.

She watched him slip out of the room on silent feet before turning back to the chairs to see Sergei watching her silently. The other man was also awake. Calen motioned to the other stranger, and they both left without a word.

Alone with Sergei, she felt a rush of emotion, a large part of which was anxiety. Why did he look so serious? Why couldn't he smile at her?

"Is the baby okay?" she asked worriedly.

Sergei's face softened. "Yes, here, see for yourself."

He helped her sit up before placing the infant in her arms. Their son was fast asleep, his long dark lashes over soft baby cheeks.

"He already looks so different," she marveled.

His little cheeks had filled out and the red cheeks had faded to a soft blush.

"Yes, he's been on formula, and he seems to like it. I think we should introduce some breast milk, but we should buy it online. I've been doing some research on medically vetted sources," Sergei said in a distressingly businesslike tone.

Taken aback Eva frowned. "I had planned on breastfeeding, remember?"

Sergei shook his head. "You've lost too much blood, and are recovering from surgery."

"Did the doctor say that?" she asked suspiciously.

Sergei scowled. "You need to focus on regaining your strength. Breastfeeding will be too strenuous for a while yet."

Eva blinked. "I...are you mad at me?"

Did he blame her for getting kidnapped? Why was he so distant and cold?

"Yes I'm mad, but no, not at you," Sergei said tightly before sitting on the bed next to her. Her took her hand and pressed it to his heart. "Although it will be a long time before I can forgive you for scaring the hell out of me."

Then he did the most shocking thing she'd ever seen. The ice man burst into tears. Sergei covered his face with one arm, and Eva's apprehension crumbled. Tears stung her own eyes.

"Don't. I'm okay. I'm sorry he got me, I promise I won't ever go anywhere without you ever again," she said, clutching at his chest with the hand he had pressed against him.

"That wasn't your fault," he said, wiping his tears on his sleeve with a rough gesture. "It was mine, an oversight in your security, one that won't happen again. What I was actually referring to was your drastic way of getting off the *Angel's Folly*."

"Oh."

"Yes, oh. If you ever do anything like that again, I'm going to...well, I don't know what I'm going to do. I can't threaten you, cause I can't stand the thought of your being hurt again. You've already done enough damage to yourself. Promise me you won't ever take a risk like that again. Please, just sit tight and wait to be rescued."

Eva frowned at the implication that she should act like a damsel in distress, but she didn't say anything. There was no need to make Sergei feel worse right now by arguing with him. And she *had* gone a little too far.

Of course, that hadn't been her intention. She had just tried to make it look scary enough to freak Karl out enough to take her to the hospital. And it had worked. But she'd lost so much blood that she'd been barely conscious when she'd been found. The helicopter ride to the hospital was a blur. She had a faint recollection of being rushed into surgery and then nothing else.

"Eva, I'm waiting. Promise me you won't ever take such a risk again."

"I promise the next time I get kidnapped, I will wait for you to rescue me," she said, hoping to lift his heavy mood with a little humor.

"Don't joke," he said, scowling briefly and squeezing her hand tight.

"I'm sorry," she said. "I'm just so glad to see you again. Thank you for sending your friends."

Sergei gave her a resigned smile. "I just wish it had worked."

Eva leaned against him, tired now. "It was a near thing, but when I couldn't leave with the baby, I had to get out of there," she said in a low voice, running her hand over his chest. "All I could think about was coming home to you."

"And all I could think about was getting you back. Both of you," he said, pulling her close before the baby let out a squeal.

"Ooh, look he's awake," she said excitedly. "He's so beautiful," she added, bending her neck to kiss the baby's brow.

"Yes, he is," Sergei said staring at the two of them for a long moment before shifting to wrap an arm around her. "What are we going to call him?" he asked. "We can't keep calling him the baby forever."

"No, we can't. I've been thinking about it and really, I don't think we have a choice," she said in an apologetic tone.

Sergei's head drew back a little. "Do you want to name him after your dad?"

"God, no. Dad always disliked Wallace and hated being called Wally. I was thinking of more recent events," she said with a meaningful raise of her brows.

Understanding dawned and Sergei's features cleared before he snorted slightly. "If you insist."

"I think I do," Eva said before turning to the baby. "Hello, Ethan Patrick. I'm your mommy," she whispered before kissing him again.

The baby snuffled and waved his tiny hands in the air, making her laugh. His thick dark lashes lifted, and his blue eyes fixed on her. And that was all it took. She was in love.

Again.

EPILOGUE

"*Don't you dare give that baby beer, Sergei.*"

Sergei's face flashed with guilty surprise as he spotted Eva in the doorway. He was holding a bottle with an exclusive microbrew label to the baby's lips. Ethan Patrick, who looked about three months older than his actual five months, was grabbing at the bottle with chubby hands and chortling happily, as if he knew how much it was upsetting his mother.

Giancarlo, who was visiting for the week, was leaning over, taking a picture of the father-son bonding moment with his camera phone. Next to him, Alex watched laughing. He was bouncing his own son, Alex junior, on his knee.

They were back on Alex's Greek island palazzo enjoying the last of the September sunshine, only this time they were visiting as guests. He and Eva made their home in Manhattan in a large brownstone that Sergei had renovated with enough security to rival Fort Knox. Eva had spent most of the summer recovering from her ordeal, and Sergei had wanted to take her somewhere special to celebrate being well again.

Alex had insisted on everyone getting together at the villa, but

Calen's little girl had come down with a bad cold and he and his wife Maia hadn't been able to travel.

"I'm not letting him taste it," Sergei protested as he tried to take the bottle away from the baby's surprisingly strong grip. "It's just for the picture."

"Uh huh," Eva said, her tone still sharp and suspicious.

Using two fingers, she pointed to her eyes and then back at him in the unmistakable 'I am watching you' warning, before she walked away to join Elynn on the terrace for lunch.

"She's like a tiny little tyrant," Gio observed with a laugh.

"About him, definitely," Sergei said with a wicked grin, letting the baby taste the beer again. "But it's great. I'm so glad to see her up and energetic that I sometimes intentionally make her a little mad just so she'll yell at me. I find it reassuring."

Alex shook his head. "You have an odd way of going about this whole happily ever after thing."

Sergei just laughed in reply. Gio leaned back and studied the two of them with a distant smile. Thinking that perhaps his last single friend was on domestic bliss overload, he was about to launch into a bracing pep talk. Gio really needed to start dating again. But then he got distracted by Ethan Patrick taking a swipe at Alex junior.

It got competitive after that, and he and Alex set aside their drinks to stage a baby wrestling match. Despite the age difference, they were near to evenly matched. Ethan Patrick was a very big boy.

Eva often said, quite smugly, that it was because she'd been able to breastfeed after all. In the end, her bloodloss hadn't been an issue and Sergei had been overruled by the lactation nurse he'd hired shortly after they left the hospital.

"I want five more," Sergei said as they watched the adorable violence unfold.

Alex looked at him questioningly. There had been some question as to whether or not Eva would be able to have another child after what had happened.

"So is that in the cards?" he asked cautiously.

"Yes. Eva's fully recovered, and there was no permanent damage. She had another checkup before we came out here, and the doctor said we can have more kids," Sergei said before changing the subject a little abruptly.

It wasn't that he wasn't relieved. He really wanted more children somewhere down the line, but since he got Eva back, he hadn't been willing to risk hurting her in any way. They hadn't had sex for six months, despite the fact the doctor had given them the all clear weeks ago.

Though they had agreed to take things slow during her recovery, lately Eva had started watching him expectantly when they were alone. She had started wearing sexy short nightgowns and giving him a lot of suggestive little touches.

But whenever he got aroused, the mental image of her lying in that hospital bed would flash in his head and he would march himself straight into a cold shower.

He had never been cleaner.

Later that night, he joined Eva in their room after checking on Ethan Patrick. Alex had set up a nursery for them next door so they could have some privacy, but the moment he saw his angel in a tiny black nightie he wished he had the baby to use as a shield.

"Damn," Eva said suddenly.

"What's wrong?"

"I put this on before I put the baby to bed, and I didn't notice he spit up on it a little," she said before drawing the brief silk gown over her head.

Sergei froze. Underneath the gown Eva was wearing a black lace demi bra and the smallest black g-string he had ever seen.

Since having the baby, her body had changed in ways that drove him absolutely crazy. Her waist was back to pre-baby size, but her hips were a little fuller and her breasts...oh God. He could feel IQ points dropping away as she went into the bathroom for a washcloth. She stayed in the doorway, dabbing at her breast with the towel, taking her sweet time to remove the baby spit.

Sergei stared at her slack-jawed until he realized Eva had been speaking to him for some time.

"What?" he asked blankly.

She smiled suggestively and cocked a hip. "I was asking how you liked the view."

"Uh," he answered stupidly. There wasn't a single coherent thought in his head. "Like?"

Yes, he liked. He more than liked. *Shit.* "I...I'm sorry. I need to take a shower," he said hastily.

He made a move to the doorway, but Eva was still standing there all glowing soft skin and lush curves. Stopping short, he ended up backing away.

"You can't," Eva said, regret on her angelic features as she came toward him. "It's broken."

"The shower's broken?" he asked, moving away until he backed into the bed.

"Yes."

She kept advancing, biting her lip to stop from laughing when he grabbed a pillow and held it in front of him like a ward against temptation.

"Since when?"

It had been working this morning. And just after lunch.

Eva shrugged nonchalantly. "Since I broke it."

"How did that happen?" he asked, genuinely puzzled.

"It wasn't easy. Took forever to take apart without the proper tools," she said with a perfectly straight face.

She grabbed the pillow from his hands and tossed it away. Breathing heavily, Sergei fisted his hands at his sides.

"Angel stop," he said in a near panic as Eva pushed him onto the bed and climbed on top of him. He inhaled deeply, and her clean soap scent hit him, triggering a chain reaction that had him hardening like steel. "I don't want to hurt you," he whispered urgently.

"Sergei, this is okay. The doctor said so. And so did the one I saw for a second opinion. And the one after that for the third opinion you insisted I get," she said, stroking his face gently before kissing him softly. "I'm all right now. I know you are worried about me, but I'm perfectly fine, and I miss being with you."

She stroked his chest with her hands and rocked forward, her silky panties teasing his rock hard erection.

Sergei's paper-thin resistance crumbled, and he grabbed her with both hands, flipping them over until he was on top. With frantic hands, he tore at her bra and panties until they were lying in shreds at their sides.

Eva tried to work him out of his clothes at the same time, but he had the advantage, and all she could do was work a few buttons of his shirt open. He took over, tearing at his pants until he was free.

Sergei groaned as the head of his cock made contact with Eva's softness. With a herculean effort, he stopped to look down into her flushed eager face. Too overcome to notice he had stopped, she tried to make them come together with a wanton little move of her hips. Muscles corded in his neck, Sergei pinned her hands down with his own.

"Angel if this is painful, if you feel any discomfort at all, stop me. You're my whole world," he said urgently. "You and our son."

Eva put both of her hands on either side of his face while looking into his eyes gravely. "I love you, too," she whispered.

The relief and rush of emotion were almost painful in their intensity. Inexplicably, he felt like crying, but Eva moved underneath him and his lust took over. With excruciating slowness, he pushed inside, giving her every opportunity to stop him.

Instead, she urged him closer by wrapping her legs and arms around him until he was flush against her. He tried to hold still to give her time to adjust but, despite the fact she was pinned beneath him, she twisted and writhed until they were rocking together in concert.

"You had a baby, you're not supposed to be this tight," he groaned, making her laugh wickedly before she flexed around him, squeezing him so hard it hurt.

He retaliated by moving faster and harder. His faster strokes made the heat rise too quickly, but it was all right, because Eva was right there with him. Shifting positions so that she was on top and in control, he focused on giving her everything he had.

His hands roamed over her body while his mouth tasted and licked from her lips to her breasts. Above him she rocked, twisting up until just the tip of him was still inside before sinking back down. The pulsing pleasure nearly blinded him.

"Eva, I can't wait," Sergei whispered urgently as his cock began to jerk inside her.

He was helpless to stop his release. With a little cry, Eva ground down on him, her orgasm triggered by his own. She rode him through the last of the spasms before collapsing on his chest. Burying his hands in her hair, he held her tight as their breathing calmed and their bodies cooled.

It was a very long time before he was able to speak. "I do love you. More than anything," he whispered, aware he hadn't actually said the words out loud yet.

But Eva had already fallen asleep, lying on top of him.

That was all right though. He could tell her again tomorrow.

The End

Continue the Singular Obsession Series with Gio's story, the Roman's Woman, a Readers' Favorite Five Star read!

Elizabeth Butts for Readers' Favorite wrote:

"This is a very hot and spicy book; you will fly through the pages while feeling just a teensy bit warm (okay, a LOT bit warm) because of the sexy scenes that are scattered throughout. However, The Roman's Woman is not just an erotic novel. No, this book has substance, great characters, beautiful descriptions of emotions, and internal battles. Author Lucy Leroux does a beautiful job…"

Thank you for reading this novel! Reviews are an author's bread and butter. If you liked the story please consider leaving one.

Subscribe to the Lucy Leroux Newsletter for a *free* novella!
www.authorlucyleroux.com/newsletter
or keep up with her L.B. Gilbert releases
www.elementalauthor.com/newsletter

APPENDIX

RUSSIAN TO ENGLISH TRANSLATIONS

[1] Russian for best friend

[2] Russian for I want to make love to you/sleep with you. Do you want me?

[3] I love you, angel.

ABOUT THE AUTHOR

A 7-time Readers' Favorite Medal Winner. USA Today Bestselling Author. Mom to a half-feral princess. WOC. Former scientist. Recovering geek.

Lucy Leroux is the steamy pen name for author L.B. Gilbert. Ten years ago Lucy moved to France for a one-year research contract. Six months later she was living with a handsome Frenchman and is now married with an adorable half-french 5yo who won't go to bed on time

When her last contract ended Lucy turned to writing. Frustrated by a particularly bad romance novel she decided to write her own. Her family lives in Southern California.

Lucy loves all genres of romance and intends to write as many of them as possible. To date she has published twenty novels and novellas. These includes paranormal, urban fantasy, gothic regency, and contemporary romances with more on the way.

www.authorlucyleroux.com

amazon.com/author/lucyleroux
facebook.com/lucythenovelist
twitter.com/lucythenovelist
instagram.com/lucythenovelist
bookbub.com/authors/lucy-leroux